Maybe Matt's Miracle

By Tammy Falkner

Night Shift Publishing

MW00889508

For all of you who have been affected by cancer.

Copyright © 2014 by Tammy Falkner
Maybe Matt's Miracle
First Edition
Night Shift Publishing
Cover design by Tammy Falkner
ISBN-10: 1499221819
ISBN-13: 9781499221817

All rights reserved. No part of this book may be reproduced or
transmitted in any form or by any means, electronic or
mechanical, including photocopying, recording, or by any
information storage and retrieval system without the written
permission of the author, except where permitted by law.

This book is a work of fiction. Names, characters, places, and
incidents either are products of the author's imagination or are
used fictitiously. Any resemblance to actual persons, living or
dead, events, or locales is entirely coincidental.

Skylar

Today would be a beautiful day if not for the casket and the three children with wet faces and red eyes sitting beside me on the front pew. The service hasn't started yet, and people keep wandering up to look at my half sister, Kendra. Some of them whisper soft words to her and reach out to touch her cold hand. I touched it, too. That was the second and last time I would ever touch her. She's the sister I never got to meet until the day she died.

I startle as the pew shakes. Seth, the oldest of Kendra's children, jumps to his feet and cries, "Grandpa!"

Grandpa? What? He has a grandpa? I look up and see my very own father. He's here? Huh? He wraps Seth up in his arms and squeezes him tightly. He sets him back and looks into his eyes. "How are you holding up?" he asks quietly.

Seth's eyes travel toward the casket. "We're okay," he says. He swallows hard. I can hear it from where I'm sitting.

Dad takes Seth's face in his hands and stares into his eyes. "Everything is going to be fine," he says. "She's in a better place." He looks over Seth's shoulder toward me. "And you have Skylar now," he whispers. Seth nods.

A better place? When can I go to a better place? Anywhere would be better than this church where my dad is paying homage to his illegitimate daughter.

Dad walks over to me and kisses my cheek. "How are you, Sky?" he asks. He's not nearly as friendly with me as he is with the grandchildren I never even knew he had until a few days ago.

"Fine," I bite out.

Dad sits down and motions toward Kendra's girls with a crook of his finger. The little one, who is three, scrambles into his lap, and the older one, who is five, leans into his side. He drops an arm around her and holds her close. He knows these kids. He knows them a lot better than he knows me. That chafes at me so badly that it makes me squirm in my seat.

Dad's brows scrunch together in subtle warning. I stop moving.

I really need to learn that look, now that I'm a mom.

Yes. I'm a mom. My dad came to me about a week ago and asked for my help. And *bang*—instant motherhood.

"Skylar," Dad says quietly. "I need for you to do something for me."

I look up from my manicotti and force a grin to my face. I should have known that he wanted something. He never would have invited me to lunch otherwise. "Did you get another speeding ticket?" I ask. I'm a brand-new attorney, as of last month.

"No," he says slowly. He won't look me in the eye. "It's about Kendra."

I drop my fork, and it clatters loudly against my plate. I scramble to catch it, and then brace myself with my palms on the table. "What about her?" I ask.

I know who Kendra is. She's the daughter my dad had with his mistress. I found out a few years ago, when my mother went on a drunken bender and unburdened her soul. And burdened mine.

Kendra is the daughter my father loved. Her mother was the woman he loved. It didn't matter that my father was married to my mother. It didn't matter that he had three kids with my mother. It didn't matter that we were the perfect family with the house on the hill and a summer home at the Cape. Our family was only perfect until we found out he had another one. One he actually loved.

He had a whole other life with Kendra's mother, right up until she died. They shared an apartment together, and they had a daughter. Dad went back and forth between our house and theirs for many years, but he was never really present when he was at ours. My mother was too resentful. So he stayed away more and more. With them.

Then suddenly one day he was back. His eyes were rimmed with red, and he retreated to his study with a bottle of Glenlivet. He didn't come out for days. When he finally emerged, my mom walked around for a week singing, "Ding-dong, the bitch is dead." Kendra was already an adult at that point, and married.

But I had my father back after that day. I didn't understand at all how it had come to be. I didn't know at the time that he had another daughter. Another woman he had loved. Another life. But he did. And now he wants to talk about her?

"Kendra is dying," he says. His eyes fill with tears, but he won't let them spill over. He blinks furiously, his face reddening.

"Oh," I say. How am I supposed to respond to that? Ding-dong, the bitch is dead... "What happened?"

"She has cancer. She found out when she was pregnant with her youngest daughter, Mellie." He wipes his eyes with a cloth

napkin and motions for a waiter to bring him a drink. "I got her into a really wonderful chemical trial, but she wanted to wait until Mellie was born." He heaves a sigh. "If she hadn't gotten pregnant, she might have made it. She could have gotten an abortion, but she refused. She waited too long. The cancer is going to win, and she doesn't have anyone to take the children."

I can't breathe. My chest stills, and I feel like I'm going to pass out. Dad shoves a glass of water at me, and I raise it to my lips, sputter into the rim of it, take a sip, swallow, and inhale. I take another deep breath. And I wait. Because there's more. There's always more with my dad.

"She has three children. Seth is sixteen. Joey is five. And Mellie is three." He covers my hand with his and squeezes it. "They don't have anyone but me. And I can't take them." He sits back and rubs the bridge of his nose. "You know how your mother is," he explains.

Yes, and I know how my mother was betrayed. Yes, I know how my mother found out about his mistress. Yes, I know how my mother hates the ground they all walk on. Sometimes I think she hates me, too. It's hard to tell. I really don't think she loves anyone or anything.

He looks me in the eye. "I need for you to help me. They're your nieces and nephew, no matter what your mother has taught you."

I am stunned. Absolutely stunned. "You love them," I say quietly.

He nods. "I do."

"You love her." The words fall on the room like cracks of thunder.

"I do."

I lean back against the chair. "Can I ask you something?"

He nods. It's a quick jerk, but I see it.

"What did they give you that we couldn't?" I ask. I don't even cry. I just ask it. I always wanted to know.

"Your mother made it really hard for me to be a part of our family," he says. "After she found out—" He raises his hand to stop me when I open my mouth to complain. "Wait," he says. "Hear me out."

I nod. I couldn't talk if I wanted to.

"I loved you and your brother and sister. But I loved Kendra's mother, too, and I should have divorced your mother and made a clean break."

"Without us," I say.

"No, I would have taken you with me if I could. But I couldn't. Your mother would have ruined me financially, and I could get over that, but she would have gotten custody of you all. And I couldn't just leave you with all that hatred, without at least trying to be a buffer." I don't remember him as a buffer. I know him as that man I never knew. He balls up his fist and squeezes tightly. "That's why I never left completely. Your mother is more than a bit vindictive, as you know." He scrubs a hand across his perfect white hair. "Sometimes I think she would have been okay with it if Kendra's mother was white."

What? Kendra's mother's not white? My father had an affair with a woman of a different race?

"If you do this for me, your mother is going to be very angry at you."

No shit. She'll hate me. But I think she already does anyway.

"I understand if you say no," he says on a sigh. "But they don't have anyone else."

"Where is their father?" I ask.

He shrugs. "Fathers," he says, enunciating the word. "Seth has a dad who sees him once or twice a year, and the girls' dad has a new family and not enough time for them."

"So, what do you want me to do?" I ask. I throw my napkin into my plate. My manicotti is churning in my stomach.

"I want you to go and get them."

"Did you ask Tim? Or Lydia?" They're my brother and sister and both are older than me.

He shakes his head. "They have families of their own."

"And I don't." *Shit, I don't have anyone. No one but a boyfriend I almost never see. My mother is a nutcase, and my father's heart lies with another family.*

"You're single. You would be wonderful with them." He lowers his voice and looks around the room. "You won't look at them like they're unwanted, biracial children. You'll love them. I know you will." He stares at me. "Will you at least meet them? Please? I know it would be a challenge. You'd have to learn a lot, but Seth is sixteen. He helps to take care of the little ones. Hell, in two years, he can take custody himself. That's what he wants."

Dad's pleading with me.

"I've never asked for anything before," he says.

He's right. He's never asked for a good night kiss. Or any of the things fathers want. Well, he probably asked for them from Kendra.

"I'll go," I say. They're just children, after all. And children need to be loved. I wasn't, but I can make it better for Kendra's kids, can't I? There's a tiny little piece of me that wants to make my father proud. To make him love me.

He deflates like a balloon, his body relaxing. "Oh, thank God," he says. He lays a hand on his chest. Then he gets up, lifts me by my elbows, and pulls me to him. I can't remember ever getting a hug from my father before, and I don't know what to do with it. He holds me like that, breathing into the hair on the top of my head for a moment. Then he sets me back. His eyes are wet with unshed tears. "Thank you," he says. "Thank you so much."

I nod. I can't do anything more. I feel like somebody took my insides and shoved them up my throat.

I'm jerked from my memories when someone sits down on my left. I look up and instantly recognize Matthew Reed. He was a friend of Kendra's from the cancer center. I went to visit, right before Kendra died, and to get the kids. Matt was waiting with her. He stayed with Seth so they could be there when she took her last breath. I took the little ones home; I didn't think they needed to remember their mom that way.

His blue eyes gaze into mine, and he sticks out a hand to shake. He doesn't say anything. I look up at him. He's wearing a blue turtleneck covered up by a black button-down shirt, with a pair of really nice trousers and a suit coat. He tugs at the top of the turtleneck, and I get a tiny peek of his tattoos.

"You clean up nicely," I say. I smile at him because I don't know what else to do.

"Thanks," he says quietly. His blond hair is held back with a leather band at the nape of his neck, but a piece falls forward, and he tucks it behind his ear. He has a row of piercings up the shell of his ear, and I count them in my head. I have a suddenly insatiable desire to see his hair hang loose around his face.

He looks down at my black skirt and my white blouse. "So do you."

I think I was wearing something similar the last time I saw him, but I smile anyway. He squeezes my hand and pulls his fingers from my grasp. I probably shouldn't have held his hand so long. I'm an idiot. He leans across me and reaches for my dad's hand. "Mr. Morgan," he says with a nod. "I'm so sorry for your loss."

Dad nods his thanks and grips Matt's hand tightly, and then swipes a finger under his nose. He goes back to talking to the girls, and they're snuggling closer and closer to him as he murmurs softly to them.

Matt reaches past my dad and bumps knuckles with Seth. Seth smiles at him, but then the preacher walks to the front of the church, they close the casket—thank God—and the service begins.

Matt takes my hand in his again, and I feel tears sting my eyes. I blink up at him, and he smiles softly at me. He squeezes my hand gently and listens to the pastor. But he doesn't let me go.

Matt

"She looks lonely," Emily says as she elbows me in the side. Emily is my brother Logan's wife, and she holds a little piece of my heart. But sometimes I want to elbow her back when she pokes me with her scrawny limbs. "You should go check on her," she whispers vehemently. She raises her elbow again, and I grab it before she can jab me.

"Fine," I bite out. I get up, stepping on my four brothers' feet as I scoot past them. Of course, I'm in the center of the aisle and have to go by all of them. Reagan, Pete's girl, reaches out and squeezes my hand as I walk by her. I love Reagan, and Emily, too. But Emily is a little more outspoken. Reagan is famous for her tender touches, and Emily is the opposite.

I adjust my suit coat and tug at the turtleneck I borrowed from Logan. He gets free clothes from Emily's parents, who own Madison Avenue, the upscale clothing company. I feel like a monkey dressed up in a coat and a top hat. Like the ones that dance at carnivals. *Dance, monkey, dance.*

I drop into the open seat beside Skylar, Kendra's half-sister, and I reach out to shake hands with her. She holds on a second too long, and I don't mind it. She looks tired. Her dad is sitting beside her, but there may as well be an ocean between them. It's only a few inches, but even I can feel the divide.

I shake his hand and bump knuckles with Seth. Seth and I were both with his mom when she died. We shared the most difficult moment of his life, and it's something I will never, ever forget.

I watched Kendra take her last breath, and all I could think was how lucky I was that it wasn't me dying there in that bed. It could have so easily been me. Kendra and I were in the same chemical trial, but I got better and my cancer went into remission. Hers didn't.

She died.

I'm alive.

I look down at Skylar. She looks nothing like Kendra. Kendra was biracial, so she had skin the color of sweet coffee, and she wore her hair natural but short. Skylar is light skinned, blond, and blue eyed. She has rhinestone-encrusted sunglasses pushed up on top of her head, holding her hair back from her face. It hangs halfway down her back in soft waves.

The preacher starts to speak at the front of the church, and Skylar closes her eyes. She squeezes her hands together in her lap, and I can't tell what's going on in her head. I wish I knew.

I reach out and take her hand in mine without even thinking about it. I tuck our twined fingers down on the seat between us, and I give her a gentle squeeze. She looks up at me and blinks slowly, her blue eyes startled. But then they soften and she blinks at me again, and this time she really looks at me. She squeezes my hand back, and I don't let her go. I hold it until both our palms start to sweat.

I get so wrapped up in the feel of her hand in mine and the soft drone of the preacher, that it startles me when a cough jerks me out of my trance. I look up and see a tall man looking down his nose at me. He nudges my knee. "I think you're in my spot," he says.

I look at Skylar, and she is just as shocked as I am. She pulls her hand from mine and wipes it on her skirt. I scoot over, and he settles down beside her. He drops an arm around her shoulders, and she leans over to press her lips to his. It's a quick kiss, one that makes me wonder how often he does it and if it's always quite that chaste.

Great, now I'm thinking about how it feels to kiss her. Shit. Where did that come from?

Finally, they roll the casket from the church, and we all follow to the graveside. I am a pallbearer and so are my brothers. My brothers are really good for things like that. I volunteered them when Mr. Morgan called to ask me to do it.

I take the carnation off my lapel, lay it on top of the casket, and go to stand with my brothers behind the crowd.

Emily threads her arm through mine. "Who is the guy?" she asks, nodding toward the man who's standing with Skylar.

I shrug. "I have no idea."

"Does she have a boyfriend?" Reagan asks.

My brothers are silent. I wish Logan and Pete would tell their girls to shut it for a few minutes and quit being so nosy. I tap Emily on the tip of her nose, and she scrunches up her face. "Stop being so curious," I tell her.

I wrap my arm around Reagan and pull her to me. I like it when she goes all soft against me, because when she's not soft, she's ready to take my head off with a karate chop. I have been on the wrong end of a startled Reagan before, and I don't particularly want to go there again.

"You okay?" she asks quietly.

I heave a sigh. "I guess." I shake my head. "I still can't believe she's gone," I say.

Reagan kisses my cheek and then stops to wipe her thumb across the lipstick she must have left on my skin. She smiles. "I'm glad you got better," she says quietly.

I squeeze her. "Me, too."

But shit. I feel guilty. Kendra left behind three children.

I see Skylar walking toward us, and Emily and Reagan step back. The three-inch-high heels of the shoes Skylar's wearing sink into the earth, and she totters a little because of it. I reach out to help steady her with a hand on her elbow. She stops in front of me.

"Thank you for being there with her," Skylar says quietly.

"She was my friend," I explain. I don't know what else to say.

She looks into my eyes. "Was she in a lot of pain?" she asks. She shakes her head. "I tried to talk to Seth about it, but he pretty much pretends I don't exist."

I shove my hands in my pockets. "What do you mean? He's not giving you a hard time, is he?"

She shakes her head again. "No. He's perfect. He takes his sisters to day care in the morning and picks them up after school. He feeds them, and he bathes them. He won't let me do anything. I think I'm just a placeholder." She blows out a heavy breath.

I scratch my head. I don't know how to tell her what I want to say.

"What?" she asks, her delicate brow arching.

"Kendra asked him to make it easy for you," I admit. "When she was dying, she told him some things about how to be a good man. Always open car doors. Carry a handkerchief on dates, because you never know when she'll cry. Never let her pay for dinner." I take a deep breath. "And she told him to make it easy for you."

Her mouth opens like she wants to say something but nothing comes out. She's speechless. She closes it tightly, pressing her lips together. "What else did she tell him?"

"Just normal stuff about dying," I tell her. It was soul-wrenching to watch. I'd finally had to leave the room so I wouldn't upset them both with my sobbing. I missed some things as a result.

"I don't know what to do with kids," she says.

"They don't really need much," I say. "Just for you to love them."

"I'm trying," she says.

I want to lay my hand on the back of her hair and smooth down the length of it. I bet it feels like silk.

"I, um, should have introduced you to my boyfriend," she says. "Do you want to meet him?"

I shake my head. I see him talking with Mr. Morgan. Skylar's dad doesn't look like he's impressed.

"When you, um, took my hand..." she says. "I should have told you."

"Why?" I look down at her. She comes up to my shoulder, even in her heels.

"I, um, didn't want you to get the wrong idea."

This time it's me raising my brows at her. "Why did you think I took your hand?"

Her face colors. "I'm not sure," she says.

I wrap my hand around her wrist and give her a soft squeeze. "I took your hand because you were trembling," I say. "That's all." She's trembling now, too, but I let her go.

"Oh," she breathes.

She has her phone clutched in her free hand, so I take it from her and add myself to her address book. "Do me a favor?" I say.

She looks up at me and then back down at the phone.

"Call me if you need anything. Anything at all. I promised their mom."

"Okay," she replies. "Thanks for everything." Her blue eyes meet mine, and I have never seen anyone look quite so lost. But then her eyes narrow as her gaze shoots past me. "Shit," she suddenly spits out.

"What?" I ask, looking over my shoulder toward the sedan that just pulled up.

"My mother is here," she says. She squares her shoulders, and I suddenly see a spark that wasn't there a moment ago. "Can you watch the children for a minute?" she asks.

"Why?"

"Just because," she says. She grits her teeth and looks up at me. "Promise me. No matter what, don't let her anywhere near the children."

What the fuck? I look back at the sedan. The door opens, and an older and much harsher version of Skylar gets out.

"Okay…" I say slowly. Skylar nods her head, steels her spine, and walks toward her mother.

The rigidity of her posture makes me think of my own mother's the time that Johnny Rickles stuck a "Kick me" note on my back and then watched all the other kids laugh. My mother went ballistic when she saw it. It's a look that says danger will have to go through her before it gets to the children, and I think I just met Seth, Mellie, and Joey's new mom for the very first time. Her name is Skylar Morgan, and she's tiny and gorgeous and awesome.

Skylar

I don't know why she's here, but I do know that she can't stay. Mom pushes the black-veiled hat from in front of her eyes and smiles at me. "Good afternoon, darling," she says, leaning forward just enough to not touch me as she places an air kiss near my cheek. Her breath reeks of scotch, and she sways a little on her feet.

"What are you doing here?" I hiss. I crowd my mother back toward the car until she's standing in the open door. Her driver looks uncomfortable, and I immediately feel sorry for him.

"I came to pay my respects, dear," she says. Her voice drips honey, but my mother has no sweetness about her.

"Get back in the car, Mother," I say. I make a hasty motion with my hand.

"This is no way to treat your mother," she says. Some of the sweetness has left her voice, but the mask isn't coming off. Not yet, anyway.

"Mother," I warn with a growl.

She heaves a sigh. "I just wanted to pay my respects," she says again.

"Send a card," I say.

She looks across the cemetery toward the grave, and her eyes narrow. "Are those the children?" she asks. Her face puckers as though she smells something bad.

"No," I say.

"Then be a dear and tell me which ones they are, darling," she says. "I want to meet them."

"No," I bite out.

"Rachel," my father clips out as he quickly strides toward us.

"Oh, hello," Mom chirps.

"Get in the car, Rachel," he says. He takes my mother by the elbow and shoves her inside.

"But—" she sputters. He closes the back door on her and addresses her driver, who stands at attention near the car.

"Drive," he says.

"Yes, sir," the man replies, and he slides into the driver's seat.

"I'll call you tomorrow," Dad says. "I need to get her out of here," he explains.

I nod. "Why did she even come here?" I ask, more to myself than to him.

"Because she is not in control of this part of my life," he grinds out.

I look up at Dad. "Do you ever wonder what your life would be like if you hadn't married Mother?" I blurt out. No idea where that came from.

He presses his lips to my forehead really quickly. "Never, because then I wouldn't have you."

My gut clenches, and my head spins. "What?"

"Skylar, I love you," he says. Then he slides into the car with Mother, and they pull out of the cemetery. I watch until their taillights fade in the distance.

"Everything all right?" a voice asks as it moves toward me. I look up and see Matthew Reed and four people who look remarkably like him.

"Fine," I say, my hand waving breezily in the air because I don't know what to do with it. "That was just my mother trying to insert herself somewhere she shouldn't."

Matt's eyes narrow, but he doesn't say anything. He points to the men next to him, introducing each in turn. "My brothers—Paul, Logan, Sam, and Pete." Each of them reaches to shake my hand. There are three women with them, too. "And this is Logan's wife, Emily, and you already know Reagan." I met Reagan by accident the day Kendra died. We shared a car ride.

The last one, a pretty, black-haired girl with tattoos up the side of her neck, steps forward, holding out her hand. "Friday," she says.

"It's Saturday," I say.

She laughs. "No, my name is Friday," she clarifies. She leans into the biggest of the brothers—I think his name is Paul, but there are so freaking many of them—and he wraps an arm around her shoulders. "I work with these big lugs in the tattoo parlor."

"Tattoo parlor?" I say. I must sound like a parrot because all I seem to be able to do is repeat what everyone else is saying.

"Reed's," Matt says. "We all work there."

"Oh," I breathe. I am usually so much more eloquent than this. At least I hope I am.

I look around the brothers and see Seth standing with his sisters. Each of them holds one of his hands. Everyone else has left the cemetery already. Have we been here that long?

Matt motions from one brother to another. "We were going to go and get a pie," he says. "We thought you might want to go with us."

New York pizza is one of my favorite foods. "I don't know," I hedge. Seth has walked closer with his sisters, so I look over at them. He looks hopeful. I haven't seen him look interested in anything at all, aside from his sisters' well-being, in a week now. I raise a brow, asking him what he'd like to do.

He nods. Then he looks away, almost like he's afraid to feel hopeful. He looks toward the casket being lowered into the ground.

"We'd love to join you," I say.

Joey looks up at Seth and asks, "Will Mommy come?"

Seth has been trying to tell the little ones all week that Mommy is gone, and they can't seem to grasp the concept of death. They keep expecting her to walk through the door.

"No," Seth says, and I see him swallow hard. "Mommy can't come."

"Maybe later," she says quietly, her face falling. He picks her up, and she puts her head on his shoulder. Mellie takes his hand, and we walk toward the funeral cars.

"Rico's is just a couple of blocks away," Matt explains, looking at the car like it's going to bite him. "Do you want to meet us there?"

"We'll walk with you," Seth says, and they all start in the direction of the pizza parlor. I look around, thinking I'll see Phillip, my boyfriend, but he must have left. That doesn't surprise me, not in the least. I pull out my phone and send him a quick text message.

Me: *Where are you?*

I shove my phone back in my pocket.

We all fall into a line, with me and Matt walking side by side at the back end of it.

"How are things going?" he asks.

"Terrible," I admit, and I feel the dreaded tears sting my eyes. Matt pulls out a handkerchief and offers it to me. I take it and dab at my eyes. "It's just hard. The kids don't know me, and Seth's not really interested in letting me get to know the little ones. He won't even let me read them a bedtime story. He cooks, he cleans, he does laundry, he does everything, and I have never felt more useless in my life." I look up and realize Matt's listening. He's really, really listening.

"Seth has been taking care of his sisters for a really long time," Matt says softly. "He's used to doing it all by himself. He did it when his mom was in chemo. And he did it all through her treatments. It's normal for him. He doesn't mind it because it's what he knows."

"The little ones keep asking when she's coming back, like she's on vacation or at the office." My throat is so thick that I feel like I'm going to choke.

He winces. "That's got to be tough," he says.

"I just wish I knew what to do from here," I admit. I have no idea how to be a mom. I don't know what to do for fevers, and I can barely change a diaper. Thank God the littlest one is almost potty trained. Although I am learning diapering out of sheer necessity. You put one on crooked, and you're screwed.

"Are you going to keep them?" he asks.

"I don't know what I'm going to do," I admit. "I just don't know. I don't have to go back to work just yet. They're letting me work from home. Well, not my home—Kendra's home."

"You're still staying there?" he asks.

I nod. "For now. I thought it would be better for them to have someplace familiar, surrounded by their toys, their own beds, and even their mom's things. At least for the moment."

Matt takes my elbow in his grip and stops. "Skylar," he says.

"What?" I look into his blue eyes and am almost startled at the intensity of his gaze.

"Can you love them? Really love them? Because there's no shame in admitting you don't want them or can't take care of them. They deserve better."

"They do deserve better than me," I whisper. "But I'm all they have." I snort, just because I can't help it. "Honestly, Matt," I say, "I can't even keep a houseplant alive. What am I thinking?"

He brushes a lock of hair from my forehead. "Do you want to know what I think?" he asks.

"What?" I breathe. We're in the middle of a crowded street, but I have never felt quite so separated from the rest of the world.

"I think you can do it. I have faith in you."

"Why?" I ask. "You don't even know me."

"Because you care," he says. "That's all kids need. For someone to care."

"Do you have kids?" I ask.

He shakes his head as a veil falls over his eyes. "No. Can I borrow yours sometimes?"

I laugh. "Kind of like a cup of sugar?"

He shakes his head. "I wouldn't bring the cup of sugar back. The kids on the other hand…" He raises and lowers his hands like he's weighing his words.

I laugh.

"I can't have kids," he says. "Or at least the chances are slim." He puts up a hand when I open my mouth to ask a question. I know he had cancer, but I don't know what kind or what his prognosis is. "Not being able to have something really has a tendency to make you want it more." He points to Seth's back. "See, you got three at once, and I can't even have one." He chuckles and nudges my shoulder with his. He keeps walking, and I stay beside him. "How does your boyfriend feel about them?" he asks.

I shrug my shoulders. "We haven't really discussed it."

"Don't you think you should?" His brow furrows as he looks down at me.

"That's complicated."

Matt takes in a deep breath. "I have a confession to make," he says. "Do you want to hear it?"

"Of course."

"In the church, when I took your hand, it wasn't just because you were trembling."

My heart lurches, but now we've arrived at the restaurant. He ushers me through the door with a hand at the small of my back, and the time for small talk is over. Crap.

Matt

My brothers are pigs. I have known this for a long time, but it's never more evident than when they're all in one place. And in public. Sam and Pete are having an arm wrestling match in the middle of the table while we wait for the waitress to bring the check. Mellie and Joey have fallen asleep. They're draped across Seth at angles that don't look remotely comfortable, but I think he's used to his sisters being all up in his space. His hand trails down Mellie's back absently, and he looks down at her fondly, his smile soft. I go and sit down next to him.

"How's it going, Seth?" I ask.

He shrugs and looks everywhere but at me. "Fine," he says.

I nod and wait a moment. I'm pretty sure no one is paying us any mind, so I say what's in my heart. "I remember when my mom died. People kept asking me if I was okay, and I told them I was, but I really wasn't. Not even close."

His gaze jerks to meet mine. "Your mom died?"

I nod. I hate talking about Mom because then I have to talk about Dad, too. "My mom died. I was a little younger than you. Then not long after that, our dad left, too." I sweep my hand toward my brothers. "Then it was just the five of us."

Seth heaves a sigh. "Sucks," he grunts out. Then he lets his head fall back, and I finally see it. I see some of the exhaustion.

"Sucks ass," I reply. "But all you can do is play the cards you're dealt." I point toward Skylar, where she's talking with Reagan, Emily, and Friday. She's so damn pretty when she smiles that she takes my breath away. But if there was ever a woman who was out of my league, it's Skylar Morgan. "How are things going with your aunt?" I ask.

"Fine," he clips out. He looks at her, but there's more curiosity than fondness.

"You getting to know her?"

He shrugs.

"You should let her help you some," I suggest. "She mentioned that she's feeling a little left out."

His gaze shoots up to mine again. "She did?"

I nod. "Do you hope she'll just hang around until you don't need her anymore?"

"I don't need her now."

"You can't do it all by yourself, Seth. No one can."

He points to his chest. "I can."

"You're sixteen years old."

His face clouds, and it's honestly the most emotion I have ever seen on the kid's face. "I know how old I am. I also know that I promised my mom I'd take care of them."

"Would it hurt to accept some help?" I ask. I nudge his shoulder. "When does wrestling start?"

"Next week, but I'm not going out for it." His brow furrows. "I don't have time."

"How much time do you need?"

He sighs heavily. "It's two hours every day after school. Matches on the weekends and one night a week. Mellie and Joey are already in day care all day. I can't put them with a babysitter, too."

"You don't have to put them with a babysitter. Leave them with their aunt." I point toward Skylar, and she catches me, her eyes narrowing. I shake my head at her. She gets it, but she's still curious. "She's their legal guardian, Seth. Not you."

His voice is quiet when he speaks, so quiet that I can barely hear him, but I make out the words. "I'm afraid if I ask her for too much, she's going to leave. Then we'll all go to foster homes and be split up. No one else wants us." His jaw ticks as he clenches his teeth. "Do you know they asked my dad to take all of us?"

I didn't know that. "And?"

"And he said he'd take me, but he wouldn't take Mellie and Joey." He looks down at them, his gaze softening, but he's still angry. "Can you believe that? He'd give them to someone else. Anyone else. My mom would shit a brick if she knew." He shakes his head. "Sucks."

"Sucks ass," I say again.

Seth grins. "Sucks ass," he repeats.

Pete walks in front of me, and I reach out and shove his hip. He looks down at me. "Are you guys talking about my ass?" he asks. He looks down at his butt, making a big deal of it. "I mean, damn, I know it's pretty, but still."

I place my shoe on his butt and kick him to the side. He walks over and hides behind Reagan. "Look what he did, princess," he says. "He kicked me." He wraps his arms around her and says, "Go kick his ass for me, will you?" He shoves her in my direction. Everyone knows that Reagan is a martial arts expert and she's flipped me over her shoulder more than once in practice situations.

I hold up my hands in surrender. "Please don't," I say. "I had cancer," I remind the crowd. I still get brownie points.

Reagan laughs. "You can't pull the cancer card anymore," she says. "Two years with a clean bill of health." She holds up two fingers. "Remember, we had a party to celebrate?" She flops down beside me, and I put my arm around her and pull her over to kiss her forehead. There was a time when she couldn't have been in a crowded room without being anxious and nervous, but she's not like that now. Not since her attacker was caught and put in jail. He died there, so she didn't have to face him in court. Reagan is much more self-assured, now that the mess is behind her. Sure, some things still get to her, but most of the time, she's just Reagan. She's Pete's girl and part of the family.

I notice they're all getting to their feet. "Did you guys pay the bill?" I ask.

Paul nods. Skylar is trying to push money at him, but he refuses. I have to remind myself to pay him for their part of dinner later. She protests, but he ignores her, just like he should. She huffs and shoves the money into her purse.

"Thank you for inviting us," she says. She goes to Seth and starts to take Mellie from him, but I reach around her and pick up the sleeping girl instead. Mellie wraps her arms around my neck and her legs around my waist, and she clings to me like she's a Velcro monkey. My heart stutters a little. I like this feeling. I like it a lot, and my heart aches because I will never have this.

"I can take her," Skylar says, holding out her hands.

"I got her," I say, and Seth stands up with Joey wrapped around him. I hitch Mellie a little higher, and she makes a snuffling noise against my neck. I don't have any desire to put her down.

"We'll see you at home?" Paul asks, shooting me a questioning glance.

I nod. He rushes all our brothers out the door as Reagan, Emily, and Friday say good-bye to Skylar. I hear some murmured words about calling them if she needs help, and she smiles at them and goes in for a round of hugs. We step out onto the sidewalk, and she says to me, "I can carry her. The apartment's not far." She raises her hands again, and I turn my body away, blocking her.

"I'll carry her home," I say. I would feel like a heel if I let her, and she would never be able to carry Mellie all the way in those heels she's wearing, anyway. And secretly I'm glad I've got the opportunity to spend some time with the kids.

She lets us into the apartment, and Seth walks toward the room the girls share, if the two beds are any indication. He pulls the covers back and drops Joey onto the sheets. He pulls her coat off and tosses her shoes to the side, and then pulls the covers up over her. I do the same with Mellie, and I'm glad they didn't have to take baths or change into jammies, because they're not related to me and I wouldn't know what to do with that.

"Thanks for the help," Seth says quietly.

"Anytime," I reply. He turns to walk out of the room, but I grab his shoulder. "Seth," I say. "You're not alone, kid."

He looks into my face. "I know," he replies softly. "Good night." He turns out Mellie and Joey's light and pulls the door closed behind us.

"'Night," I say.

I blow out a heavy breath as I walk back out to the living room. Seth disappears into his room without even a comment toward Skylar.

I jerk my thumb toward Seth's room. "You always get the silent treatment from him?" I ask. Makes me want to jerk a knot in his ass, but he's not mine. And I don't think he's doing it to be disrespectful. I think he's doing it to ease her burden to a point where it's nonexistent. I don't know if I should jack him up or give him a medal.

She shrugs. "I don't mind." But her voice is small. "The girls all tucked in?" she asks.

"Yeah," I say. I follow her to the kitchen. I would like to say it's just so that I can talk to her, but it's kind of because I like the view of her ass. She's kicked her heels off and is padding around in her stockings. I wonder if they're thigh-highs with one of those little garter belt things. I swipe a hand down my face, trying to wipe my thoughts away. She has a boyfriend.

Skylar pulls a bottle of wine from the fridge and pours a glass. "Have some?" she asks.

I'm not really a wine drinker. "No, thanks."

Her eyes narrow, and she reaches into the fridge and pulls out a beer.

"Now that I will take," I say with a laugh.

"Kendra must have liked beer," she says. "That was in the fridge." She holds up her glass. "Do moms drink wine?" she asks.

"Mine did," I say. I follow her into the living room and sit down on one end of the couch. She sits on the other.

"Was your mom a good mom?" she asks.

"The best."

"Lucky you," she says with a noise from the back of her throat. "I was raised by nannies and cooks and housekeepers. A constant rotation of them." She lays her head on the back of the couch and looks up at the ceiling for a moment. Then she drains the last of the wine in her glass and sets it on the side table. She yawns, covering her mouth delicately. "Sorry," she says. "Long week." She smiles, and my breath catches until I remember it's supposed to go in and out.

"I should go," I say.

"You don't have to leave," she says. "It's nice to have someone to talk to."

I settle back again. I don't want to leave. I like this quiet silence with her, and I don't know why. "Do you want some unsolicited advice?" I ask.

She snorts. And it's so damn cute that I can't keep from grinning. "I'll take all the advice I can get."

"Tell Seth he should go out for wrestling."

Her eyebrows shoot up. "Wrestling?" she asks.

I nod. "He loves the sport. He was a regional champ last year."

She sits up a little. "When does it start?" she asks.

"Next week."

"Why didn't he tell me?"

"Umm…" I don't know how much to tell her. "He's afraid that if he gives you too much work to do, you'll leave them, and then the state will put his sisters in foster care."

She growls and sits forward. "And you got all that from him at dinner?"

I nod and raise my beer to my lips. "I've known them longer," I say.

"How long did you and Kendra date?" she asks.

I choke on my beer. I cough into my closed fist for a minute. "What?"

"You and Kendra," she says again. "How long had you been going out?"

"Oh, we weren't like that," I rush to say. "We were just friends."

"Oh," she says. Then silence settles over the room. Finally she says, "So, wrestling, huh? Isn't that a little barbaric?"

I smile. "Nope. It's all strategy and strength and conditioning. It's good for him."

"What if he gets hurt?"

"He's a boy. He's going to get hurt."

"You have all the answers, don't you?" she says.

Unfortunately, I don't have any answers. About anything. "If he wrestles, he'd have to go straight there after school every day. That might give you some time to get to know Mellie and Joey when you pick them up."

She nods. "Sounds like a plan."

"Everyone needs a plan," I say with a grin. She smiles, and I feel this little flutter in my heart.

I hear a door open behind us, and Seth comes out of his room. He looks over at us, his gaze shooting from Skylar to me and back. "Everything okay?" he asks.

Skylar sits up and rests her elbows on her knees. "Matt was just telling me about wrestling," she says.

Seth groans and throws his head back, sending me a look like he wishes I had kept my mouth shut.

"I think you should sign up," she says. Her voice quivers a little.

"What about the girls?" he asks.

"What about them?" she replies. "I'll just start picking them up every day."

Seth scratches his head. "You're okay with that?"

She nods and smiles at him. "I'm fine with it."

Seth smiles at her, too. "Okay," he says.

"Will you let me know when your games are so I can come watch?" she asks.

"Matches," Seth and I both say at the same time.

She laughs and holds up both hands in surrender. "Matches," she repeats. "Sorry," she says, but she's laughing, too. "So, can I go to your matches?" she asks.

Seth nods. "Sure." He looks toward the kitchen like he wants to get free. "I'm just going to get some water and go to bed," he says.

"Good night," Skylar calls.

He looks back over his shoulder and says quietly, "'Night, Aunt Sky."

He walks away, and I look over at Skylar, only she looks a little shell-shocked. Like a stiff wind could blow her over. "You okay?" I ask.

She laughs and shakes her head. "Did you hear that?" she asks.

"He's going to wrestle?" I'm slightly baffled.

"No," she says quietly. "He called me Aunt Sky." Her eyes are a little misty, I realize, so I squeeze her knee. She covers my hand with hers and looks up at me. Her gaze shoots straight to the center of me. "Thanks for your help." Suddenly, her phone chirps from her pocket, and she lets my hand go to reach for it. "My boyfriend," she says. She doesn't look very happy to be hearing from him.

"I should go." *She has a fucking boyfriend, numbnuts,* I remind myself. I get to my feet and throw my beer bottle in the recycling bin. She follows me to the door. "Call me if you need anything?" I suggest. *Or if you don't need anything,* I want to add, but I don't.

She leans heavily against the edge of the door. "I will," she says. And I believe her. I just hope something goes dreadfully wrong so she'll actually call me. No loss of life or limb or anything drastic. Maybe a leaky sink or a stopped-up toilet. "'Night," she says.

"'Night," I reply. She closes the door, and I stand there for a moment because I can't think of anywhere I'd rather be.

The door suddenly opens, and Sky sticks her head out. She bumps into my chest, and I steady her by grabbing her elbows. I try to wipe the grin off my face, but it's almost impossible. "Did you need something else?" I ask over a laugh.

"You're still here," she says against my chest. The heat of her breath does funny things to my insides. And the rest of me. "I wanted to ask you something," she says, her voice all breathy.

She leans a shoulder in the doorway and looks up at me, her eyes so blue and clear that I could fall into them and stay there. She bites her lower lip between her teeth and then says in one big rush, "You mentioned when we were walking into the restaurant that you didn't take my hand just because it was trembling. I was wondering…um…why else you might do that."

I reach up and tug the length of leather that was holding my hair back and let it fall around my face. Then I make a big production of tying it back up, but I really just want to buy myself some time to figure out how to answer her. I grin. "I did mention that wasn't the only reason, didn't I?" I ask, still stalling.

She nods, still worrying that lower lip. Her cheeks are rosy, and her eyes are bright.

I don't know the right way to respond, so instead I bend down and kiss her cheek. I linger, letting her breath blow across my shoulder as I take in the scent of her. It's clean and girly, with a hint of citrus, and so damn breathtaking that I can barely stop sniffing her. I take one last inhale and whisper, "I did it because I like you." She shivers lightly, and I see the hair on her arms stand up. I force myself to walk away. It takes everything I have in me not to turn around and look at her again. But I don't. I keep walking.

###

I let myself into our apartment and stop short when I see someone sitting on the couch talking to Paul. My brother gets up, looking uncomfortable as hell. "Look who dropped by," Paul says, pointing toward our guest. My euphoria ends immediately. All the good thoughts I had when I left Sky are suddenly dashed against the wall that is treachery and deceit.

His name is Kenneth, and he used to be my best friend. Right up until the moment that he fucked my fiancée, April. "Ken," I bite out. "What the fuck are you doing here?" I ask.

Paul gets between us, like he could keep me off him if I really wanted a piece of him. Not hardly.

"Well," Ken says. "I...um...I was hoping we could talk." He looks toward Paul like he doesn't want to say anything in front of him.

Paul steps up beside me. "Do you want me to leave?"

I shrug. I can kick Ken's ass just as well with him in the room as I can with him out of it. "Do whatever you want," I say. I reach into the fridge and take out a beer, pop the top by resting it on the edge of the counter and slamming it. Then I flick the metal top toward the trash can. "Score," I whisper to the room as it shoots inside.

I go over to the couch and plop down on it, resting my feet on the coffee table as I start to channel surf.

"Call me if you need me," Paul says, and then he disappears into his room. Like I'd have to call him. He's going to have his ear glued to the door until Ken leaves.

Ken sits down on the couch across the room, his ass perched on the edge. He rests his elbows on his knees and leans toward me.

"Why are you here, Ken?" I ask. He may as well tell me so we can get this uncomfortable meeting over and done with.

"Well," he says. He stops and scratches the back of his head, running his hand up and down over and over. His discomfort makes me feel a little better about the whole situation, actually. I let him stew. "I wanted to tell you about the wedding," he says slowly, enunciating carefully.

I pretend nonchalance, although I feel anything but. "Who's getting married?" I ask.

He had better fucking not say him and April.

"Well, I asked April to marry me," he blurts out, looking even worse than a moment ago. He winces like he's afraid I'll hit him. Hell, I still might.

"Congratulations," I deadpan. I try not to put any feeling into my voice at all, because if I did, I would be yelling and screaming and crying out like a wounded bear, because I feel like someone just shoved a red-hot poker in my gut.

"I wanted to be the first to tell you," he says. "Considering the situation." He wrings his hands together.

"Considering the fact that you fucked my girlfriend," I say, then take the last swallow of my beer. That one might go to my head since I drank it so fast. But I really don't care.

"S-she was h-hurting," he stutters. "After your diagnosis and all, you know?" He looks at me like he's waiting for confirmation. I'll confirm that he's an ass. A lying, cheating, no-good, lame-ass best friend. "We kind of just fell together."

"You tripped and fell right in her pussy, did you?" He holds up a hand and starts to stutter, but I keep on talking, as though I don't care. "I completely understand. Happened to me a time or two. Probably the same nights it happened to you." I snort.

"Matt," he says. "I know I've told you I'm sorry before, but please know that we didn't intend for this to happen. We never wanted to hurt you."

I was hurt for a while, but now I'm beyond that. Pissed is a much better color on me than hurt. "How many times do you want me to congratulate you?" I ask.

He sighs. "I just didn't want you to hear it from anyone else," he says. "I handled things poorly, but I still have the utmost respect for you as a friend."

"Thanks," I bite out.

"Hey, I hear that you're in remission," he says. He smiles as if he's happy for me. "I'm so glad you're doing well."

"Thanks," I grunt. Apparently, I have turned into a caveman. A caveman who doesn't give a fuck.

He gets to his feet. "Well, I should probably go." He reaches out a hand toward me. It hangs there in the air between us until he finally gets the hint that I wouldn't touch him with a ten-fucking-foot pole.

"When's the wedding?" I ask as I stand up, too. I'm a glutton for punishment, apparently.

"Next weekend," he says.

I lift my brow and snort. "That soon, huh? You must have been planning it for a while."

He starts to scratch the back of his head again. "Um…not really. Well, we were planning it, but we decided to move the date up. Um…" He looks into my eyes like he's hoping to soften the blow. "April's pregnant."

My breath stutters from me. I close my eyes and inhale through my nose because I feel like I'm going to throw up. I force my eyes open and walk to the door. It's all I can do not to put my foot in his ass and kick him through it.

"Can…um… It's really important to April that we have your blessing."

"You didn't need my blessing when you fucked her," I say. "Why do you need it now that you knocked her up?"

"She feels terrible about the way things happened," he says.

"Good," I bite out. "She should." She should hate it. She should hate herself because she fell into someone's arms while I was getting shot full of chemo and almost fucking died.

"She's not a bad person," he says. "She just made a mistake. We both did."

"A mistake happens once," I explain, holding up one finger. "Not dozens of times." And those are only the ones I know about. "After the first time, it's a choice, not a mistake."

"She just didn't know how to deal with the situation."

"You mean like standing by my side?" I hold up my hands like I want him to answer. But I really don't. Not at all.

"I'd like us all to be friends again," he says. He's almost pleading. And it would make me laugh if it didn't make me want to cry.

"Never gonna happen," I say. I open the door and motion for him to walk through it. In two seconds, I'll start to count to ten.

He brightens for a second. "Hey, Paul was telling me you're seeing someone."

Paul did what? "So?"

"So, I think that's great. I'm happy for you." He claps a hand on my shoulder and squeezes until I stare down at it, contemplating how I'm going to break each of his fingers. He jerks his hand back. "I think you should bring her to the wedding. It'll be like old times. What do you say?"

I just glare at him.

"Well," he says, smiling as if he's solved world hunger in one night. "I'll be sure April sends you an invitation. We'd love for you to be there."

The little devil on my shoulder taunts me. "Hey, how did April feel about your fucking her best friend?" I ask. Rumors are fun, when they're not about you.

A muscle in his jaw ticks. "That was a mistake."

"You make a lot of those, don't you?" I ask.

"I'm human," he says. He hitches his waistband higher.

He's a human with no morals or conscience. Can't say April didn't get what she deserved with him, though.

"If you come to the wedding, I'd appreciate it if you didn't mention that best friend thing to her." He looks everywhere but at me. I point toward the hallway, and he goes in that direction.

I don't say anything more. He waves as he goes out the door, and I slam it behind him. It hits so hard that the walls vibrate. Paul comes out of his room.

I get another beer from the fridge and repeat my opening procedure, singing "Score!" in a vehement whisper when the top sails into the trash.

"You okay?" Paul asks.

"Fine," I bite out.

"You sure?"

"Yep."

"You don't look fine."

"Fuck you very much."

Paul heaves a sigh.

"How much did you hear?" I ask.

He winces. "All of it?"

I go and sit on the couch, not saying anything that's in my head. Truth be told, I would be tearing shit up if Paul wasn't here.

"I can't believe they want you to come to the wedding." He snorts.

"Why did you tell him I'm seeing someone?"

Paul grins. "Seemed appropriate at the time. Bastard was being all smug, telling me how wonderful his life is."

"So you made up an awesome life for me."

Paul shrugs. "Didn't seem like it would hurt."

It does fucking hurt. My life might be lonely, but it's mine. It's all I've got, and when you've come close to losing your life like I have, you appreciate every single thing about it.

"Are you going to the wedding?" Paul asks.

I shrug. "Don't know." I play with the tassels on a pillow, wrapping them around my finger over and over.

"Maybe it would be good closure," he says.

"It's already closed."

"It's not."

I lean toward him. "You want to talk about closure, Paul? Then let's talk about you and Kelly. Let's talk about the fact that you're still fucking your baby mama, even though you're both fucking other people, too. Let's talk about closure on that, shall we?"

Paul presses his lips together. Then he gets up and goes to his room, closing the door softly behind him. He doesn't punch me, which is what I deserve. He just walks away. I think I hit way too close to home.

My heart aches for what I just did to him. But it was the only way to get him to drop it.

Closure. Fuck closure. That wound is still open and festering and painful and raw and so damn irritating that I don't know what to do with it. Will it ever get better? I don't see how.

Skylar

I had just closed my eyes when my phone buzzes in my pocket. I never did hear back from Phillip after the funeral. He just left. But that's very much the way he is. He's there one minute and gone the next. And then gone for a really long time. I take my phone out and see his smiling face on the screen. Do I have to answer it? I mentally steel myself and pick up.

"Hello?"

"Skylar, hi," he says. I can almost see his toothy grin in my mind's eye, and it makes me cringe. It shouldn't be that way, should it?

"So nice of you to finally reply to me," I toss out.

I can hear the *click* of his dress shoes against the pavement. "Sorry about that. I had to get back to work. I'm just leaving the building now." I hear the slam of a door and imagine him getting into his Mercedes.

"Working late?" I ask.

"Yeah," he says very softly. He gets quiet for a moment and silence falls over the cell waves.

"So what's up with you?" I ask.

"Big case at work," he says.

"Oh, tell me about it."

"You know I can't."

"We both work for the same firm, Phillip, for God's sake."

"About that," he says.

I sit up. Phillip is a managing partner at my firm. He holds my future in his hands.

"We had a board meeting today to discuss your situation."

"Oh, really." I try not to add a *pffft* at the end of my comment, and almost succeed, but I feel like someone just jerked the air from me.

"We decided you need to take some family leave time to get things settled on your end."

I sit all the way up and cross my legs criss-cross-applesauce style. "I don't think that's your decision to make."

"I think it's in your best interest, Sky," he says softly. "You need to get settled with the kids, hire a nanny, decide where you're going to live…"

"Well, eventually, we'll live at my apartment. We're just here temporarily, while the kids adjust."

There's silence on the line.

"Why don't you just say what you want to say, Phillip?"

"I never signed on to be a dad, Sky," he says.

"I didn't exactly sign on to be a mom," I remind him.

"Yet you let your father talk you into this harebrained idea."

"It's not an *idea*. The kids don't have anyone else." I pull the phone back and stare down at it for a moment. "Are you breaking up with me? Over the kids?"

"I'm giving you time to figure things out," he says.

"I don't need time to figure things out."

He pauses. "I was going to tell you today, but you were busy with your mother."

"You were going to tell me at the funeral?" I screech. "Is that why you came?" I should have known it wasn't because he cared about me or my family.

"What are you going to do, Sky?" he finally snaps. "You're going to raise those children? Those kids who don't look anything like us? You're going to parade them around in public? You're going to take them to the Cape and on vacation and you're going to be their mom? Why don't you just hire a nanny, for Christ's sake? Your father has enough money."

I get up and start to pace back and forth across the floor. "I can't fucking believe this," I say. "I never took you for someone who gives a shit about race. When did you become this guy?"

"I'm the same guy I have always been!" he shouts at me. "You're the one who has changed. I want someone who can work by my side and play by my side and just *be* by my side. I don't want kids between us, particularly if they're not ours."

Silence falls again. I stop in front of the dresser to look into the mirror. There's a weird sense of peace on my face.

"It's not like we ever have sex anymore, anyway. We can't seem to find the time." He sounds like a four-year-old.

It has been a while.

"We're just not at the same place," he says.

"We're not talking about proximity," I spit back.

"Will you at least consider a nanny?" he asks.

I don't even need to think about it. I was raised by a constant parade of nannies, and I will not do that to these kids. I don't have a single person in my life who can sit with me and tell me stories about my childhood because *no one was there*. "No," I bite out.

"Why not? This isn't even your responsibility!" he shouts.

"I may not be their mom, but I'm their aunt. I'm their Aunt Sky, and I'm all they have. They don't have anyone else, and I know what that feels like. I will not leave them alone. I will be here for them, whenever they need me, for the rest of my life."

To tell the truth, I've been kind of brooding about my situation because I couldn't find my footing, but I have it now. It's solidly beneath me.

"I will teach Seth to drive, I will take Mellie to dance lessons, and Joey will do gymnastics." Okay, I sound like a lunatic now. "They can do or be whatever they want to be. Because they won't be alone." I point my finger at nothing and jab into the air with it. "They will never, ever be alone as long as I'm here. Do you understand me? Never!"

My voice is cracking, and I can't catch my breath. But I need for him to know how I feel about this. Sometimes I open the door to the girls' room and just watch them breathe as they sleep. It's really the only time I've been able to get close to them. "I didn't get to count their fingers and toes when they were born, but I can count them every day when they come home from school. I can be their Aunt Sky, and someday, when I've earned their trust and I'm lucky enough for them to love me, maybe, maybe then they'll want to be my family."

I want a family. I want those kids.

"Sky, think about what you're doing," he says. "You're emotional. You need to sit down and think this through. Don't do something you'll regret. Make a list of the pros and cons if you need to."

"Pro: they're amazing." I start to tick items off on my fingers, even though he can't see me. "Pro: if they'll let me love them, I'll be the happiest woman on the face of the earth. Furthermore, I'm not emotional. I'm perfectly rational."

He scoffs. "You don't sound rational."

I hold up another finger. "Pro: you've already dumped me, so now I can tell you that you're really lousy in bed, Phillip. Awful. You're selfish. If I never have to see your penis again, I'll be a happy, happy woman. Giddy, in fact."

"I'm not bad in bed…"

"You're selfish. And I almost never get to come, Phillip. You know this."

"I didn't," he mumbles.

"Never." I grin at myself in the mirror. "My pros are *far* outweighing my cons. I see orgasms in my future without you, Phillip. Lots of orgasms."

He hisses at me. "Con: people will look at you funny for the rest of your life when you parade those kids in public. They'll never see them as yours. They'll see them as some poor orphans you adopted. Or, even worse, they'll assume that you are their mom."

"That's not a con. It doesn't bother me that they're biracial. I love the color of their skin, their eyes, and their hair." Although I do need to learn how to make those little pom-pom knots for the girls.

The texture of their hair is a lot different than mine. "I love it because I love them."

"You just met them last week!" he yells.

"But I feel like my heart has known them forever." The sound of Mellie's laughter makes me soften. The look of pure surrender on Seth's face as he takes care of the girls makes me melt. And Joey, when she gets all dirty when she eats, I think it's adorable. "I love these kids. And I will fight with my dying breath to take care of them. So don't ever tell me that they're not good enough for my life. In fact, I think it's the other way around. I'm not good enough for them." Finally, a tear tracks down my face. I have a lot to learn, but I can do it. "But I will be."

"If your mind is made up," he clips out.

"Unequivocally," I toss back.

The line goes dead. And it's only then that I let myself crumble. I rest my palms on the dresser and put my weight on them, biting my lower lip as a sob racks me.

"Aunt Sky," I hear from the doorway.

I look up and swipe my fingertips beneath my eyes. "Seth," I say. God, I hope he didn't hear any of that.

"Are you all right?" he asks quietly. He walks into the room. I look away because I still want to cry.

Seth reaches out and wraps his arm around me, pulling me against him. He has me in a weird kind of headlock, but it feels nice. He holds me close to him. He's already inches taller than I am. I force myself not to sob but for a moment. "How much of that did you hear?" I ask as I pull back.

"I didn't hear anything about orgasms," he says with a grin. He swipes a hand over his mouth.

A chuckle erupts from me. "Well, that's good."

"And I didn't hear anything at all about Phillip's junk." He shudders.

"Even better." I look up at him. "I'm sorry you heard all that."

"I'm not," he says, and he suddenly looks like a young adult. "I'm glad I heard it."

"Well, I'm not. I'll try to be quieter next time."

He sits down on the edge of my bed. "I've been really worried," he admits.

I sit down beside him. "Me, too."

"But I'm thinking that since we don't have a mom and you don't have a family, we can make this work." He doesn't look at me, and I sense a little tremor in his voice.

"I think we can make it work, too."

He puts his arm around my shoulders. "I have one question for you."

I assume he wants my resume, which is wholly inadequate, particularly since Phillip thinks he just put me on leave. It will be a cold day in hell... "What?" I ask.

"Did you mean it when you said you wanted to teach me to drive?" He grins at me.

I laugh. It feels good to laugh with Seth. "Yeah, I meant it." I bump his shoulder with mine. "Our groundskeeper taught me."

"That's sad," he says, his eyes narrowing.

"Yeah." I nod. "It kind of is."

Matt

I wake up the next morning knowing that I have to apologize to Paul. I was way out of line last night, and I can't just let it go. I wait around for him to wake up. He usually goes to the tattoo parlor before I do, but his bedroom door is still closed. He doesn't have Hayley, his five-year-old daughter, this week. She's with Kelly, her mom. He sometimes sleeps in when he doesn't have to get up with her. She rises with the sun, and although it's a-fucking-dorable to see her padding around in her jammies, a man needs some sleep sometimes. We work really late at the shop, so we don't always get eight hours.

Looks like Paul is making up for lost time.

Logan lives with Emily, Pete lives with Reagan, and Sam went back to college late last night on the bus, so it's just Paul and me in the apartment now. It seems quiet. Too quiet sometimes. I'm used to the TV blaring because Logan doesn't know it's turned up too loud—he's deaf—and Sam and Pete, the twins, throwing one another all over the furniture. Now it's just me and Paul, two old guys, and a whole lot of quiet. I don't think I like it.

I hear Paul's door open and then the splash of him going to the bathroom. We're guys. We don't have to close the door when there are no girls here. He comes into the kitchen then, his blond hair sticking out in one hundred different directions, and he scratches his belly, his flannel pajama bottoms showing off the tattoo of Kelly's name. I am well acquainted with it, since I put it on him. And it's a damn fine tattoo, if I do say so myself. Me, I don't have any women's names on me anywhere, and I'm pretty sure I never will.

"'Morning," Paul mutters, pouring himself a cup of coffee.

"'Morning," I say back. I open the paper and stare down at it, but I can't see the words on the page. I can feel Paul's need to dump his bowl of Honey Graham Oh's over my head. Hell, I deserve it.

"Sorry about last night," I mutter.

He doesn't look up from his cereal. "Don't worry about it."

"I was an ass."

"I should have kept my mouth shut."

"I should have agreed with you. You were right. It's not done."

He talks around a mouthful of food. "If it was done, you wouldn't have been acting like that dickwad punched you in the gut."

"Yeah."

"What does she see in him?" he asks.

"He wasn't dying?" I guess.

He finally looks up at me. "No excuse."

No, there's no excuse to cheat.

"And you were right about me and Kelly." He keeps eating, not looking up at me.

"I don't want to be right about that."

"Too bad. I didn't know you guys knew that we still do that."

I shake my head. "Nobody knows but me."

"I hope we aren't too obvious." He winces.

"No, I saw you two together when Logan was in the hospital. The way she looks at you…" I watch his face. "And the way you look at her."

He finally lifts his gaze. "We just keep falling into bed together. That's all." He shrugs. He looks really uncomfortable, and that's not usually how I think of Paul. "It's easy. And comfortable."

I wouldn't know what that's like. I laugh to myself.

"What?" he asks.

"You talk about sex with Kelly like it's your foot sliding into an old shoe."

He snuffles.

"But just like an old shoe, exes can be comfortable but fail to support you the way you need."

"Ding, ding, ding," he cries, like he's ringing a bell in the air.

"Huh?" I have no idea what he's talking about.

"Did I ever tell you why we split up?"

He never did, but I have a pretty good idea. I shake my head anyway.

"She didn't want you guys."

"What?" Now that was the last thing I expected.

"She was pregnant with Hayley, and I was almost twenty-one. Mom and Dad were gone, and she didn't want you guys. I wanted to marry her. But she didn't want my family."

"She made you choose?"

He gets up and slams his bowl into the sink a little too hard. "There wasn't a fucking choice. You guys were my life, and I was all you had. No choice."

Paul stepped into fatherhood the way some people step into college, into a job after school. He gave it everything he had. We're only a year apart, but I never could have done what he did. He gave up everything, even his own happily ever after, for us. God. Now I feel awful. We ruined his life.

"I couldn't have raised them without you," he says. "Where I was weak, you were strong. And where I was strong, you were weak." He's right. We did complement each other.

"You gave up full time with Hayley for us." Now I'm pissed.

"I am Hayley's father, and I always will be. I have her half the time, and it works out well for the two of us."

It does. It really does.

"What about now that they're all out of the house?"

"What about it?"

"Now that everyone is taken care of, why don't you take care of yourself? Go get yourself a real life. You and Kelly keep falling together. Why not make it permanent?"

He shakes his head. "I don't love her."

"But—"

"I like her. We're friends. But that's it." He shrugs. "And she's seeing someone. It's getting pretty serious."

"When was the last time you guys…?"

He grins. "Yesterday."

I roll my eyes. "Then it can't be very serious with this other guy."

"Just the fact that there's another guy means it's not serious with me." He heaves a sigh. "And I don't love her. That's one thing I'm sure of. Because the thought of the woman I love sleeping with another man should tear me up inside, but it doesn't. There's something wrong with that."

"Okay." I don't know what else to say to him.

"So, about April," he says.

"I don't want to talk about April."

He glares at me. "Too bad."

This is Paul. This is what he does. "What do you suggest?"

"She's getting married, man. It's time to get over her."

I throw up my hands. "I'm trying."

"You should go to the wedding. Get it all out of your system. Take a hot chick with you."

"Where am I going to get one of those?"

He looks at me like I've gone apeshit. "Dude, you can find tail anywhere."

Maybe I've been looking in the wrong places.

Skylar

I spend all day Monday working out my employment issues. I had a meeting with my immediate supervisor, who rushed to assure me that my job was not in jeopardy, that my situation was discussed during the meeting, but only to the extent that they all wanted to know if there was anything they could do to support me through this transition. What an asshat Phillip is. And what's worse is that I almost believed him.

I couldn't be happier that this situation forced me to cut my ties with him, particularly when I walk around the corner and find him by the water cooler, standing much too close to another one of the first-years. She looks a little frazzled when she sees me, and she very quickly walks in the other direction.

Phillip starts toward me but I wave him away. "Don't even think about it," I warn. I keep walking.

He follows me all the way to my car without saying a word. He doesn't speak until after he watches me fumble with a box of papers and my trunk. He doesn't offer to help me. Not once. Would Matt stand there and watch me while I struggled with a box? Something tells me he wouldn't. I really shouldn't compare anyone to Matt, though, since I truly don't know him.

"You're going through with it, aren't you?" Phillip asks, folding his arms across his chest.

"Going through with what?" I ask, blowing my hair from my face.

"Those kids," he spits out. "You're keeping them."

I laugh. "They're keeping me, actually," I say.

"I never took you for stupid."

I snort. His face turns red. "The only stupid thing I ever did was pick you. Asshole," I say under my breath as I get in my car. I pull out while he stands there watching me. It's all I can do not to put the window down and stick my middle finger out to flip him off. But I'm a mom now. Moms don't make public spectacles of themselves, do they? Probably not. I settle for doing it in my head. It'll do for now, too, because he looks pissed.

I turn the radio up loud as I drive across town. I should feel bad about our breakup, but I'm not heavyhearted. Not at all. Not like I should be. I actually feel free. And I have to admit that I feel a little bit hopeful. I have a feeling Matthew Reed has something to do with that.

Heck, I just broke up with someone I thought I was in love with. I shouldn't be having feelings for Matt. It's too soon. Plus, I have too much going on in my life to add a new boyfriend to it. What man in his right mind would want me and my three kids? I snort to myself as I walk into the day care to get the girls. One of the other moms scrunches her nose up at me and ushers her kid by me quickly, taking a wide berth. I guess moms aren't supposed to snort out loud, either.

Seth told Joey and Mellie that I would be picking them up from school today, but I'm not completely sure they know what's going on when I walk in the door. Joey hides behind her teacher's skirt, and Mellie sticks her thumb in her mouth. I drop down to their level and say, "Hi, girls," with a soft voice. A soft voice won't scare them, will it? Crap. I am terrible at this mom stuff.

"Mrs. Morgan?" the teacher asks. I called her last week and talked with her on the phone about our situation. She was very nice and really understanding.

I stick out my hand. "Miss," I say to correct her. I'm definitely not married, and it doesn't look like I ever will be now.

She shakes my hand and steps to the side to get Joey out from behind her. Both the girls are still in day care, and they combine the classes at the end of the day on the playground. The girls apparently stick to one another like glue. Is that normal? Heck, normal is just a setting on the dryer, right? I wouldn't know normal if it bit me on the butt.

"Miss Morgan, if I can make a suggestion…" The teacher grimaces.

I look up at her. Joey and Mellie still aren't coming toward me. I live in the same house with them. Joey pulls on her teacher's skirt and says quietly, "Is my mommy coming to get me?"

Pain slices through me. I don't know how to explain death to the little ones. Seth doesn't either, apparently.

The teacher squats down and says, "Now, we talked about this, didn't we, Josephine?"

Heck, I didn't even know that Joey's real name is Josephine. What kind of a mother am I?

Joey just blinks up at her.

"Mommy's gone, and she's not coming back," the teacher says.

Joey's eyes fill with tears, and I step around the teacher to pick her up. She comes to me, heavy and limp like a wet dishrag when I lift her. She lays her head on my shoulder and snuggles in. "I'd appreciate it if you didn't discuss their mother with them," I bite out. I'm sure the teacher has good intentions. But, God, she was a little cold, in my opinion.

"They need to understand that she's gone," the teacher says.

I hold up a finger. "Shh," I hiss in a crisp warning. The teacher purses her lips.

"Mommy wouldn't leave," Mellie says. She comes forward and takes my hand, her fingers wet from where they were just stuck in her mouth, but I don't care. She's touching me of her own free will. It's me and the girls against the world.

"That's right," I say to her. "Mommy would never leave you on purpose."

"Don't give them hope that she's coming back," the teacher warns.

"Shh," I slice out again.

She stops talking.

"Mommy can't come back," I explain. "Mommy didn't want to go, but she didn't have a choice."

"Mommy will be back," Mellie says quietly.

"Mommy loved you both so much," I tell them.

"Both the girls need new clothes," the teacher interjects.

I turn back to face her. "What?"

"Seth had been taking care of them for quite some time, so I didn't say anything, but their clothes are getting too small. Mellie's shoes are too tight, and Joey's pants are about four inches too short. Children grow, Miss Morgan. A lot."

I bite my tongue because I can't think of anything nice to say, and I have been a lawyer long enough to know that no response is probably better than saying what's on my mind. Because what's on my mind is that I want her to take a long walk off a short pier.

When did I become such a barbarian?

"Thank you for letting me know. I'll take care of them," I say instead. "I appreciate it." They do have to come back here tomorrow, after all.

I look down at the girls. "Who wants to go shopping?" I ask.

Mellie looks up and smiles. "Me," she says. And I hear a softly whispered "Me" from right beside my ear.

Matt

It's around seven in the evening when my phone rings. I'm outlining a tattoo on a client at Reed's, so I can't answer it. Friday walks over and motions toward my pocket. "Do you want me to get that?" she asks.

I lift my gun and stand up so she can get in my pocket. "Please," I say.

"Better be careful or Paul's going to get jealous," she teases as she fishes around in my pocket.

Paul makes a noise. He's been trying to get her in his pockets for as long as I can remember. "I think he's already green with envy," I say loudly.

"If green is the new red," she tosses back. She pulls my phone out and puts it to her ear. We didn't carry phones for a long time because we simply couldn't afford it. But last Christmas, Emily's dad bought us all new phones, since he has more money than God and nothing better to do with it. He said we were too hard to keep up with without them. But I think it was more Emily's doing than his.

"Matt's phone," she chirps. "Hey, Seth," she says, her face scrunching up. "Yeah, he's here, hang on." She presses the "speaker" button on the phone.

"What's up, Seth?" I ask.

"Matt?" Seth asks, and he sounds a little breathless.

"What's wrong, Seth?" I ask. I set my gun down and start to pull off my gloves.

"Have you talked to Aunt Sky today?" he asks.

"No," I reply, the hair on the back of my neck immediately standing up. "Why?"

"Today was the first day she was supposed to pick up the girls, and I just got home and no one is here. It's getting late, is all."

"I haven't talked to her," I say. "Do you want me to come over?" I'm already making my way to the front door and Pete is taking over with my client.

"Call us if you need us," Paul says to my back. Like he has to remind me. With a glance over my shoulder, I wave at him, and he nods.

"Did you call her phone?" I ask.

"Yeah, but it's going directly to voice mail. And the texts I sent say delivered but not read."

"Her battery is probably dead, Seth," I say. I'm not worried at all. Well, maybe a little.

"She should have called to tell me where she is," he murmurs, and I can imagine him scruffing his hair in frustration.

"She probably thought you wouldn't be home yet," I say. "I'm on the way to keep you company. You feel like a pizza?" Teenage boys always feel like pizza.

###

I stop to order a couple of pies at Rico's really quickly, and take them with me. When I get to the apartment, I see Sky unloading the girls from the car in front of the apartment. She's found a spot and is ushering them along. She has bags and bags of stuff in her hands.

"Need some help?" I ask.

She looks up and blows her hair from her face with an upturned breath. "Matt," she says, but a pleasant smile tips the corners of her lips, and it's enough to take my breath away. *She has a boyfriend, asshole. Don't get any ideas.* "What are you doing here?"

I grin, because it's how I'm feeling inside. "Seth called me freaking out when you weren't home," I admit.

Her face falls. "Oh," she says. She frowns. "Why would he do that?"

I shrug. "He was worried."

She slams the door of the car, even though there are still more bags in there.

I look through her window. "Let me help with those."

She shakes her head. "I'll come and get them later," she says. "After I calm Seth down, apparently." She looks ruefully at me. She holds up the bags. "We went shopping."

"I can tell," I say. I motion toward Mellie and crouch down. She climbs onto my back and holds on tightly. I stand up and swing her around the way I would my niece, and she squeals and laughs. I still have pizzas in one hand, so I set them on top of the car.

"Do me," Joey cries, clinging to my leg.

I scoop Joey up too and spin them both in circles.

Sky laughs. "I think they like you," she says quietly. There's a look of longing on her face.

I jostle them both. "Yeah, they like me." They both squeal as I spin them around again. "I mean, really," I tease. "What's not to like?" I arch my brow at her, joking with her like I would with a woman I might be interested in. But there hasn't been one of those in a long time.

Her face colors, and she's so damn pretty. But she doesn't say anything. Her eyes travel, though, from the top of my head to the tips of my feet, staying in some places longer than others. Is that interest I see in her eyes? She licks her lips and looks away.

"Careful," I warn quietly.

She shakes her head, like she wants me to shut up. So I do. For now.

I follow her into the building, with the girls still clinging to me since I'm holding on to them and the pizzas, and they're still squealing when I walk through the door of the apartment with them.

"Look what I found," I say loudly as we step into the kitchen. Seth spins around, his face hard, and he starts to open his mouth. I can just imagine what's about to come out, so I cut him off. "Your Aunt Sky was nice enough to take the girls shopping this afternoon," I say. I meet his eyes and give him a subtle warning to keep his trap shut.

He glares at me and leans around me to say to Sky, "You could have called so I wouldn't worry."

"I didn't think you'd be home yet." She glances at her watch. "I didn't mean to worry you, Seth," she says. She's sincere. And knows she worried him needlessly. "I'm sorry about that," she says quietly.

I give Seth a look, and he heaves a sigh. He walks to her and wraps her up in a weird hug, like the ones I've seen him give his mom a hundred times. He picks her up off the ground a little. "I was worried about you, too," he explains.

She smiles, and it's beautiful. "Thanks," she says. "My phone is dead, too. I'll be sure to keep a charger in my car from now on. I'm not used to having to check in." She starts to put bags down. "I took the girls shopping for some new clothes," she says. She looks up at Seth. "I hope that's okay."

He looks a little chagrined. "That teacher of theirs has been harping about their clothes for a week."

"Girls," she calls. "Come and show Seth what you got while I go unload the rest."

Seth looks up at me and then down at the many bags that are scattered all over the place. "There's more?" he asks.

I grin and swipe a hand down my face. I saw all the shit that was in the back of her car. "Lots more," I say. Sky walks toward the door, so I jerk a thumb in her direction. "I'm going to help your aunt," I say.

He grins at me. "Helping? Is that what they're calling it now?"

Sky is already out the door, and I really want to go with her. "She has a boyfriend," I say.

He shakes his head. "Not anymore. He dumped her yesterday. It wasn't pretty."

So she doesn't have a boyfriend? My heart leaps. Hot damn. "Did she cry a lot?"

He shakes his head. "But there was a weird discussion about orgasms, his junk, and him being selfish in bed." He shudders. "Way more than I wanted to hear."

"Way more than you should be repeating, too," I warn.

He grips my shoulder. "You need all the help you can get, man," he says, giving me a squeeze. He grins.

I flip him the bird in a way that Joey and Mellie can't see and follow Sky into the hallway. She's still waiting at the elevator, so I jog up to her and stop, a little breathless. I'm not sure if my lack of air is because I'm so fucking relieved she's unattached or from the quick jog, but my bet is it's the former. And I'm okay with that.

Skylar

Goodness gracious, he's handsome. Matt's wearing a gray T-shirt and jeans, and his hair is pulled back with a rubber band. He's so tall that I have to tip my head to look up at him. He grins down at me. He's breathing a little hard, and I have to admit I am, too.

"How was your day?" he asks. The elevator dings beside us, and we step inside. He hitches his hip against the rail and crosses his arms in front of his chest.

I ran out of the apartment because I was a little overwhelmed with emotion. It's pitiful that a kid can make me lose my tight grip on reality just by being nice to me. But when Seth grabbed me and told me he was worried because I was late, I realized that I'm part of a family, and like the Grinch who stole Christmas, my heart swelled to twice its size. Then it cracked and my eyes filled up with tears and I had to get out of there before I lost my shit.

I swipe my fingertips beneath my eyes and smile a watery smile at Matt. I wish he had given me a few minutes to myself, but it's too late now. I get to look like an idiot in front of an attractive man.

Who am I kidding? He's hot as hell. And I'm about to start sobbing. Why is it that I get all teary every time this man is around?

"Sky?" he asks quietly. "What's wrong?"

"Nothing," I croak. I clear my throat because there's a lump the size of Texas in it.

He walks toward me and touches my chin with gentle fingers, tipping my face up to his. "Then why are you crying?"

"Because I'm a girl," I squeak out, like that's an excuse.

"Liar," he says. He cups my face with his palm, his fingertips tickling the skin in front of my ear, brushing back and forth.

"You'll think it's stupid," I say.

"Try me," he tosses back.

"No." I sniffle. I square my shoulders. "I'm fine, really. It's nothing."

The doors open on the lower level, and we step out, but instead of walking toward the front doors, he takes my hand and tugs me with a quick jerk into the stairwell. He closes the door and sits down on the lowest step. He pats the spot beside him. "Take a break for a second."

I gingerly sit down next to him. He scoots closer until his hip touches mine. I scoot away from him, but he scoots even closer. I look up, and I can't keep from grinning at him. "You're in my space," I warn.

"I like being in your space. I kind of want to be all up in your space," he says, his voice teasing and playful. But then he pats his shoulder. "God didn't give me broad shoulders just to hold up my T-shirts." He uses his hand to push my head onto his shoulder. He's quiet for a moment, but then he says, "Let me take some of your burden, Sky. Tell me what's wrong."

He sits quietly and just breathes. He doesn't say anything more. I sit there and take in the scent of him. It's woodsy and manly and clean. It's Matt, and I like it. I don't want to cry anymore. I want to climb into his lap and kiss him. "Oh God," I moan.

"Nope. I'm just Matt," he says with a chuckle.

I punch his shoulder playfully. He pretends to fall to the side, but he pops right back up, getting even more in my space.

"Is this about your boyfriend?" he asks quietly.

I shake my head. I had almost forgotten about Phillip. "No," I start. But I can't get the words together. "Never mind."

He sits quietly, and then he starts to whistle. He's not letting me off without an explanation.

"It's just that I never had a family." There. I said it. Now he can pity me. "So when Seth was worried, not just about his sisters but about me too, it made me feel a little emotional." I shrug. It sounds even more stupid now that it's out of my mouth. "That's all. I know it's stupid."

He doesn't say anything. He just nods.

"I just am having a hard time finding my place in this situation. But I think I'm finding it, and it feels good."

He arches his brow. "So, that was a good cry?" he asks.

"That was a very good cry." A grin tugs at the corners of my lips even though I'm still feeling really emotional.

"Okay," he says with a nod. He pats his shoulder. "You want to cry on me some more? I kind of like having you touch me." He grins and opens his arms in invitation. "I'm really good at hugs, too."

I bite my lower lip, trying not to grin.

"I'll pretend it's a chore if it'll make you feel better. I'll even groan out loud."

This time I laugh. I can't help it. He's so damn sweet.

"Is that a no?" he asks, deadpan.

"I'm not usually this emotional," I say.

He shrugs. "All women say that. It usually precedes an episode of batshit craziness."

"Are you calling me crazy?"

He shakes his head vehemently. "Definitely not." He smiles. "There are a lot of words I would call you. *Crazy* isn't one of them."

Now I'm intrigued. "Do tell."

"You're fucking gorgeous as hell," he says. His eyes drag up and down my body.

Heat creeps up my cheeks.

"And you're smart. And loyal. And you've bitten off more than you can chew by taking on three kids that aren't even yours."

I like that he thinks I'm smart. And loyal.

"And you're not mine." He gets to his feet and reaches down to take my hand. "So we had better get out of the stairwell before I do something stupid like kiss you."

He pulls me up, and I brush off my butt, trying to figure out what to do. "You want to kiss me?" I ask.

"More than anything," he says quickly.

I grin and look away from him. "Good." I open the door to the stairwell and walk through it.

"What's that supposed to mean?" he asks my retreating back.

"Nothing," I toss over my shoulder. My heart feels a lot lighter than it did a few minutes ago, probably because there are about a million butterflies fluttering around in my gut. My belly flips when I meet his gaze. "I'm glad you want to kiss me, is all." I shrug again.

"So can I?" he asks softly. He's following me to the street and toward my car now. I beep the locks so I can open the door. I start to pull bags out and load him up.

"Can you what?" I ask.

He grins. "You know what."

I drop my voice down to a whisper. "You might have to spell it out for me, Matt."

"I W-A-N-T T-O K-I-S-S Y-O-U," he spells out, laughing.

I laugh, too. "Good," I say again. I get out the last of the bags. He's carrying most of them, so my load is pretty light. I step up onto my tiptoes and kiss him really quickly on the cheek. "Thanks for helping with the bags. And for the pizza. And for rushing over when Seth called you. I'm sorry if he ruined your night."

"You can make it up to me," he says. He puckers his lips.

I can't keep the smile from my face. "You coming up?" I ask.

He holds up the bags like he has no other choice.

"Run while you can, Mr. Reed," I say, and I try to take a bag from him.

"I don't think so," he says.

My belly does that little flip again, and I can't help but wonder where this is going.

Matt

Her cheeks are a pretty pink color, and she avoids looking at me in the elevator. I let her walk in front of me down the hallway because she has absolutely the prettiest, most perfect ass I have ever seen and I want an excuse to look at it. She's wearing her business suit again—a pencil skirt, heels, and a pretty top.

She looks over her shoulder at me and draws her lower lip between her teeth, her face growing even rosier. I go hard immediately. If she doesn't quit it, I'm going to have to hang out in the hall before I can go inside. I take a deep breath and stop looking at her ass. Instead, I look at the bags and bags of clothes she piled me high with. They're dripping off my arms, and I have shoe boxes stacked in my hands.

"Did you buy the whole store?" I ask as she opens the door.

She holds up four fingers. "I bought out four stores. Little girls are expensive." She shrugs and says, "I got some things for Seth, too. I just hope they fit. I had to guess his size."

He's going to love that. The kid hasn't had anyone to take care of him in a long time. I have a feeling she could have bought him a pink fur coat and he would have taken it with pride just because she gave it to him. "I'm sure whatever you got will be fine."

She opens the door, and I start to divest myself of bags. The heavy one filled with jeans left grooves on my wrist, and I hold it up for her to see. "See what your shopping trip did to me?" I ask playfully.

She takes my hand in hers and turns my arm over, appraising it closely. Her hands are soft, and her fingernails are manicured to perfection. She drags her forefinger across my wrist. "I'm so sorry, Matt. Look at you: you're wounded!" She laughs loudly. It sounds so pretty coming out of her lips. It's unfettered and not at all restrained. I fucking love it, particularly when she tips her head back and then she gets to laughing so hard she snorts. But that just makes her laugh even louder. "What can I do to make it up to you?" she asks.

I hold my wrist up and stick out my bottom lip. "Kiss it and make it better?" I suggest.

She lifts my wrist up high and presses her lips to my skin. I'm afraid I'm going to melt into a big, old, sweaty ball of funk right there on her carpet, but as soon as her lips touch me, she blows a quick raspberry into my skin. It makes me laugh, and I grab for her, pulling her to me.

But just then, a naked child streaks out of the bathroom. It's Mellie, and I cover my eyes as she runs by. Seth chases after her, carrying a towel. He growls at her playfully, though, and she dashes behind the couch. She starts to run by me, and I reach out really quickly and grab her, holding her squirmy little naked body far away from me. Damn, but she's slippery. She laughs and wiggles her feet, kicking wildly, and it's all I can do to hold on to her.

"Come here, you," Seth growls, and he wraps Mellie up in a towel. She giggles all the way down the hallway until I hear the door shut.

Sky lays her hand on my chest, brushing down it. "You're all wet," she says, shaking her head.

"It's fine," I say, brushing her worry aside. "It's just a little water." I rub my hands together. They're still slippery. "And soap." I laugh.

"Let me get you a towel," she says and starts toward the kitchen. "I'm still learning where things are." She opens drawer after drawer. She finally finds a hand towel and holds it out to me. "Sorry she got you wet. Not to mention streaking naked in front of you."

"Are you kidding?" I ask. I fucking love this stuff. I have missed this commotion in my own house since the younger boys left. "It's fine."

"I would give you a T-shirt to change into but I don't have one your size," she says. She grimaces. "Sorry."

I make like I'm going to pull this one over my head, and her eyes dance toward my abs, growing wider when she takes in the tattoo to the left of my belly button. "Wow," she breathes. She covers her mouth with her fingertips.

My tat is a green frog. But it's not just any green frog. My brother Logan is an amazing artist, and he drew it for me. It's a frog on a lily pad with flowers floating all around. On top of the frog's head is a crown of thorns. I really love it, but I feel kind of raw and exposed now that she's seen it. "Want to kiss my frog?" I ask, since I'm feeling so out of sorts.

She licks her lips.

"Don't do that," I warn. My voice sounds gruff even to me.

"Do what?" she whispers.

I step toward her, glancing really quickly down the hallway to see where the kids are. "Don't lick your lips at me, Sky," I say.

She does it again. "Oops," she breathes, but she's grinning.

I want to kiss her, but I need to know what I'm up against. "How's your boyfriend?" I ask. I know Seth said they broke up, but I want to hear it from her. I won't touch someone who is dating someone else. I have had enough heartbreak in that area to last a lifetime.

"What boyfriend?" she asks.

"Don't give me hope if there is none," I sing. But I'm serious. Totally serious.

"We broke up."

"Are you devastated?" I want to know how she's feeling. About all of it.

"Elated," she says instead.

Thank God. A shiver crawls up my spine, because I'm seriously interested in this woman. "You sure you're done with him?"

"Positive." She nods. Her eyes don't leave mine.

"I'm going to make you fall in love with me," I warn.

"You can try," she says quietly.

I lean down and kiss her cheek really quickly just before Mellie runs into the room. She skids to a stop at my feet, sliding into the room on her footed jammies. She grabs onto my legs with one arm and slips her palm into Sky's hand with the other. Sky brushes a strand of hair from Mellie's face, a soft look in her eyes that I didn't expect from her.

"Anybody want to play bowling on the Wii?" Seth asks as he walks into the kitchen. He looks from Sky to me and back. "What did I miss?" he asks.

"I got you a bunch of stuff today at the store. Why don't you check it out?" she asks.

His brow arches. "You got stuff for me?" He grins and whoops and goes to rummage through the bags.

He is a teenage boy, and I do have experience with those beasts. The girls, not so much. When Sky's not looking, I chuck him on the shoulder and warn, "Even if you don't like it, pretend you do. Don't hurt her feelings."

"Are you kidding?" he asks. He holds up a T-shirt. "These are great." He tries his shoes on, and they fit. She bought Vans, so she couldn't go wrong there. He loves them. "You shouldn't have, Aunt Sky," he says. He gets up and goes to her. She's grinning from ear to ear. He picks her up and spins her around. "Thank you," he says.

She squeals. "I have to get used to that hugging thing you do," she says.

"Why?" he asks. He looks confused. I have a feeling Sky didn't get much affection as a child. But these kids were steeped in it.

"It's just…not something I'm used to," she says.

Seth's face falls. "Do you want me to stop?" he asks. "I hugged my mom all the time."

"If you stop, I'll have to ground you or make you wear a funny hat to school or something. Hell, I don't know how to torture you, but I'd come up with something." She laughs, but I can tell she's uncomfortable.

He wraps his arm around her shoulder again and squeezes her. She squeaks a little, and he laughs. "You're like a little mouse," he says. "Do you whisper when you're angry, too?"

She punches his shoulder. "You'll find out if you keep it up."

Sky kicks her shoes off and pads around in her stockings. She gets a slice of pizza and goes to sit on the couch. The kids start a game of Wii bowling, and they con her into playing. "I've never done this before," she warns.

"It's easy," Seth says. He motions her forward. "Come on. I'll show you."

She gets up, grinning, and I reach for the front of the TV to turn the sound up. Sky pulls her arm back, right as I turn back to walk to the couch, and suddenly the controller flies out of her hand and smacks directly into my nose.

"Ugh!" I grunt out.

Sky puts her hand over her mouth and gasps. But then she runs toward me when she sees the blood dripping down my face. I walk into the kitchen because I don't want to get blood on the carpet.

"Oh thit," I swear, when I see that the kids didn't follow us. She sits me down in a chair and puts a towel under my nose. "That hurts wike a mudder fudder." I sound like I'm all stopped up with a cold, but the blood is still dripping, so I pinch my nose closed.

"I'm so sorry," she says as she drops down in front of me. She rests her forearms on my thighs. I can smell the pizza she just ate on her breath, and I really, really want to kiss her, but I have blood all over my face and hands. "I'm so sorry," she says again. "I didn't know it would fly out of my hand like that."

"You hab ta wap it awound your wist," I say.

"I have to wrap it around my wrist?" she repeats.

"To keep it fwom fwying."

"Crap," she says again. "I am so sorry."

She already said that. She gets up and goes to get a wet towel. She cleans my hands and wipes gently beneath my nose. My nose hurts like a son of a bitch. I jerk my head back, but she just follows, probing and prodding.

"I think the bleeding has stopped," she says. But I let her continue to fuss over me, just because I like it. "Do you want some ice?" she asks.

Yeah, but I need it for my dick and not for my nose. "Pwease," I say. Her face is only inches from mine. But then she goes to the fridge. She comes back with a small bag of ice. She'd probably get offended if I shoved it in my pants, so I lay it against my nose, instead. I brace my chin with one hand and hold the ice with the other.

"I really didn't mean to hit you," she says. She looks so worried that I have to let her off the hook. Hell, I lived with four brothers. I have had more nosebleeds than I could ever begin to count.

"I'll wiv," I say.

She leans close and kisses my cheek. I want to turn my head and press my lips to hers, but I don't.

"You in lub wif me yet?" I ask.

She laughs and turns her head away, closing her eyes. Her giggle is so damn cute. She winces.

"I gwess dats a no," I say.

I lift my shirt and wipe the edge of my nose, since she took my wet towel. When I do, her eyes go to my frog prince, and she leans forward and presses her lips to him. She looks up at me, her blue eyes wide, as she holds her lips there for a second. Then she makes a loud smacking noise and pops back up, grinning. "There. All better?"

Fuck no. We're just getting started.

Seth sticks his head into the room. He smirks at me and shakes his head. "Dude," he says. He laughs. "That's the saddest thing I've ever seen."

I throw down the ice. "Dat's it. I'm going to kick your ath at bow'ing, Seth. You are going down." I follow him into the other room, take a controller, and try to pretend like she didn't just rock my world.

Skylar

I am so into the game that I don't even realize how late it is until Mellie climbs into my lap and falls asleep. I know she's asleep because I feel drool slide down my leg. I sit up, careful not to jostle her, and pull her into my arms. She makes a sleepy little murmur beside my ear and burrows in closer. I take a deep breath and soak it in, because these moments are few and far between.

"Okay, that's it," Matt says, and he bends over to turn off the Wii. "I think there has been enough butt-kicking for one night." He shoves Seth's shoulder. Seth shoves him back and they tussle on the floor. He pins Seth down and grins. "How was wrestling today?" he asks.

Seth sits up, brushing his hair back into place. "It was okay. We have practice matches on Wednesday night." He looks up at Matt. "You want to come watch?"

Matt lies back on the floor, acting like he's winded after wrestling, but I think he's shocked that Seth asked him. He picks up a ball and starts to toss it up in the air and catch it. "What time?" he asks.

Seth shrugs like it doesn't matter. "Seven, I think," he says. "So you want to go?"

Matt sits up and nods. "If it's okay with your aunt," he says. Matt winks at me, like Seth can't see him. Seth does, though, and shakes his head.

"Quit scamming on my aunt, man," he warns.

"It's not scamming. It's…" He stops and looks at me. "Hell, I don't know what it's called." He looks a little uncomfortable. He throws the ball into Seth's chest, and Seth falls back on the floor, clutching his belly.

Joey walks up and sits down on Seth's stomach, bouncing and laughing when he groans. "Why are you still up?" he asks. He looks at the clock. "It's past your bedtime."

He grabs her hands and stands up, tossing her over his shoulder. She squeals. He comes over to me and dangles her in front of my face. "Kiss Aunt Sky good night," he says.

She leans forward, takes my face in her hands, and kisses my cheek. "'Night, Aunt Sky," she says quietly.

Seth points to my lap. "I'll be back in a second for that one," he says.

"Actually, I'll take her," I say. I stand up and lift Mellie gently into my arms. She cuddles closer to me, and I realize she's been sweating against me when the cold air hits where she was lying. But I wouldn't change it.

Seth shrugs. "You sure?" he asks, cocking his head to the side.

I nod and smile at him. "If you don't mind. I'd like to put them to bed."

Seth nods toward the girls' bedroom. "Sure," he says flippantly, and he starts in that direction.

He pulls back the covers and flies Joey around like an airplane, making a humming, blowing noise with his mouth until she lands between the sheets. She giggles, and he leans down to kiss her cheek. "Good night," he says. Then he comes and helps me tuck Mellie in. She's out cold, and she barely makes a move as he covers her. I turn to walk out the door, but Joey calls out and I have to turn back.

"Aunt Sky?" she says.

I turn back. She's snug as a bug in a rug in her blankets, and I can't think of anything she might need. "Do you need something?"

"She's going to make you stay as long as she can, asking for kisses and water and everything she really doesn't need," Seth warns. He points a finger at her and says, "Go to sleep."

I walk back over to the bed and sit down on the edge, tucking the blankets even more tightly around her. She pulls her arm out and lays her hand on my forearm. "If you see my mommy," she whispers, "will you tell her good night?"

My heart clenches in my chest, and I have to close my eyes and take a deep breath. But then I lean over and whisper in her ear, "You can talk to your mommy anytime you want, and she'll hear you. So you can tell her good night, yourself." I tweak her nose playfully.

"She can hear me?" she whispers.

I nod my head. "She can hear you, even though she's not here anymore." I blink my eyes furiously because it's all I can do to sit there without sobbing. When did I become such a crybaby? The same time I became a mom, apparently. "She'll never leave you. I promise."

"I'll tell her myself," she says. She smiles and rolls into her pillow, her eyes closing.

"Good night," I say, and I kiss her forehead, lingering for a moment to take in that little-girl smell.

Seth is waiting for me in the hallway when I come out. "Wow," he breathes.

"What?" I ask. I avoid his gaze because he looks like someone just jerked a rug out from under him.

He shakes his head. "Sometimes it seems so easy to go on without her, and then other times, the memories and all the small things about her just swamp you, you know?"

I don't know. I've never had anyone who loved me like their mom loved them. I don't know what it's like to lose your anchor. To suddenly float rudderless. "You can talk to her, too, you know," I say. He follows me to the kitchen. "She's still here for you."

He shakes his head again. "I like to think that, but I'm not sure I believe it." He heaves a sigh. "I feel kind of alone."

My heart sinks. I felt like we were finally getting somewhere, but maybe I'm not able to give him what he needs. "I'll try harder," I say.

He pulls me into his arms and squeezes me, his forearm wrapped around my head again in that awkward embrace. But I like it.

"Everything okay?" Matt asks from the doorway. He lifts an eyebrow at me.

I step back and brush my hair back from my face. "Fine," I say, smiling at him. I don't know why, but it feels natural having Matt around. We have this odd kind of chemistry that makes my belly flutter but comforts me at the same time. He brings a sense of peace with him. I can't define it, but I know I want more of it.

He walks up to Seth and wraps his arm around the boy's head, taking him in a gentle headlock, and gives him a noogie. Seth shoves at him, but he's smiling. "I'm going to bed," Seth says.

"Already?" I complain. I look at my watch. "It's early yet."

He glances quickly at Matt, and Matt ducks his head and grins. "I'm tired," Seth says, and he fakes a yawn and a stretch. He's grinning, and Matt swipes a hand down his face to hide his own smile. Seth kisses my forehead, bumps knuckles with Matt, and goes to his room.

I don't know what to do with myself all alone with Matt, so I start to load the dishwasher with today's dishes. Matt picks up plates and cups from the table and helps me.

"Careful, or I'll get used to having you around," I warn playfully.

He looks directly into my eyes. "Good. That's what I'm going for."

My breath hitches, and I have to turn away so that I'm not facing him. I lay my hands flat on the counter and take a breath. But then I feel Matt's length behind me. His palms lie flat on the counter beside mine, his arms bracketing my body. I can feel him from the top of my head to the heels of my feet, he's that close.

"You in love with me yet?" he whispers quietly.

A grin steals across my face, and I'm so glad he can't see it. "Nope," I say past the lump in my throat.

He brushes the hair from the back of my neck and presses his lips there. I'm suddenly glad he's behind me, because my knees might just give out. His lips are soft and warm, but insistent. He kisses the side of my neck, and I tilt my head because it feels so damn good.

"Someday, you're going to want to marry me," he murmurs.

"You're awfully sure of yourself." My voice quavers only a little. I'm quite proud of that.

"Mmm hmm," he murmurs, and his lips gently slide up the side of my neck.

Suddenly there's a noise behind us, and Matt jumps back. He's across the room in nothing more than a second. I turn around and look up to find Seth standing in the doorway. He looks from me to Matt and back to me over and over. Finally, he snorts and says, "Dude, you should just kiss her already. God." He walks to the fridge and gets a bottle of water, and then he leaves the room.

Matt grins. "I should probably go."

"Don't," I say quickly. I squeeze my eyes shut. When I open them, he's looking at me intently. "I mean, if you need to go, you can. But if you want to stay for a bit…"

"I want to stay," he says quickly.

"You want a beer?" I ask. I think there are still a few in the fridge.

"No," he says. "Thanks, though."

I pour myself a glass of wine so I have something to do with my hands.

He gets himself a bottle of water and follows me to the couch. I sit down on one end, and he sits on the other. He's much too far away, in my opinion, but he's too close at the same time. *What am I doing?*

I pull my feet up onto the couch, my knees pointed toward the TV, and Matt stares at my legs. I tug my skirt down a little. He groans and lays his head back, but he's grinning. "You don't know how hard it is to sit way over here while you're over there," he says.

"Yes, I do," I admit.

His gaze jerks to meet mine. "You're feeling it too?" he asks. His eyes are so blue and so deep that I want to fall into them and stay there. *Don't ever look away from me, Matt.*

I nod and bite my lower lip to keep from grinning. "Why don't you have a girlfriend, Matt?" I ask. And I really want to know, because it's unfathomable to me that he's single. He's handsome, and he's so kind.

He shakes a finger at me. "There's a story there," he says.

I settle into the sofa a little deeper and turn so that my feet are pointed toward him, my legs extended. My toes almost touch his thigh. But then he lifts my feet and slides under them, scooting closer to me. "I was in love with a girl. For a long time."

"What happened to her?" I ask. He starts to tickle across my toes, and then his fingertips drag down the top of my foot. It's a gentle sweep, and it feels so good that I don't want him to stop. His fingers play absently as he starts to talk.

"When I got the diagnosis," he says, "she couldn't deal with it."

"Cancer?" I ask.

He nods. His fingers drag up and down my shin, and he slides around to stroke the back of my knee. I don't stop him when his hand slides beneath my skirt, although I do tense up. He smiles when he finds the top of my thigh-highs, and he unclips the little fastener that attaches them to my garters. He repeats the action on the other side, his hands teasing the sensitive skin of my inner thigh as he frees the stocking and rolls it down. He pulls it all the way over my foot, and does the same with the other side. I am suddenly really glad I shaved my legs this morning. I wiggle my toes at him, and he starts to stroke me again. I don't ever want him to stop.

"This okay?" he asks. But he's not looking at my face. He's looking at my legs.

"Yeah," I breathe. "Keep talking. You got diagnosed…"

"I got diagnosed, and the prognosis wasn't good. I went through chemo and got a little better. But then I needed a second round. Things didn't look good, and we were flat broke. I couldn't work at the tattoo parlor anymore because my immune system was too weak, so I had no money coming in. I was poor and sick, and she didn't love me enough to walk the path with me." He shrugs, but I can tell he's serious. "She cheated with my best friend." He shrugs again. "And that's the end of that sad story."

"You still love her?" I ask. I don't breathe, waiting for his answer.

He shakes his head and looks up. "I did love her for a long time. And I haven't been looking for a relationship. I haven't dated anyone since her. But I'm not in love with her anymore. I know that now."

"Why now?" I ask.

He looks directly into my eyes and says, "Because I met you, and I feel really hopeful that you'll want to go after something real with me. I know we just met and all, but I was serious about making you fall in love with me." He laughs. "Then you hit me in the nose tonight, and I knew it was meant to be."

"What?" I have no idea what he's talking about.

"When my brother Logan met Emily, she punched him in the face. And when Pete and Reagan first started dating, she hit him in the nose." He reaches up and touches his nose gently. "So, when you hit me tonight, I just knew it was meant to be." He grins. "I hope you feel the same way, because I really want to see where this thing is going to go."

"So the women your brothers fell in love with, they committed bodily harm to them and that's how you guys knew it was real?"

"We kind of have a rule. If a woman punches you in the face, you have to marry her." He laughs.

"I didn't punch you."

"Same difference," he says. "That's my story and I'm sticking to it."

I set my wineglass on the side table when I realize it's empty.

"I do want to talk to you about something, though," he says. He's quiet and serious and he stops rubbing my leg. He wraps his hand around my ankle.

"Okay," I say hesitantly.

"With all the chemo, the chances of my ever having kids are slim." His eyes are full of pain. "There's probably no chance at all." He jerks a thumb toward the hallway. "Would you be satisfied with three kids and no more?"

I lay my head back and laugh. "You think I need more than three?"

"I just want to be completely honest with you. I can't get you pregnant. So if you wanted to have a baby, I'm not the guy for you, and I don't want to get my hopes up."

I gesture to his lap. "Everything...works? Right?" Heat creeps up my cheeks. He lifts my foot and presses it closer to his zipper.

"Everything works," he says quietly. He's fully hard against the side of my foot, and I feel like my face is aflame with embarrassment, but he doesn't seem to mind.

"I have a question for you now," I say. I don't even know how to phrase it, but I have to ask. "My kids," I say. "They're not blond-haired and blue-eyed. Would that be a problem for you?"

We're totally putting the cart before the horse here, and I feel stupid even asking these questions of a man I just met, but I like him. I like him a lot.

"Your kids are perfect," he says. "I would be honored to spend time with them."

"But, like…" I drop my face in my hands. I can't get what Phillip said to me out of my head. "But…would you be okay being with them in public and having people think they're yours? And mine?" I gesture back and forth between us. "Not that I'm trying to give you my kids or anything, but we're sort of a package deal."

"I like the package," he says. "And I'd be honored for anyone in the world to think those kids were mine, if we ever got to that point in our relationship."

"This is a relationship?" I ask. I'm grinning like a fool, though.

"Not yet," he says. "Right now, I'm just a crazy guy you just met, who divested you of your stockings and wants to touch your feet." He looks down at my toes and tickles them. He looks me in the eye. "So, now you want to fall in love with me?" he asks. "You did hit me in the face, so I'm obligated to marry you at some point."

I toss my hands up. "Or we could just hang out," I say with a laugh.

He nods. "That sounds nice." He smiles at me.

"So why hasn't some lucky woman snatched you up yet?" I ask again.

"I have issues." He chuckles, but then he sobers. "I do have some trust issues. And, while I am in remission, I live each day knowing I could get sick again. I don't like wasting time because it's one of the only things in life we can't get more of. So, I know I'm moving really fast and I'm probably scaring the shit out of you, but that's how I roll. I love hard when I love, and I hope you're okay with that."

I scoff. "Don't tell me you're in love with me when you just met me. I'd have to call you a liar."

"No, I'm not in love with you…yet. But for the first time in a long time, I want to chase this feeling and see where it goes."

"So, I'm the chasee, huh?" I ask. My heart thrills at the idea of it.

"Oh, I plan to chase you. Provided that you'd welcome my advances." His hand slides up and tickles the back of my knee, and I'd welcome just about any advances he wants to lay on me. "Just one more thing," he says.

"What?" I ask.

"Once I fall in love with you, don't ever cheat on me. If you want to be done with me, tell me. But don't lie to me or cheat on me. It'll make me hate you. And all I want to do is love you. Someday. When we're both ready."

I'm ready now. But at the same time I'm not. "Deal," I say.

He lays his head back against the sofa and tilts it to look at me. "So, can I keep playing with your feet?" His eyes are full of all sorts of things I don't understand, but I like it. I like it a lot.

I sit forward and pull my feet out of his lap. He pouts until I put my bottom in it instead. I take his face in my hands and look into his eyes. "I like you a lot," I whisper.

"Not in love with me yet, though?" he whispers back, but his hands wrap around my hip and lock beside me, holding me close to him.

"Not yet," I say.

He rubs his nose against mine in gentle little sweeps up and down, his eyes closed. My lips are so close to his that I can almost taste him. But suddenly, he picks me up and plops me down on the couch. He stands up, adjusts his jeans, and kisses my forehead. "I have to go," he says quickly.

"What?" I sputter. I was about to kiss him.

"Thanks for letting me hang out with the kids tonight. It was a lot of fun bowling with your family."

I suddenly feel empty, and I don't like it. "Thanks for dropping everything when Seth called you. And for the pizza." *And thanks for flipping my world upside down.*

I stand up and follow him to the door. He looks down at me from the doorway and brushes my hair back behind my ear. "I want to kiss you."

"You totally should," I toss back.

He shakes his head. "Not yet," he says. "Are you working from home tomorrow?"

"No, I have to go in to the office." I have a big case that I've been working on, and we need to have a team meeting.

"When can I see you again?" he asks.

I can't bite back my grin. "When do you want to see me again?"

"Every day, all day." He laughs. God, when that man smiles, he could knock me to my knees. "Can I call you?"

I nod.

"Good," he says.

He turns and walks away from me. I step out into the hallway and call toward his back. "That's it?" I ask.

"For now," he calls back, but he's laughing. He waves at me as the elevator doors close, and I sag back against the wall.

That wasn't very nice. But I'm grinning when I go back into the apartment.

Matt

God, that was hard. I've never wanted to kiss anyone so much in my life. But she's not ready for me. I can tell. She's not ready for the kind of want I have inside me. Hell, I'm not sure I'm ready for it, either. But I want to be, and that's a good place to start.

I have a little spring in my step on the way back to Reed's. I feel bad leaving the way I did earlier, right in the middle of a tattoo. But Seth needed me, and to be honest, I wanted to see Sky.

It's hard to admit that with everything I've been given in life, I haven't appreciated it enough. I've gotten second and third chances that most people will never have. But even after all that, I've just been coasting. She makes me want to do more than coast. She makes me want to pedal hard.

I walk into the shop, and I'm glad when I just see Logan and Pete. Logan is two years younger than me, but he's wicked smart. Pete's the youngest, barely twenty-one, but he's in a serious relationship just like Logan, and I want to pick their brains a little.

"Everything okay?" Logan asks. Logan is deaf, but his speech is excellent, so he speaks to us. When we talk back to him, we sign and speak at the same time so he doesn't miss anything. Logan didn't talk for years, not until he met Emily and she made him open his mouth. Now he rarely shuts up.

"Fine," I reply. "I just went over to Skylar's."

Pete's eyes narrow at me. "What the fuck happened to your nose?" he asks.

I look in the mirror over the sink. The skin under my eyes is a little purple, and I imagine there's a good chance I'll have two black eyes by tomorrow morning.

"Skylar hit me," I say.

Pete snorts. "Shut the fuck up," he says when I just look at him. "She really hit you?"

"It was an accident," I say. "We were playing Wii bowling, and the controller flew out of her hand." I touch my nose. It actually hurts like a motherfucker.

"You'll have to marry her," Logan says. "It's a rule." But he's laughing. I'm not.

"Yeah, I am kind of headed in that direction," I say. I don't look at either of them because I feel like they'll see right through me. They always have been able to.

"What?" Logan rolls his chair over toward me so he can look directly at me.

"You saw what I said," I say.

He arches his brow. "I just want to be sure I saw it right."

I shove his chair with my foot, and he skids across the floor. "You saw it right."

"Already?" Pete says. He sits down across from me. "You just met her."

"How long was it before you knew you wanted Reagan?" I ask. I can't shove Pete away because he's not on wheels.

"Seconds," he says. He doesn't even blink.

I look at Logan. "And you?" I ask.

"I never wanted Reagan," Logan says. Pete punches him on the arm, and he throws up his hands in surrender. "Minutes." He looks at me. Logan has this way of looking into your soul. He has to read people based on their body language, and I'm afraid he's reading all of mine. "Wow," he breathes. "You like her that much."

I nod. "Yeah." I scoff. "I'm not in love with her or anything"—I might as well be honest—"but I can't get her off my mind."

"You done her yet?" Pete asks.

"Done her?" I repeat.

He makes a crude gesture with his hands. "Done her," he says again.

"God, no," I breathe. "I haven't even kissed her."

"Wow," Logan says again.

"Would you stop saying that?" I gripe.

"You want to kiss her," Pete says.

"I want to do all sorts of things with her," I admit. "But she's special."

"Wow," Logan says again.

"Cut it out!" I shove his shoulder.

"I remember when I brought Emily home. She slept in my bed for a long time before we ever had sex. It wasn't about that. It was about those quiet, intimate moments. Those were what mattered. They fed my soul." Leave it to Logan to hit the nail on the head.

"Yeah," I say. "Like that."

"I wanted to fuck her, too, but not until I knew it was permanent." His comment is crass, and someone else might find it crude and uncaring, but I find it honest.

"Same here," Pete tosses out. "That's how you know she's the right one. When you would take hearing her voice over getting your rocks off."

I nod. I don't know what else to say. Pete shoves my shoulder. "I'm happy for you?"

"Are you asking me?"

He shrugs. "Sort of. I don't know what to tell you. If she's the one, you'll know it."

"What about April?" Logan asks.

"What about her?" Why would he bring April up now?

"Not too long ago, she was still on your mind. That changed?" Logan asks.

"Yeah. A lot." I tug the rubber band from my hair and let it fall around my face. I run my fingers through it to buy myself some time. "I don't know how to explain it."

"That's the beauty of love," Pete sings.

"I'm not in love with her," I challenge.

"Not yet. But there's a possibility."

"Yeah." A lot of possibility. I grin.

"Doesn't she have a boyfriend?" Logan asks.

I shake my head. "Not anymore. They broke up."

Logan's eyes narrow, but he doesn't say anything.

"She gave me the impression that he didn't like the idea of raising biracial kids." I wince because I don't even like saying it out loud.

"How do you feel about that?" Logan asks.

"Kids are kids," I say. We have been exposed to so many types of people, and with Logan's disability, we learned early what's important in life. And now that Pete's working with disabled kids and kids from the youth detention center, he often brings them home and we're exposed even more. It doesn't matter what your outsides look like; it's your insides that count. "I want them almost as much as I want her," I admit. "I'd be honored to have a place in their lives. Any place they'll let me have."

Logan still looks flummoxed.

"Stop looking at me like I've gone apeshit."

Logan shakes his head. "I'm just surprised," he admits.

"Me, too."

Pete claps a hand on my shoulder. "When do we get to meet her again?" he asks.

"Bring her around you guys?" I blow out a breath. "You have to be crazy. You'd scare her away."

But in all honesty, I wouldn't want anyone who couldn't accept my brothers exactly as they are. They're loud and rude and they fart a lot, but they all have hearts of gold. And they're mine. "I'll ask her." I look around the shop. "Are we done for the day?" I ask.

"We?" Pete protests. "I didn't see your ass doing tats tonight." He shrugs into his coat. "I'm going home," he says. But before he leaves, he looks at me and stalls.

"What?" I ask.

He grins. "I'm just so happy for you," he says, then laughs. "I really am."

"Shut up," I grouse.

He leaves, and it's just me and Logan. He stops speaking and starts signing. *She's the one, huh?* he asks.

Maybe, I sign back. *I don't know.*

He nods. *Good.*

Good what?

If anybody deserves a happily ever after, Matt, it's you.

Shut up, I grouse again. I don't know what to say to that.

He laughs. *I'm going home. You should, too.*

I nod and help him lock up. Then he leaves me in the street with a fist bump and a quick *I love you* sign. I flash it back at him, and he walks away.

I take my phone out of my pocket and scroll to Sky's number. It's late, but I want to hear her voice. It's stupid, I know. But it is what it is.

"Hello," she says, her voice hesitant.

I lean against the building because my knees wobble when I talk to her. It makes me giddy. "Hi," I say quietly.

"Hi," she breathes back.

"Were you asleep?"

"No, I was just thinking."

"About what?"

"You," she admits. My heart starts to beat harder.

"Good thoughts?" I ask.

I can almost hear her smile through the phone. "Very good."

"I just wanted to say good night." It sounds stupid aloud.

"I'm glad you called," she replies. "Really glad."

"Can I call you tomorrow?"

She laughs. "You better."

"Good night, Sky," I say.

"'Night, Matt."

I disconnect the call and put my phone in my pocket. No one is up when I get home. I'm not even sure if Paul is home. I go into my bedroom and get ready for bed. Just as I slide between the sheets, my phone rings. I see that it's her number.

"Sky?"

"Yeah," she admits.

"You okay?"

"I just wanted to tell you good night," she says quietly.

"I think you already did that." But inside, my heart is beating like a tattoo gun.

"Oh," she says quietly. She laughs. "Sorry."

"You tired?" I ask.

"Not at all."

So we talk late into the night. We talk until my eyes are droopy, and I still don't want to hang up the phone.

Skylar

I need toothpicks to hold my eyelids open today. Matt and I talked until really late last night, but every time I got ready to hang up the phone, he would ask me something else. It was always something thought provoking and deep. And he answered my questions, as well.

I now know that he likes any kind of ice cream with chocolate chunks in it. He loves nuts. And he has this crazy passion for life that I didn't know even existed. His family is important to him, and mine is, too. He asked me out on a date for Friday night, but I put him off because I don't know yet where Seth will be on Friday.

But I do want to go out with him. I want to spend some time alone with him with no kids in the other room. I want to kiss him and see if this passion is all in my head.

It's almost lunchtime, and I have successfully avoided Phillip the whole morning. He approached me once, but I turned my back on him, and he went the other direction. I have been working really hard on a case today, getting my paperwork ready. I stop and press the heels of my hands into my eyes. I really shouldn't have stayed up so late last night.

The buzzer on my phone goes off. "Yes," I call.

"Sky," the receptionist says quietly. I pick up the handset.

"Yes," I say again. "What's up?"

"There's a really hunky guy standing in front of me, and he's asking for you," she whispers into the phone.

What hunky guy would be asking about me? "What does he look like?"

"He's about six two," she starts.

"Six three," I hear someone say.

"Oh, six three," she says. "He's a big one." She giggles.

My heart jumps. "What color is his hair?"

"Blond. And long."

It's Matt. Oh shit. It's Matt.

"I'll be right there," I say. But my heart is thumping like crazy. What is Matt doing here? I hunt around under my desk for my shoes and slide them on. Then I straighten my skirt and run a hand down my hair to smooth it. A minute ago, I had it held up with a pencil.

It's just Matt, I tell myself. *It's Matt.*

"Do you want me to send him back?" the receptionist asks. She laughs again. "Or I can just keep him?"

Definitely not. He's mine. "I'll be right there," I repeat. I look down at my business suit. I hope I look all right. I guess it's too late now to worry about it.

I walk into the reception area and find Matt leaning against the glass doorway. He turns to face me and smiles. "Hi," he says quietly.

I walk toward him, my legs shaky. "What are you doing here?" I ask, but I'm grinning, too. I stop in front of him, one move short of leaning into him for a hug. The receptionist is watching really closely.

"I came to see if you want to go to lunch." He shrugs. He's wearing black jeans and lace-up boots. A black T-shirt is stretched across his broad chest, and it's tucked neatly into his jeans. I can see his tattoos. A piece of hair has fallen from his ponytail, and I want to reach up and tuck it behind his ear.

"How did you find out where I work?" I ask. I motion for him to follow me. *Thank you*, I mouth at the receptionist, and she winks at me and gives me a thumbs-up. I shake my head, and Matt walks quietly behind me.

"I texted Seth," he says.

"Traitor," I say, but inside, I'm thrilled.

"Did I come at a bad time?" he asks. He looks down at his wrist, even though there's no watch on it. "I can come back later."

"No, no." I don't want him to leave. Ever. I lean against the edge of my desk. "I'm glad you're here."

His voice is deep and soft when he responds. "I've been thinking about you all morning." He shrugs, looking a little sheepish. "So I figured I'd drop by. I totally understand if you're too busy, though." He looks into my eyes. "I might cry if you send me away, but I'll go."

I'm not going to send him away. Not a chance. "I don't want you to go," I say.

He grins. "Good." He looks around my office. "Do you have time for lunch?"

"Oh!" I cry. "I thought you were just going to stand there and let me look at you. You actually want to go somewhere?"

He laughs. "Yeah. I told you. I'm going to make you fall in love with me. Lunch is step one."

"What's step two?" I ask impulsively.

"If I told you, it wouldn't work."

I nod. I want it to work. "Don't tell me."

"Guy's got to have some secrets." He smiles. "Can you leave with me for a little while?"

I hold my thumb and forefinger about an inch apart. "Just for a little while." I motion toward my desk. "I have a big case I'm working on."

"You can tell me about it over lunch."

Yes, I can. Because I'm going with him.

I get my purse and put it over my shoulder. I'd follow him just about anywhere right now. I walk toward him and step up onto my tiptoes. He bends down a little and puts his cheek in front of me. I groan, but I kiss it quickly. He covers the wet spot with his hand. "I'm going to hold it there the rest of the day," he says.

"You use these moves on every woman you meet?" I ask.

He shakes his head. "Just telling you how I feel," he says. He looks into my eyes, and I see nothing but sincerity.

He opens the front door for me, and his hand lands at the small of my back to guide me through it. Goodness, I'm ready to melt. After we're through the door, he reaches for my hand and threads his fingers through mine. I look up at him.

"This okay?" he asks.

I nod, and we continue that way to the corner bistro.

"You're quiet," he says as the waiter seats us. It's a busy place, but the food is amazing, and a lot of people from our office come here. I slide into the booth, and he slides in beside me.

I startle a little. "Oh," I breathe.

"This okay?" he asks. He tucks a lock of hair behind my ear.

"Yeah," I say. "Fine."

He looks at the menu. "What's good?" he asks.

Do I have to behave and pretend to count calories? Or can I get what I want? I look into his face. I just can't gauge him.

"What?" he asks, but he's smiling.

"Will you be disgusted if I get the really fattening Reuben with chips?"

His brow furrows. "Why would that disgust me?"

I lay a hand on my stomach. "I'm starving."

The waiter comes back, and Matt orders two Reubens with chips and sodas. "I think you're pretty damn adorable, you know that?" He turns a little to face me as a server delivers our drinks.

"Right back at you," I say, lifting my straw to my mouth. I take a sip, and he watches me closely. "Do I have something on my face?"

"Just a smile," he says. "I like it."

I grin even more. "Me, too."

"So Seth has a match tomorrow," he reminds me. "Do you care if I go?"

"Seth invited you, didn't he?"

He nods. "But I don't want to be where I'm not wanted."

I look into his eyes. "You're wanted," I say. My heart starts to thump.

"Ditto," he says. "I love wrestling. All my brothers wrestled. Including me."

"Didn't you say Seth is pretty good?"

He nods. "Regional champ for his weight last year," he says. "He's really good. Good enough he might be able to get a scholarship."

"Wow," I breathe. "That's pretty amazing."

"Their mom left money for college, right?" he asks.

I nod. The waiter brings our food, and Matt is apparently comfortable with eating and talking. "There was an insurance policy that's very generous," I tell him. "Enough to take care of them."

"She was pretty good about planning," he says. "Your dad helped her a lot, too, with managing money."

"What did she do for a living?" I ask. I really don't know much about my half sister. Not much at all.

"She was an attorney. I think she practiced criminal law."

"Putting away the bad guys."

He nods. "When she could."

"I don't do anything quite that sacrificial."

"What kind of law do you practice?" He is giving me all the attention he's not giving to that sandwich.

"IP law," I tell him. "Intellectual property."

He nods. "You'll have to tell me about it sometime."

"I'd like that."

He grins. He looks over my shoulder toward the other side of the room. "Your boyfriend is here," he says, not looking at me.

I look over my shoulder and see Phillip with some of my colleagues. He raises his glass in my direction. If I were closer, I'd throw my soda at him.

"You guys didn't end things well, did you?"

I shake my head, pretending to be really engrossed in my sandwich. But I really don't want to talk about Phillip.

"Are you sad?" he asks.

"Only that you're talking about it," I toss back.

He grins. "Point taken." His voice drops to a sultry growl. "When I finally get in your bed, I promise not to be selfish," I say.

My heart stalls. "You have been talking to Seth," I say. "I'm going to have to have a chat with him about privacy."

Matt stills. "Sorry. I was just teasing. I won't do it anymore. Seth very offhandedly told me about your breakup. He wasn't ratting you out or anything."

"That's good to know."

"You're mad at me."

"Embarrassed that you have intimate knowledge of my sex life." I finish off my pickle and dust my hands together. "I do have to get back to work," I say.

"Fuck, I messed it up," he says, tossing his napkin onto his plate. He reaches into his back pocket and pulls out his wallet. He peels off enough cash to cover the bill and a generous tip and leaves it on the table.

"Let me pay for half," I protest.

"I invited. I pay." His hand lands at the small of my back again.

"So if I invite you, I get to pay?"

"Nope," he says. "I'm the guy. I pay."

Phillip watches us closely as we walk by him toward the door.

We walk quietly toward my office building. Matt doesn't reach for my hand, and he doesn't say anything. I turn to him when we get to the steps of my office. "Thank you for lunch," I say.

"I'm sorry I ruined it."

"You didn't ruin it. I'm just not comfortable talking about it. Not now."

"I crossed the line. Forgive me. Please?" He's not touching me, and I can feel the divide between us.

"Nothing to forgive." I step onto my tiptoes, and he leans down toward me. I kiss his cheek, and he straightens up and smiles at me.

"Thanks," he says.

"Thank you. I mean it."

I leave him standing on the steps.

My heart has already sunk all the way down to my toes.

I drop heavily into my desk chair. My phone buzzes, and I press the "speaker" button. "Yes?"

"Um…" the receptionist says.

"What is it?" I bark.

But then my office door opens, and Matt steps through.

"He's on his way to you," the receptionist says.

"Thanks for the warning," I mutter.

Matt closes my office door behind him and approaches me. I stand, and he tips my chin up toward his face. "I forgot something," he says. He's breathless, and his eyes search mine. "I forgot to tell you that I want your heart more than I want your body," he says. His eyes are flitting all over my face. "I fucked that up, but I'm not done yet. And I know how to say I'm sorry."

"Matt—" I start.

But he cuts me off. "I want you more than I've ever wanted anything, and it's difficult to even walk when I'm around you, because my dick gets so hard I could pound nails with it."

Heat creeps up my cheeks, but he doesn't stop.

"I shouldn't have gone there with you yet, but I can't help it. I'm fucking dying to be inside you. I'm fucking dying to hold you close to me, hopefully when we're both naked." He grins. "But even more than that, I want you to love me. I want you to love me a lot, and I went about it the wrong way. Please forgive me." He finally stops and draws in a deep breath. "Please."

"Matt..." I say.

"When I saw your boyfriend, all I could think was that I could satisfy you so much more, mainly because I was jealous as hell that he's been close to you. Maybe I was trying to get him off your mind and put myself there. Or maybe I'm just an idiot. It's probably the latter. I admit it. I'm an idiot when it comes to you. But that's okay with me. I hope it's okay with you, too."

"Matt," I say again.

"Forgive me," he urges. "I won't ever do it again."

I bracket his face with my hands. "Would you shut up for a minute?" I say.

He breathes out a sigh. "Okay."

"I'm not mad. Well, a little annoyed that Seth repeated something to you that he overheard in a private conversation. That's about me and Seth, though, not about you. I'll deal with him about that. And no, I'm not mad at you. There's nothing to forgive."

He doesn't say anything. He just looks into my eyes.

"Really, Matt," I say to assure him.

"You completely shut me down, which I deserved. But I already miss you."

"I haven't gone anywhere." I laugh.

A knock sounds on my office door. I look up to see my boss, who has poked her head in the crack and is holding a sheaf of papers. She looks at Matt and then smiles at me. "You ready to meet?" she asks.

"I'll be right there," I say. "Just give me a minute." She leaves.

"Fuck," Matt says. "You have to get back to work."

I nod. "I do."

He stares at me for a moment, like there's something on the tip of his tongue that he wants to say.

My boss pops her head back into my office. "How long will you be?" she asks.

"Margie," I say. I motion toward Matt. "This is Matt." I look into Matt's eyes. "My friend."

Margie smiles and walks to Matt with her hand stuck out. "Nice to meet you," she says. He shakes hands with her, and she leaves again.

"Friend, huh?" he says with a smirk.

"Yep," I say.

"I like that," he tells me.

"Me, too." I can't bite back my grin.

"Can I call you later?" he asks.

I nod, and he kisses me really quickly on the cheek. He leaves, and I miss him immediately. I'm still going to kick Seth's ass, though.

After my meeting, I go back to my office to find a flower delivery on my desk. I open the card and find that it reads, "Are you in love with me yet?"

Not yet. But I'm close. Really close, despite the fact that these feelings scare the shit out of me. My heart is overruling my head.

Matt

Fuck. Fuck. Fuck. Fuck. I fucked that up. I stop outside her office and look back toward the door. I want to go back in there and continue to apologize, but now she's in a meeting. I already barged in when I shouldn't have. Fuck.

There's a florist on the corner, so I drop in and order flowers for her. Girls like flowers, right? I don't go overboard, because I just can't afford to, but I get her a pretty red rose and make arrangements for them to take it to her with a note. Is she in love with me yet? I snort. Not even close, particularly not after what I said.

I don't know what I was thinking. I'm not that guy. I'm not overtly sexual and out of control. Well, with her I might be a little. Last night when I reached up and unhooked her stockings, I almost came in my pants. And when she asked me if everything worked and I pressed the side of her foot against my dick, oh my God, I could barely stand it.

But I want so much more from her. Someone bumps into my shoulder, and I look up. Her ex-boyfriend smirks up at me. I am a few inches taller than him and I like that. "Pardon me," I say. I turn to walk away when what I really want to do is flatten him.

"Pardon you for what?" he asks. "Fucking my girlfriend?"

I crack my knuckles really quickly because what I'm about to do is going to hurt. He doesn't even see it coming. I punch him directly in the face, and he goes down like one of those blow-up clowns that falls over when you hit it. He lies there, rubbing his jaw. "Don't ever talk about her like that again," I say.

I shake out the pain in my hand. It hurts, but it's a good hurt. I'd be willing to make it hurt a lot more if he'll get up and say something else. I adjust my jeans over my thighs and squat down next to him. People are stopping in the street to look at us, but I don't care. He's lying there in his fancy suit, looking like a jackass. Probably because he is one. He's a stupid motherfucker if he thinks he can talk about Sky like that. I stick out my hand.

"Want some help getting up?" I ask.

Warily, he reaches for my extended palm. He lets me pull him to his feet, and I make a production of brushing him off. "That's enough," he says.

"Yeah," I warn. "It was. Don't let it happen again."

He knows what I'm talking about.

"If you'd wanted her, you could have kept her. You didn't. So step aside like a man."

He nods, rubbing his jaw.

"Sorry I hit you, man," I say. I'm not. I'd do it again. But maybe now he'll keep his fucking mouth shut. "You're done with her, right?" I ask. With my history, I have to know.

"Yeah, I'm done," he says. "Still don't like it. But it is what it is."

I want so badly to ask why it fell apart, but I need to get that information from her.

"She's pretty damn awesome. But she has some issues."

I hold up a hand to stop him. "Don't tell me anything."

"She's never had anyone who loved her."

"She does now." Fuck me. Where did that come from?

"Yeah, I can tell." He rubs his face again. "I was just going to give you shit and warn you off her." He chuckles. "Got to respect a man with a right hook and decency on his side." He sticks out his hand to shake. "Best of luck to you."

I take his hand and squeeze it tightly. Not tight enough to hurt him, but tight enough to warn him. I'll take him out if he does anything to hurt her.

"Daddy issues," he says.

"What?"

"I may not love her enough, but I like her. And there's one thing I know: she has daddy issues. Get through those and you might have a chance with her."

I don't know why he's telling me all this.

He goes on. "She holds back. She's willing to settle for less than she deserves because it's what she knows. Or at least she did with me. Then she was willing to chuck it all for some kids she just met. So she's not the one for me. But that doesn't mean you can't get in there."

Oh, hell. Now I know more than I wanted to know. I make a mental note to throw out everything he just said because it's all probably bullshit. And he's still a dickwad.

But what if it's not bullshit?

Shit. Now I'll think about it.

"Thanks." I don't know what else to tell him.

He waves at me and goes into the building.

I walk to the subway so I can go to work. It's not thirty minutes later that my phone buzzes.

Sky: *You hit him?*

Me: *Yep.*

Sky: *Seriously?*

Me: *Yep.*

There's a long pause that makes me worry. But then my phone dings.

Sky: *Thank you.*

I grin. I can't help it.

Me: *My pleasure.*

Sky: *Can I ask why you hit him? He wouldn't tell me.*

Me: *Because he's a douche.*

Sky: *What did he say to you?*

Me: *Something he shouldn't have.*

Sky: *Was it about me?*

Me: *Yep.*

Sky: *Tell me what it was. Please.*

I heave a sigh and throw my head back.

Me: *He accused me of fucking his girlfriend. So I hit him.*

Sky: *But...you're not.*

Me: *I plan to.*

Long pause.

Me: *After I make you fall in love with me.*

Sky: *This is too fast, Matt.*

Me: *I almost died. Twice. I don't like to waste time.*

Sky: *Oh.*

Me: *I like you. And I think I could love you.*

Sky: *It's too fast.*

Me: *It scares the shit out of me, too, if it makes you feel better.*

Sky: *It does.*

Sky: *Are you coming over tonight?*

Am I? I almost feel like I need to distance myself a little.

Me: *I have appointments for tats at five, eight, and ten. So, I can't tonight.*

Sky: *:-(*

Me: *I'll see you tomorrow at Seth's match.*

Sky: *Would it be weird if I tell you I miss you already?*

A grin steals across my face.

Me: *Not if you mean it.*

Sky: *Thanks for the flowers. They're lovely.*

Me: *You in love with me yet?*

Sky: *Can I like you for a little while?*

Me: *Please do.*

Sky: *Talk to you later.*

Me: *Yep.*

###

It's almost ten thirty when I realize my last appointment is not going to show up. I have been counting the hours, wondering if I could get out of here and go see Sky before she goes to bed. I still don't like the way we left things.

"Oh, just go see her," Logan says, motioning toward the door. "Get the fuck out of here. You've been watching the clock all night. Go." He makes a pushing motion with his hands. "Out. You're making me sad with all the pining."

"Are you going home soon?" I ask.

"Yeah," he says as he motions toward a tattoo that's almost done. "Just a few more minutes." He points toward the front of the store, where Friday is sitting with a book open in front of her, studying. "Friday's still here. So get out of here."

We have a rule about leaving no one alone in the shop. "You sure?" I ask. My heart starts to beat quicker.

"Get out," he says. He goes back to work on the tat.

I grab my coat from the hook on the wall, put it on, and get out the door quicker than I ever have before. I can be at Sky's before eleven if I hurry. I won't even stay long. But I want to see her.

I rush to her apartment building and take the elevator up. I step up to her door and knock quietly so I won't wake the kids. I hear soft footsteps, and my heart trips a beat. She opens the door, and she looks so fucking pretty, in her baby-blue jammies and fuzzy slippers, that I do the only thing I can think to do. I draw her in to me. With a gasp, she falls against my chest. I can't get close enough to her fast enough, so I grab her bottom tightly in my hands, hitch her higher against me, and then spin us both so I can press her against the wall. I look into her startled blue eyes for a moment, and then I press my lips to her open mouth. She freezes in my arms, and I press more insistently, kissing her softly but fully. I draw her lower lip between mine and give it a gentle suckle.

She doesn't kiss me back, not completely, and I can't figure out what I'm doing wrong. She murmurs against my lips, but I don't want to lift my head long enough to pay attention. But then I hear a cough behind us. I look over my shoulder and see a gentleman sitting on the couch. His knee is jumping, and his face is a little bit red.

Oh, fuck. Her father is here.

I just gave her a really bad kiss. Our first kiss. In front of her dad.

"Matt," she says quietly, tapping my shoulders with her open palms. "Can you let me down?"

I step back and set her on her feet. "Fuck," I breathe.

Skylar

Oh, Matt. Why did you do that?

My father's face is bright red, and he looks like he wants to wring Matt's neck. I've never seen Dad act like this. Not ever.

"Mr. Morgan," Matt says, nodding toward my dad. "I didn't realize you were here," he says. Then he throws his hands up, like he doesn't know what to say next.

"Apparently," my father grunts out.

Matt looks at me as though he's waiting for direction. I cover my mouth with my hand to hide my smile. But I can't stop thinking about that kiss. As awful as it was, it was perfect, and all I want to do is get rid of my dad so we can do it again and do it better. "Dad came to check up on the kids," I say.

"And you," Dad says. He's still grunting. And his face is as red as a tomato. He's never checked up on me in my life, though.

"Me and the kids," I correct.

"It's late," Matt says. "I should probably go." He starts toward the door. But the last thing I want is for him to leave.

I thread my fingers through his and give his hand a tug. He looks into my eyes, and I swear I can see the depths of his soul. I see his longing and I see his confusion and I see his need. "Don't go," I say softly, squeezing his fingers. "Stay."

He nods. I lead him to the couch, and he sits down. He's uncomfortable as hell, and it's really kind of endearing to watch.

"I was just telling Dad about the wrestling match tomorrow." I sit down beside Matt, and he lifts his arm to lay it on the back of the couch behind me, mainly because I press myself up against his side and don't give him any choice. I snuggle into him and pull my feet up onto the couch. I bite back my smile because I don't want anyone to know how giddy this makes me, just being this close to him. On purpose.

"Are you going to see him wrestle, Matt?" Dad asks. He's staring awfully hard at Matt, but Matt just nods.

"I'm planning to, sir," he says. "I love to watch the matches."

He looks down at me, and I smile up at him. Matt surprises me when he leans down and kisses the tip of my nose. I scrunch my face up playfully at him, and I feel a chuckle rumble through him.

"I went to a few last year," Dad says.

Wait. "You did?"

He nods. "I go every chance I get. Seth is really good."

That floors me. He never came to my dance recitals. Or my gymnastics meets. Or anything I had going on. But he's making an effort with these kids, and now that these kids are part of my life, his efforts make me happy, for their sakes. They deserve to have people in their lives who care for and love them. "I know Seth will be happy to see you there."

"Are the kids in bed?" Matt asks.

"You probably should have asked that before you attacked my daughter," Dad barks. "It's late."

Matt nods. "I know."

"What happened to your nose?" Dad asks.

Matt grins. "She hit me." He jerks a thumb at me.

"Smart girl," Dad says, and he smiles at me. He's never looked at me with such fondness, and my heart lurches at the atrocity of it. Dad motions from Matt to me and back. "How long have you two been seeing one another?" he asks.

Matt arches a brow at me. "Not long," I chirp.

Dad nods. "I guess I should be going," he says. He stands up and shrugs into his jacket. I get up and walk him to the door. Matt goes, too, and he reaches out to shake hands with Dad.

"Don't disrespect my daughter," Dad says.

"Yes, sir," Matt says. He dips his head and jams his hands into his pockets, looking a lot like Seth did today when I scolded him about confiding in Matt.

Dad leans forward and pulls me into a quick embrace. This is new, too. I don't remember him doing it before. Or at least not in a really long time. "Good night, Dad," I say. "Thanks for stopping by."

"I'll try to do it more often," he says loudly, talking toward Matt.

Matt nods and ducks his head even further. I giggle.

"Your mother wants to see you," Dad says. My giggle falls away.

"Why?"

He takes a deep breath. "She just does."

"I'll think about it," I tell him.

Dad leaves, and I close the door behind him.

Matt sags onto the couch and lies down, flopping his arms out like he's ready to pass out. "Oh my God," he breathes. But he's chuckling, too. His belly pulses with laughter. "Why didn't you tell me he was here?"

He has one leg on the couch and the other on the floor, so I get on my knees between his spread legs and lean down over him, holding myself up with my hands flat on his chest. Matt doesn't allow that but for a second, though. He pulls me to his chest and holds me close to him. His body rises and falls beneath me, steady and solid.

"I would have told you he was here if you had given me time." I laugh against him.

"Don't you dare laugh," he says. "This is serious. Your dad is going to hate me from now on."

"I don't care what he thinks," I say. I scoot myself a little higher, getting my lips closer to his. "That was, like, the worst kiss of all time," I whisper dramatically.

"I know," he whispers back. His hands land on my waist, and he lifts me, bringing my mouth even closer to his. He lifts the edge of my pajama top, and his warm hands touch my naked skin. "I'm never going to kiss you again. Because that one was too awful."

"Terrible," I say quietly, looking at his lips. "But I think we should try again."

Matt hooks an arm behind me and flips us over. He looks down at me. "You think this is funny?" he asks. But he's grinning, so I'm not worried.

"Hilarious," I breathe. "Don't you?"

His face lowers until his lips hover over mine. "You're so fucking amazing that you make my heart hurt sometimes," he says. My heart trips, beating hard in my chest.

"Kiss me, Matt," I whisper.

Finally, his lips touch mine. The kiss at the door was full of passion and want. But this one is soft and hot and so genuinely perfect that I squirm under him, trying to get closer. His lips slide across mine, soft and damp and silky smooth. His tongue licks across the seam of my mouth, and when I gasp at the sensation, he sweeps inside. His hips grind against mine, and I can feel the length of him pressed against my belly. He's hard and huge, but he's still so gentle. I touch my tongue to his, and when he tries to pull back, I nip at his lips until he moans against my mouth and comes back inside.

A tap, tap, tap on my arm draws me from Matt's lips. I open my eyes to find Mellie's dark eyes looking at us. Matt pulls back from me when I say something against his lips. Then he realizes Mellie is there. He sits up and crawls off me. I scramble to sit up, too.

"What's wrong, Mellie?" I ask. But then I realize what's wrong. The smell hits me, and I have to cover my mouth. "Are you sick?" I ask.

"I threw up all over my bed," she says so quietly that I can barely hear her.

Oh, hell, what am I supposed to do now? "Did you wake Seth up?" I ask.

She shakes her head, her eyes filling with tears. "His door was locked."

"Oh, it's okay," I say. I take her sticky little hand, and Matt gets up with us. "Sorry," I say to him.

"No worries."

"I'll see you tomorrow?" I say. I wince because I feel bad.

"I'll help you," he says. "Why don't you put her in a bath while I change the sheets?" He starts toward the linen closet and rummages through the stacks of sheets there, until he pulls out a set he's happy with.

"You want to help?" I ask.

He looks at me like I've lost my mind. "Of course."

If I wasn't in love with him before, I'm a lot closer now. He's not even kissing me, yet I have a thousand butterflies taking flight in my belly.

I lead Mellie to the bathroom, get her cleaned up, and put fresh pajamas on her. When I come out of her room after tucking her back into bed, I find Matt at the washing machine, starting a load of dirty sheets. Seth's door opens, and he sticks his head out.

"What's wrong?" Seth asks.

"Mellie got sick," I whisper.

"Is she all right?" He goes into her room and comes out a minute later, after checking on her. "Sorry I didn't help with that," he says sheepishly.

"It's okay. We handled it. Go back to bed," I suggest.

"Must have been something she ate. She doesn't have a fever." Seth doesn't look worried.

It was probably the five cookies I let her have after dinner. Seth told me it was a bad idea and I didn't listen. "Must have been. Go back to bed."

Seth looks from me to Matt and back and raises his brow. "Okay," he says with a grin.

"Shut it," Matt grumbles playfully. Seth nods and goes into his room, closing the door.

"He never locks his door," I say, trying to figure out why he might do that.

Matt grins. "Sometimes teenage boys need to lock their doors," he says. "Trust me, it's okay." He puts his hands on my shoulders and leads me back to the couch.

"Oh, you think he was doing *that*?" I ask. I'm still whispering.

"It's a good guess," he says with a quiet laugh.

"See," I say, throwing my hands up, "I know nothing about children."

"He's a teenage boy," he says. "You can always assume that first."

"How do you know so much?"

"Four brothers," he explains. "Remember? Not to mention that I'm a guy. We do that." He grins.

"You mean when you were younger." I watch his face closely.

His grin gets even bigger. "And older."

My face flushes with heat. He just smiles big and taps the end of my nose with his finger.

I look down at my shirt. "I kind of smell like vomit," I say.

"Yeah," he says. "I kind of do, too." I saw him wash his hands after changing the sheets, and I did, too, but still. It's not very sexy.

"Thank you for helping me."

"You're welcome. I'm glad I was here."

Matt reaches for the tail of his shirt and pulls it over his head. He's wearing a sleeveless white T-shirt under his other shirt, so he's not naked, but this one shows a lot more skin. A lot more tattoos. A lot more muscles. Matt is big and broad but tall and lean. I let out a dreamy little sigh.

"Can I stay for a while?" Matt asks.

"Yeah, but I need to change." I get up and go change into a long T-shirt and some sleep shorts. I come back out, and Matt whistles softly, staring at my legs.

"Remind me to have her throw up on you every time we make out on the couch," he says.

I smile. I can't help it. I sit down next to him, and he pulls me to his side. Then he lies down so that I'm draped across him. My hip is tucked between him and the back of the couch.

"I don't want to go home yet," he says quietly. He pulls my head down to his chest, and I press my face against it. His hand settles on the back of my head, and he starts to stroke down the length of my hair.

"Then don't go," I say quietly.

He doesn't. He just threads his fingers into my hair and drags them down my back, over and over, until my eyelids grow heavy and I fall asleep on his chest.

I wake up the next morning tucked into my own bed, the covers pulled up to my chin. I sit up and look around. Beside me on the pillow is a note. I open it up and read.

Are you in love with me yet?

Matt

I look toward the clock on the wall again, and Paul scowls at me. "You counting the minutes?" he asks.

Yeah, I kind of am. "No." I scoff.

Paul just rolls his eyes. "What time is the match?" he asks.

"Seven," I murmur as I clean up my station. "You want to go?"

Pete steps out from the back, where he was doing a piercing. "I want to go," he says. He sends the guy he just pierced to Friday, who takes his money and sends him out the door.

"I want to go, too," Friday says. She starts to pack up her things.

Paul throws up his hands and says, "Is anyone going to work tonight?"

"Nope," we all say at the same time.

Logan grins and pulls Emily to his side. She falls against him and smiles. "Want to go?" she asks him.

"And miss watching Matt get led around by his balls? Not a chance." Logan laughs when I swing at him, and he sidesteps me.

Pete keeps up the abuse. "She should just thread a string through that piercing in his dick and then she can pull him around with no fuss." He adjusts his junk playfully. "Easier on your balls, too, man," he says.

"Quit talking about my junk," I warn, nodding toward the girls.

Friday grins at me. "We all know you're bejeweled down there," she says, making a motion toward my pants. "Bedazzled."

"It's not bedazzled," I murmur. But I don't care. They all know about it already. I got mine right after Paul got his. Only Pete and Logan don't have them. Even Sam is pierced. Logan has a bar through the base of his dick. Chicken shit. "And *stop* talking about my junk." I grab Friday in a headlock and pull her against me. She squeals and bats at my hand.

"Don't mess up the hair," she warns, blocking me. "It's not easy to look this beautiful."

Truly, Friday is drop-dead gorgeous in a fifties-pinup sort of way. She wears vintage clothes and red lipstick. Sometimes I think she gets tips just by smiling at people. Both men and women love her. But sometimes…sometimes this aching sadness steals across her face. I'm not even sure anyone else notices it.

Pete types into his phone really quickly. He finally looks up. "Reagan says she'll meet us there."

Great. I get the whole family going with me to spend time with Sky. Woo-hoo. You would think at least one of them would have an appointment for a tat. Lazy bastards.

We take the subway to the school and get there just as the boys are warming up. They're running circles around the mat as I go and sit down beside Sky, who is in the bleachers with Mellie and Joey at her feet. They're both using crayons and coloring in a coloring book. They look up and grin when they see me, though. I lean over the bench and remark about their drawings, and they go at it even harder. That'll entertain them for about five minutes. I hope Sky brought more tricks in that big bag of hers.

I sit on the bench near her and then shove myself against her side very gently, until I'm pressed up along her from shoulder to knee. She grins and shakes her head, her cheeks turning red.

"Hi," I say quietly. I look into her eyes.

"Hi," she returns. She looks so damn beautiful. She must have come from home because she's wearing a pair of jeans and a T-shirt. There's a balled-up sweatshirt on the seat beside her. "How was your day?" she asks.

"Better now that I get to see you," I admit. She smiles and leans into me. I lean toward her face and whisper, "Kiss me?"

She shoves my shoulder. "Not here," she whispers. She looks around.

"Please," I say, putting my palms together like in prayer.

She leans forward really quickly and touches her lips to mine. Last night's kiss with our tongues touching and her body pressed against mine was pretty fucking amazing, but this quick touch has it beat by a mile. "Thanks," I say. I can't hide my grin, so I don't even try.

She bumps me, rolling her eyes.

"I missed you today," I tell her.

She looks up. "Thank you for the note on my pillow," she says quietly.

I tuck a lock of hair behind her ear. Most of it is pulled up into an adorable ponytail, except for one piece that has escaped. "I really wanted to climb into bed with you."

Her eyes meet mine. "You should have."

I shake my head. "I didn't want Seth to think I spent the night." That shit is important to kids.

She nods slowly.

"You felt pretty damn good, though, lying on top of me on the couch." I'm getting hard, so I had better cut this shit out.

"You make a nice pillow," she whispers.

"Just a pillow?" I pretend to pull an invisible knife from my chest.

She pokes me with her index finger. "A nice, hard pillow," she says.

"Hard is about right," I say. I look at the mat where the boys are warming up so I can look at something that's not her. I want her so bad I can barely stand it.

The boys are stretching their backs and their necks, and doing some pretty impressive rolls. Seth teams up with another boy close to his weight class, and they do some drills together. Seth flips the other boy onto his back, and I want to walk out there and show him how he should have handled it. But he's not my kid, and I'm not his coach.

Reagan and Pete sit down on the other side of Sky, and Reagan starts to talk to her. I'm glad someone is intervening because I want to drag her into a stairwell and kiss her senseless.

Pete makes a motion at me like he's threading a needle really close to his dick and then gives it a tug like he's leading it around. I glare at him, and he laughs. Paul sits down behind us, with Friday beside him, and he laughs, too.

"Shut up," I grumble.

I turn to watch the practice. Seth is really very good at what he does. But I like to watch all the kids in every weight class. Logan and Emily make their way toward us. Logan waves, and they sit down in front of us. Now Sky has Reeds on every side of her. Mellie and Joey are getting a little restless, and Joey makes her way down the bleachers without Sky noticing. She's not used to this mom stuff yet. She sees it just as Joey gets to the bottom step and gets up to go retrieve her.

"I'll get her," I say. I stand up and tromp down the steps. Joey looks sheepishly up at me. She knows she wasn't supposed to sneak off.

I scoop her up in my arms and carry her back up to Sky. She stretches out, and I blow a raspberry into her shirt-covered belly. She giggles and sticks her belly out like she wants me to do it again, so I do. She laughs, and the sound is so damn happy it takes my breath away.

I sit down and tuck her onto my lap, then pull out my phone and turn on some Angry Birds. I show her how to play it really quickly, and she starts launching birds. She moves off my lap to sit beside me, and Mellie comes to lean against her and watch. That should last them for a while.

"Why does this seem so natural to you?" Sky asks quietly.

"What?" I ask. I flinch as one of the boys on the mat makes a terrible move. "Not like that," I say to him, even though I know he can't hear me.

"All of it," she says. "You do it all so well."

I look at her. "Do what?"

"You entertained Mellie and Joey, and you're watching the match, and I'd wager you're going to educate Seth and tell him everything he does wrong when we get home."

Home? I grin. "Am I going home with you tonight?" I ask right beside her ear.

"You better," she says.

My heart stutters. "Okay," I breathe.

After a few minutes, Logan turns to talk to me. He talks and signs at the same time, and so do I. "Her dad," he says, pointing toward the door. I scoot over to separate us a couple of inches.

"Thanks for the warning," I say, and I clap my hand on his shoulder and squeeze.

You're welcome, he signs. He grins and shakes his head. Pete pulls on his imaginary string. I want to punch him.

My brothers are all into the smaller weight matches, and they're making bets on the heavyweights among themselves. Seth is about 160, if I have to guess. He's tall and lean, a lot like me, although I weigh over 200 pounds now. Paul and Logan are big and bulky, so they wrestled in the heavier classes. I was the same weight Seth is now.

Sky's dad sits down beside us, and I reach over to shake hands with him. He glares at me. But then Mellie and Joey show him my phone, and he gets interested in entertaining them. Sky leans against my shoulder, watching the matches. She hides her face when one of the boys gets slammed onto the mat.

"That's not going to happen to Seth, is it?" she whispers vehemently.

I shrug. "Maybe." I grin at her and tweak her nose. "Don't worry. He's used to it."

"He's not going to get hurt, is he?" she asks.

I take her hand in mine and give it a squeeze. "Quit worrying. He's going to be fine."

When it's Seth's turn, she pulls her hand out of mine and sits forward. She watches him closely, only looking toward Mellie and Joey every few seconds to make sure they're okay. Maybe she's going to settle into this mom thing better than she ever thought possible.

Seth shakes hands with his opponent, and the buzzer sounds. I wince because the other kid is obviously older and more experienced than Seth. His opponent has a tattoo on his neck, which means he has at least a couple of years on Seth. Seth's good, but exuberance doesn't trump experience.

Seth gets flipped over, and Sky squeals and hides her face behind my shoulder. She looks up but turns back to me every few seconds when something happens. Seth is up in points, but this kid could honestly pin him any second, unless Seth gets lucky. I think the kid is playing with him, honestly.

"Come on, Seth," Mr. Morgan calls out. Seth looks up and grins.

They grapple for a second, and damn if Seth doesn't get lucky. He gets some back points, and the clock is ticking down.

Seth holds him off and wins on points. Sky jumps to her feet and claps when they raise Seth's arm in the air. He grins and goes to shake hands with the opposing coach. Then he stops at the edge of the mat, lifts one hand toward the sky, and says something quietly to himself. Or to his mom. I'm not sure which. Then he finds a spot on his team's bench and dries off with a towel. I'm really proud of him. Not like I had anything to do with it, but that kid could have easily won if Seth didn't have the technical skills he has. He did a really good job.

Sky grins. "I think I like wrestling," she says.

"Tell that to the fingernail marks on my arm," I tease.

She drops her voice down to a purr. "I'll kiss it and make it better later."

Friday must have heard her, because she snorts behind us. Sky laughs and winks at me. She even fits in with my family. And I fit into hers.

We wait until the end of the match to collect Seth. Her dad comes over and kisses her forehead. She startles for a second, and I wonder what that's all about.

"He did really well," he says.

Sky nods. "He did."

"I have to check on your mother," he says.

Sky's eyes narrow. "Why? Is something wrong?"

He avoids her gaze. "Nothing outside the norm," he says.

"Oh," Sky breathes. She doesn't look shocked, and I have no idea what they're talking about. He waves and goes to hug Seth, and then he leaves as quickly as he arrived. Sky stands there, holding

Joey with one hand and Mellie with the other. The girls are getting tired and whiny.

"Do you guys want to go to dinner?" Paul asks.

Sky shakes her head. "The kids already ate, and they have to get to bed. But thank you for the offer. Next time?"

"Sure thing," Paul says. He puts an arm around Friday's shoulders, and they leave in pairs—Paul and Friday, Logan and Emily, and Pete and Reagan.

"Are they dating?" Sky asks, pointing toward Paul.

I shake my head. "He wants to, but he thinks she likes chicks." I snicker. "Paul is the only one who doesn't know."

"That's kind of mean."

"I think it's part of the reason why they're so tight. He has a hard time being friends with women." I shrug. "It works for them."

Seth comes out wearing shorts and a hoodie. He took a shower, though, so he's not smelly like some of the other boys. I reach out and hook hands with him the way men do. He grins.

"You did a good job," I say.

"I almost fu—" He shoots a glance at Sky. "I almost messed up that one time."

I laugh. "Yeah, you did."

We get in Sky's car and go back to the apartment, with Seth grumbling about having to sit in the backseat with the girls, but he does it. When we arrive, I pull Seth back on the sidewalk.

"Do you care if I go up with you guys and spend some time with Sky?" I ask.

His eyes narrow at me. "Would it matter if I did mind?" he asks.

"Yeah," I admit. "It'd matter a lot."

"In that case, I don't mind," he says. He punches my arm and runs into the building ahead of me, chasing Mellie and Joey into the elevator. He holds it open for us, and we all go up together.

"To the bathtub," Sky cries as soon as we get in the door. The girls scurry toward the bathroom.

"You're getting pretty good at this barking-orders thing," I tell her, drawing her toward me. I hook my index fingers in her belt loops and pull her closer.

"Kiss me," she barks, laughing.

Seth makes a gagging sound. I shoot him the bird behind her back.

"I'm going to go help the girls," he says, rolling his eyes.

I finally get to kiss her. She wraps her arms around my neck and pulls my head down toward hers. I'm almost breathless, when a naked child streaks through the kitchen. I laugh, and we spring apart.

"I'll get it," I say, and I take the towel Seth tosses me and go after Joey. I catch her and carry her back to the bathroom, all wrapped up in a fluffy white towel. I give her to Seth and look around. I realize I'm suddenly where I've always wanted to be. Now I just need to figure out how to make it permanent.

Skylar

The last time my dad invited me to lunch, he gave me three children and a new life. I'm a little worried about what he wants today. It has been a week since the wrestling match, and Dad has called four times just to talk. I am having a little bit of a difficult time adjusting to the presence of a parent in my life, particularly now that I'm an adult.

I'm working from home today, so Dad is coming to the apartment. I made a very simple lunch for us. A knock sounds on the door, and I go to let him in.

"Hi, Dad," I say when I open the door. He leans in to kiss my cheek and shrugs out of his suit coat.

I haven't made any changes in the apartment, but Dad looks around and nods his head. "The place looks nice," he says.

"Thanks?" I say unevenly.

"I talked to Seth yesterday," he says as he sits down and opens a cloth napkin in his lap.

"Oh yeah? What about?"

He shrugs. "Nothing important. Sometimes I like to call for no reason at all."

"Do you call Lydia and Tim's kids, too?" They're my brother and sister, but they're a good bit older than me, and we have never been close. I can't even remember their kids' names. That makes me feel bad for a second, but I get over it quickly. They don't know my kids' names, either.

He nods. "I do."

"So, it's just me you never had a relationship with?" The words are out, hanging in the air, before I even realize I said them. I want to jerk them back, but it's too late.

He lays his napkin down.

"When I met your mother, I was flat broke. I went to college in Virginia on a scholarship, and one day I saw your mother walking barefoot on the grass." He smiles. "She was the most beautiful thing I'd ever seen. She was wearing a green flowery sundress, and her toenails were painted pink. Her hair hung down over her shoulders, and it was a riot of curls."

I've never seen my dad get all nostalgic. I'm not sure I like it.

"I was a total nerd, and she was the most free-spirited person I had ever met. I fell in love with her in seconds."

"What happened?" I ask. I stop eating because I have never heard him like this before, and I'm afraid he'll stop. I don't want him to stop, despite the fact that this feeling is so foreign to me. I actually want to hear about their past from my dad.

"I played around with computers. That's all I wanted to do, until I met her. Then life became fun and playful. We built forts in our dorm rooms, and then we'd spend the day wrapped up inside them." His face gets a little red, and he coughs into his fist. "It was magical."

"That doesn't sound like Mom at all."

He makes a snuffling noise. "I know, right?" he says. "But she was amazing. We got married, and then your mom got pregnant with Tim and then with Lydia, and we didn't have a pot to piss in, but we were happy. So happy. Sometimes it hurts to even think back to those days. Because then things changed."

"You cheated."

His eyes jerk up to mine. "No. That was after."

"After what?"

"Your mom got pregnant a third time and then miscarried late term. Very late term. She sank into a depression and had a really hard time coming out of it. At the same time, I sold some computer software I'd written to a big company, and we suddenly had some money. We bought a house, and your mom started to settle in. But I had long hours, and she started to pull away from me more and more. She started dressing in fancy clothes and going out to lunch with friends, all of whom were really wealthy, and we were growing more and more wealthy, too."

"I didn't know about the baby."

"So, I was working all the time, some of which was to support her new need for more things, bigger cars, and jewelry." He shakes his head. "The girl I met in the grass that day was suddenly gone, and I worked really hard to bring her back. I had a limited amount of time and even less energy, but I did try. Your mom pushed me away at every turn, and finally, I realized that we were just living in the same house. We weren't in love anymore. We were nothing."

"That's when you met Kendra's mom."

He nods. "She worked in my office. It was terribly inappropriate, and I still feel bad about it. But what hurt even more was when I broke things off with her and went to confess my sins to your mother, your mom just didn't care anymore. She wanted to maintain her lifestyle and nothing more. So, I stayed in a relationship with Kendra's mother. And your mother became the woman she is today."

"Cold and heartless."

"She's not cold and heartless," he protests. "She's just…hurt, I think. I don't know. She never really got over that baby. And she never got over us. And neither did I."

"Dad," I start. "How did you two end up with me?" I'm fifteen years younger than my siblings. Like a whole new family.

He smiles. "It was crazy. One day I went home, and your mother was in the garden. She had dirt from the tip of her nose to the bottoms of her feet. Honestly, she acted a little bit nuts that day, looking back on it, but she was her old self. I don't know what happened, but it was like someone flipped a switch in her. I looked into her eyes and saw the woman I fell in love with."

He grins. "She looked up at me from the dirt pile and asked me if I wanted to help. She shoved a trowel at me, and I took off my coat and rolled up my sleeves. We got dirty together, and then the sprinklers suddenly came on, drenching us both. Your mother, with her perfect hair and her perfect everything else, would normally throw a hissy fit if she got wet or dirty, but she just flopped down on the grass and laughed. That was when I realized your mother was sober. She was completely and totally sober, and she hadn't been for a really long time.

"She'd gone through AA and been in therapy, and I hadn't even noticed it. She wasn't taking pain pills she didn't need. Her head was clear, and she was that laughing, funny, intelligent girl I met in college. But older and better. And I realized I still loved her. I worked really hard to court her and make her fall in love with me again. And she did. She let me back in."

"Did you stop seeing Kendra's mother?"

He nods. "I couldn't stop seeing her entirely, because we had a daughter together, but I did stop the relationship. She was heartbroken, but she got over it. I think she respected the fact that I wanted my marriage again, in some small way." He shrugs. "She did fall in love again and marry, and it wasn't a relationship that had to be in secret. Back then, interracial couples didn't go out in public without some pretty obnoxious stares, particularly wealthy white men who are already married. But she met a man and got married. She was happy. And I was happy with your mom." He grins. "And you were born. Your mom was ecstatic."

I snort. "You're a good liar, Dad."

He holds up his hands as though surrendering. "I'm not lying. It was like we had a new start."

I wait, because he's going to drop the bomb on me soon. I can feel it coming.

"Then when you were around five, I noticed that she was going out to lunches with her old friends, and she was suddenly pushing me away. She started drinking again, and it became all about the wealth. No matter what I did, she wouldn't get any help. But I stayed. I never left her side. Kendra's mother died, and your mom threw a party, even though that relationship had been over for years. I've never been able to forgive her for that."

"Ding-dong, the bitch is dead," I whisper.

He startles. "You knew about that?"

I nod, and tears fill my eyes. I brush them back. "She was drunk when it happened. When she told me, I mean."

"I hired nannies to take care of you because she simply wasn't able. I worked because I had to keep her in the lifestyle to which she was accustomed. Looking back, I should have forced her to get treatment. She could have been a wonderful mother to you if I had."

"All water under the bridge, Dad," I say. "None of it can be changed now." I start to clear the dishes from the table.

"Your mom is in rehab again," he blurts out.

I sink back into my chair, and the plates clatter to the tabletop. "Now?"

He nods. "Yes, now. She went. I saw her yesterday. She looks good. Like her old self. She wants to see you."

I feel like someone has let the air out of me. "I assumed you asked me to take these kids because you knew I didn't care if I ever had a relationship with Mother."

I may as well have slapped him. "I asked you to take them because you have more love to give than anyone I have ever met. They needed you."

"No, Dad," I correct. "I needed them. They don't love me yet, but they have the potential to. And I'm hopeful that one day they will, because I already know I love them. All of them."

"I had a feeling that's how this would go."

"Why the sudden interest in my life, Dad?" I ask. "Phone calls and lunches and showing up at matches… I don't know what to do with it all. I don't know why you're doing it." I pound my fist on the table, and the dishes jump. "You don't have to pretend to love me for me to love them."

"I'm not pretending, Sky. I do love you. I know I royally messed things up. But I'm still your father, and if you'll let me, I want to be there for you."

"Take, take, take, take." I throw up my hands. "That's all you ever do, Dad. You take. You took from Kendra's mother. You took from Kendra. You take from the kids because they make you feel loved. There's nothing like unconditional love from children." I squeeze my fist in front of my heart. "You took from Mom."

"Your mom has her own demons."

"And so do you, Dad. It's called being an unfaithful liar."

He opens his mouth to protest, but I hold up a hand. "Do you know that I can't have a healthy relationship with a man because I'm constantly waiting for him to leave? I'm waiting and waiting for him to take off and go away, just like you did. I'm always waiting for him to drop me. And I don't care if he does, because I never let anyone get close enough to hurt me."

Jesus Christ. Where did that come from?

I get up and finally put the plates in the sink. "I think you should go, Dad," I say. I brace my hands on the edge of the counter because my knees are about to give out.

I hear Dad shuffle around. Then he comes over and kisses my temple really quickly. "I love you, Sky," he says.

Then he's gone. And it's not until he leaves the room that I let myself break. I drop onto the couch and put my head in my hands and sob. I cry because I didn't ask for any of this. I didn't ask for him to unburden his soul all over my kitchen table. Now I know enough that I pity him, and I'd rather hate him. I'd rather feel nothing at all. There's a noise at the door, and it opens. I'm about to scream at Dad, but I see Seth come in. He stops short when he sees me.

"What's wrong?" he asks.

I force a smile and sweep beneath my eyes with my fingertips. "Allergies," I say. "Why are you home early?"

"We got out at noon today," he says. "Half day."

"Oh." He must have forgotten to tell me he had a half day. It wouldn't matter anyway, since Joey and Mellie would be gone all day regardless. Day care isn't on the same schedule. I get up and try to smile at him. "I'm going to go take a shower."

I go into my room and lean heavily against the door. How did everything get so messed up?

Matt

Paul sits across from me at the kitchen table munching on his Honey Graham Oh's. He flings an envelope at me from the mail pile. I look down at the elegant scroll. Fuck. It's the invitation.

I open it up and pretend to read out loud. "You are cordially invited to the wedding of the lying bitch and the cheating fuckhead of a best friend." I lay it down on the table and point to the envelope. "Look, she included the whole family. You guys can go with me."

"Are you going to go?" Paul asks around his cereal.

I shrug. "I don't see why I should. It's not like it matters."

He grins. "You're over her."

"Hell, yeah, I'm over her," I say. And I am. I am one hundred percent completely over her. "I am pretty damn sure I'm in love with Sky."

I've seen her every night this week. On the days when I can't go over to the apartment at night, I take her to an early lunch at work. I don't want to go a day without seeing her. We still haven't moved past the hot-kissing stage, but that's okay with me.

Paul narrows his eyes at me. "That was quick."

"Pete and Logan say that's how it worked for them." I snap my fingers. "Quick."

Paul shakes his head. "I can't say I've ever felt that."

Hopefully, one day, he will.

My phone vibrates in my pocket, and I pull it out. Why would Seth be calling me this early in the afternoon?

"What's wrong, Seth?" I ask. I'm grinning when I answer, but it soon falls from my face. He's quiet. Too quiet.

"Seth?" I ask.

"I came home from school early today," he says, his voice a whisper.

"Okay…"

"And Aunt Sky was crying on the couch."

"Do you know why?" I grab my keys and start for the door.

"I don't know. It wasn't like a little sniffle, either. She was just sobbing. Like shoulder-shaking, can't-catch-your-breath sobbing. Do you think she has her period or something?"

Her period. I snort to myself. He better not say that where she can hear him. "Where is she now?" I'm already walking down the street toward a cab. I jump in and talk to Seth the whole way to their apartment.

"She said she was going to take a shower."

"Okay, let me in when I get there."

"I don't know what to do with a crying woman," he whispers vehemently.

Neither do I, but we'll figure it out.

He lets me in when I knock, and then he throws up his hands and points toward Sky's room. I go and knock lightly on the door. She doesn't open it, so I test the knob. It turns, and I let myself into the room. I can hear water running from the shower, so I go in that direction.

She's still crying. I can see her shoulders heaving through the shower glass. All I can think is that she needs to be held. I strip down to nothing and open the shower door. She startles and then realizes it's me and jumps into my arms. She's completely naked, all wet, but she's sobbing, so I can't even enjoy it.

I close the shower door behind us, and we're both under the spray. I brush her wet hair back from her face. "What's wrong?" I ask. I turn so that my back takes most of the water.

She doesn't talk. She just shakes her head against my shoulder and holds tightly to me. She sobs into my neck, and I just hold her. I don't know what else to do for her. I'm as lost as Seth is when it comes to crying women. I think all men are. But she's fucking miserable, and I think I just need to support her.

Finally, her sobs quiet, and I realize that she has rivers of mascara running down her face. I very gently push her back under the spray and wash it away, sluicing her face with my fingertips. I pick up a shampoo bottle and lather her hair. She gets really still in my arms, but she doesn't fight me. She lets me take care of her. I rinse her hair and wash her with a soapy washcloth. I try not to look at her boobs, but it's fucking hard. They're boobs and I'm a guy, not to mention that they're fucking perfect. I force myself to skim over them and pay attention to the rest of her body. She has dimples over her ass, and I want to lick them, but I don't. Instead, I shut off the water, step out, and come back with towels.

She lets me wrap her up and dry her hair a little. I wrap a towel around my waist and pull her by her fingertips to her bed. She tugs the covers back like she's exhausted and slides between the sheets. I move to pull the covers up to her chin, but she mewls a little protest when I try to leave so I slide in behind her.

She lets me wrap my body around her. But then she surprises me and pulls her towel off, tossing it to the floor. I follow with mine. We're naked between her sheets, and oh my God, I have no idea what to do with her. I thought when this time came I would be ready to make love to her. But that's obviously not what she needs right now, not to mention that Seth is in the other room.

I brush her wet hair down between us, and she rolls to face me. "My dad came to visit today."

I don't say anything because I don't think she wants me to. Her nipples are little pinpoints pressed against my chest, but I force myself to lightly draw my fingertips down her arm instead of touching them.

"He bared his soul to me. He told me about all the awful things he and my mother did to one another and why."

Her voice is soft but not weak. Not at all. She sounds a little nasally from all the crying, and she's a little hoarse.

"He told me about how I came to exist."

I hope he didn't go into a shit-ton of detail, because that would just be gross.

"I wasn't a mistake. But what I told him might have been."

"What did you tell him?" I ask softly.

"I told him that it's all his fault that I can't fall in love with someone."

I freeze. *Where does that leave me?* "Why?"

"I'm used to being alone. If I don't count on anyone, I'll never get let down."

I can see that.

"But then you happened."

I take her leg and draw it over my hip. My dick is hard, and she's right there, but I can't do that. "And?" I ask. I run my fingers from knee to hip and skim over her naked bottom.

"And I think I fell in love with you. I'm not one hundred percent sure, but I know I like you a lot and I want to have you around. And now that I'm getting used to you, you're going to break my heart because I kind of need you, Matt. I kind of need for you to love me, too."

I roll her to her back and settle between her thighs. I balance myself on my elbows by her head so I can play with the wet hair on her forehead, brushing it gently to the side. "Done," I say.

Her eyes jerk up to mine. "Done?" she echoes.

I nod and kiss the tip of her nose. "I want to eat, sleep, and breathe you, woman," I say. I drag my nose up and down the side of hers. She shivers in my arms.

I kiss her quickly, and she scowls. "Needing me and wanting me are not the same as loving me," she says, chewing on her lower lip. Her eyebrows furrow, and I kiss the crease between them, then smooth it with my thumb.

"Are you in love with me yet?" I ask.

"Are you in love with *me* yet?" she asks me.

"Yeah," I say softly. "I am."

"Me, too," she chirps. Then she giggles, and I can feel her belly rumble beneath mine. I really need to get off her or I'm going to be inside her.

"My mom is in rehab," she says. I move over and bring her back to my chest.

"Really?"

She folds her hands on my chest and rests her chin on them. "Really," she says.

"How do you feel about that?" I ask. I trail my fingers up and down her naked back.

"That's the kicker," she says. "I feel hopeful." She heaves a sigh. "Sucks, doesn't it? No matter what they do to me, I still want them in my life."

"You want what could be," I say. "That's pretty normal."

"I want to be the kind of mom she wasn't." She blinks her pretty blue eyes at me.

"I think you're already succeeding at that." I stay quiet for a minute. "I always said the same thing. I wanted to be the dad my dad wasn't. He just took off. And I swore I would be better and do better." I mentally shrug. "Now I can't have kids, so I guess it's a moot point."

"I don't want to jump the gun or anything," she says. She winces. "But if we ever got to the point where we wanted to make this permanent…"

"I'm already there," I blurt out.

She laughs. "Do you think you might want to be a father to my kids? Like an all-the-way kind of dad? They have dads, you know that, but they're not active in their lives."

My heart swells in my chest, and I have to blink hard. "Yep," I say past the lump in my throat. "I'd adopt them, if they'd let me, and be an all-the-way kind of dad." I roll her over and settle between her thighs again. But I just want to look into her face. "And you can be an all-the-way kind of mom, and we can be ecstatically happy with the three we were blessed with. I already love them."

She brushes my hair back from my face. "You do, don't you?"

"I think I fell in love with them around the same time I fell in love with you. On day one." I laugh because I'm baring my soul here and it feels damn uncomfortable.

Sky rocks her hips under me, and I slide through her wetness. "Make love to me, Matt," she whispers.

But then there's a clatter, and the sound of screaming voices in the hallway. "Oh crap," she says, scurrying to sit up. "Seth must have gone and got the girls early." She pulls the sheet off me, leaving me bare on my back in the bed. She stops and looks down at my dick. "Um…" she says. She points to my manhood, and I swear it pulses like it's putting on a show for her. "What's that?"

"That would be my dick, and if you don't stop looking at it, I'm going to lock the door and use it to do wonderful things to you."

She scoffs. "I've seen a dick before," she says. "I meant the piercing."

"That's for you to lead me around by," I say. I chuckle.

She laughs and covers her mouth. "Does it, like, get in the way?"

I shake my head and go get my boxers. "You'll love it. I promise. It has magical powers."

She arches her brow. "All that from a piercing?"

"I was talking about my dick having magical powers." She steps into her panties, and I heave a sigh. So close to the Promised Land. "I'll show you one day when we don't have kids around."

"You mean like never," she says with a laugh.

I laugh, too, and swipe a hand down my face. "Never say never," I murmur. I put on my boxers and jeans, and then the door opens, and Mellie and Joey roll in just as I tug my shirt over my head. They jump onto the bed, and my moment with Sky is over. Or has it just begun? Hell, I can't tell.

Skylar

I park my car in the parking lot of the rehab center and drop my forehead to the steering wheel. I don't know why I'm here. Except for the fact that Dad asked me to come. I could have said no. I should have said no.

But I didn't.

I approach the desk and ask for my mom's room, but they lead me to the garden. The nurse leaves me outside the double doors and shuts them behind me. Ahead lies a large brick patio with deck chairs. It is littered with big, poufy furniture that looks really comfortable. I look around. I don't see Mom. But then a woman gets up from a lounger, and I look closely. It's my mother. Her face is stripped bare of makeup, and her hair is down around her shoulders. It's held back from her face with a clip, and I can't remember ever seeing her look so natural. Only it's not natural for her at all. It's completely *un*natural.

"Mom?" I say. She motions toward the nearby rocking chair.

She sits down and pulls her legs up, hooking her arms around her knees as if she wants to draw up inside herself. She doesn't lean forward to give me those air kisses that don't mean anything. I don't know how I'm supposed to act without them. I sit down and grip my knees tightly.

She lays her head back against the seat and tilts it toward me. "I'm glad you came," she says quietly. "Surprised, but glad." She smiles.

I'm immediately jarred because there's no malice or artifice. And instead of looking at my clothes, my makeup, or my hair, she's looking at my face. I purposefully didn't dress up today because I wanted to give her plenty to pick on, with the hope she would leave my kids alone.

"Why are you surprised?" I ask.

She shrugs. "If I were you, I wouldn't have come." She looks into my eyes, and my heart leaps in my chest, and then it gathers in my throat. I have to swallow hard to move past it.

My mother's feet are bare, and I see fuzzy slippers lying beneath her on the pavers. They have Oscar the Grouch on them, and my mind is blown. "Nice slippers," I say.

Mom smiles. "Your dad brought me those." She snorts. I have never heard any such noise come from my perfect mother's nose. "They're kind of fitting for the situation."

"Are you okay?" I ask.

She puts her feet down, sliding them into those crazy slippers she normally wouldn't be caught dead wearing, and runs her hands up and down her arms. "I'm better today. The first week was kind of hard. A lot of puking my guts out and even more time spent wishing I could."

My mom just said the word *puke*.

She narrows her eyes at me. "What's on your mind, Sky?"

I shake my head. "Nothing." If I could verbalize it, I still wouldn't. She's been fragile my whole life, and just because she doesn't seem fragile right this second doesn't mean she's not.

"Your dad comes by every day," she says quietly.

"He told me."

"Glad you two are talking," she says quietly. She's looking at me, really looking at me, and it makes me a little restless.

"Why did you want to see me?" I ask. I heave a sigh. I feel like all the air has been sucked out of me.

"I'm supposed to make amends to all the people I have wronged," she says with a shrug. She reaches over and picks up a pack of cigarettes. She shakes one free and lights it. My jaw falls open. I can't help it.

"When did you start smoking?" I ask.

She smiles and lays her head back in that lazy way again. "You can't take all my bitterness, betrayal, and hatred, *and* my alcohol and drugs from me and leave me with nothing," she says with a laugh. But there's no mirth in the noise. "I'll quit. I just need to get through this."

I nod because she may as well have slapped me.

"Your dad told me that he had a talk with you," she says. She blows out a long puff of smoke that seems to go on forever. "He told you about our history."

I nod. "He told me about the baby, and Kendra's mother."

She doesn't say anything. She just smokes, letting the cigarette dangle from her lips for a second, with one eye closed.

"He said you told him to go to hell, pretty much," she says. She smiles. It's cheeky and so beautiful.

A grin tugs at my lips. "I didn't say that in so many words."

"You told him that his choices affected the way you look at life. Men, in particular. Or did he get that wrong?"

"He got it right." I nod.

"Your dad wasn't alone in that. I am just as much to blame, if not more so." She shrugs, and a sad smile crosses her lips. "I was a terrible mother, too deeply mired in my own addictions and my own problems to parent you."

"I don't need apologies."

"Too bad," she bites out. "You're going to get them." She leans over and smudges out her cigarette. Then she touches my knee. "I'm sorry I didn't do better. I always said I would when I could, but I never got to that point. I'm sorry." Her eyes flit around, and then they land on me. "I kept telling myself that tomorrow I would change. But tomorrow never came." She blinks back tears. I have never seen emotion on my mom's face before. She's usually a vacant shell.

"What do you want me to say?"

She shakes her head. "There's no right thing or wrong thing to say. You can tell me how you feel. You can tell me to go to hell. Do what's right for you, because I never did." She points a finger at me. "You're responsible for your happiness and taking care of your heart. Only you. Other people contribute to your happiness, certainly, but you can't wait for anyone to make you happy, Sky. Nobody is going to do that for you."

She leans back again and draws her feet up.

"Now tell me how you feel," she says. "Don't hold back."

I take a deep breath, and I open my mouth to tell her that I would never be so cruel. But what tumbles from my lips is something else entirely.

"I feel like I don't even have parents," I say. "You and Dad were never around, and even when you were, you weren't. My nannies took me to dance recitals, and the household staff taught me to drive. And every time I got close enough to one of them to think they might love me, you fired them. It was cruel and harsh punishment." I lay a hand on my chest because it's suddenly aching. "I never did anything to either of you, except exist. I was quiet when you had a headache, when you were so hung over that you couldn't get out of bed. I was a perfect student. I was a drama-free teenager. I did everything just to make you like me. But you never did."

I get up and start to pace. I expect her to point to the chair and tell me how unladylike my tantrum is, but she doesn't. She just looks at me. And she's really looking at me, like I have never seen her do before. Her ears and eyes are open. Dare I hope her heart is open, too? I shouldn't. But some little piece of me still reaches for that hopeful feeling.

"I went to college and studied law, just like Dad. And I went to social events and joined committees, just like you. I attended fundraisers and made a general spectacle of myself, just to make you happy. And all I ever asked in return was for someone to love me. But you were incapable of it."

She lights another cigarette, and I see a tear roll down her cheek. She doesn't reach up to rub it away, and she doesn't hide it.

"Mother, I don't even know what to say to you. I have been so nice to you my whole life that I can't even be mean to you now, not in good conscience." I sit back down and cross my legs. "Why did you come to the funeral?" My foot starts to twitch and swing, and I half expect her to tell me to be still. But I couldn't even if I wanted to.

"I wanted to see what I was up against," she says quietly. "I've always wanted to see." She heaves in a breath. "When Kendra was small, I used to sit outside their apartment and watch him with them. He never knew I was there, but he wouldn't have cared anyway. I sent him back to her because I was so fucking miserable that I couldn't let love in, even when it was staring me in the face."

The wind blows her loose hair, and she tucks a strand behind her ear. "They're innocent, just like you were. They deserve love, and for that reason, I'm glad they have you. No one is more capable of love than you, Sky. Don't ever doubt that. You love and you forgive like no one else I have ever met."

"I haven't forgiven you," I bite out.

She laughs. It startles me, and I grip the arms of the chair so tightly my knuckles turn white. "If you forgave me just after a conversation, I would think that you were weak and tired. And you are neither of those things, Sky. You are strong and brave, and you love without restraint. I wish I could be more like you." She chuckles. "I'm planning to be more like you. I have some things I need to work through, but I'm getting there."

"What's it like being sober?" I blurt out. Yeah, I want to hurt her, but she deserves it.

"Hard," she says. She takes a drag of her cigarette and stubs it out. "Really hard. Everything hurts. Every memory. Every thought in my head hurts because it's all full of regret. I have regrets, Sky. I regret everything. I wish I could take it all back, but I can't. I know you don't trust me, and honestly, I don't trust myself. So, if you want to walk out of here and not look back, I understand."

She sits quietly, staring into the far recesses of the garden.

"I'd like to meet your kids," she suddenly says.

I start to protest.

She holds up a hand. "Not right now. When I've earned the right. I'd like to meet them and get to know them. It's sad what happened to their mother. She was a good woman."

"How would you know?" I toss out.

"I met her a few times. We would get together for lunch. One time, I got drunk over a martini or ten at our lunch, and Kendra took me home in her car. I didn't use my driver because I didn't want him to tell your father where I was going."

"What happened?" I whisper.

"She was good and kind. She took me home and held my head over the toilet. Then she cleaned me up. She tucked me into bed, and she apologized for her mother ruining my marriage." She chuckles. "But what she didn't know was that her mother didn't ruin anything. I did. I ruined all of it. I refused to let love in. And I refused to let it in because I wasn't worthy."

I can't even speak.

"When I found out she was dying, I went to her. She talked to me about the kids and her fears. She cried. I cried. I went home and told your father what happened, and I told him that he should ask you to help. That you had more love inside you than anyone I'd ever met, and that those kids would be lucky to have you. Then I went and got stinking drunk and almost killed myself on pain pills.

Because giving you those kids meant I had to give up my hatred of them. I couldn't stomach that. Your father helped me through the night. Then I did it again after the funeral. Your dad had to call 9-1-1."

"Why didn't anyone tell me?" My foot starts to twitch again.

"Would you have cared?" She stares into my face. "You might have felt a moment of displeasure, but you would have gotten over it quickly. I wasn't worth more than a passing thought to anyone, and I'd set it up that way myself." She shrugs.

I sniff back my indignation. "I would have cared."

She snorts again. "I would have been your mother that died. The woman who gave birth to you and then didn't do anything else for you your whole life."

Damn, that hurts to think about. But she's right.

"Your dad says you have a boyfriend," she says and smiles.

I nod. "Matthew," I tell her. She doesn't deserve the details.

"The one with the tattoos," she says. "He's very handsome."

"He's good and kind," I correct. Then I smile, because thinking of him brings it out in me. "And handsome."

"Do you love him?" she asks.

I nod my head. "As much as I know about love," I say. "If I have to say yes or no, I say yes. But I'm not completely sure what that means."

"I'm sorry we made you doubt yourself so much. You're worth so much more." She swipes a hand beneath her nose. "We were terrible examples."

"I don't trust him with my heart," I admit. "I'm terrified to love him."

"Afraid he'll turn on you?" she asks. "Or that he'll walk away?"

"Or that he'll love me till the end of time," I say. That's just as scary, because I don't know what to do with it.

"You should look into some Al-Anon meetings," she says. "They're for families of addicts."

"Okay," I say.

She taps my leg. "For you," she says. "Not for me."

She lights a new cigarette. I raise my brow at her.

She laughs. "I've never felt quite so exposed. It's a new and scary feeling. So, forgive me my vices. I'll quit when I get through this."

"Okay." I understand. I think.

"Don't be afraid to let him love you, Sky," she says quietly. "I was afraid to let your dad love me. I didn't think I deserved it, after the things I did when I was drinking. So I shut him out. Let Matthew in. Let him love you. Take it all in and let it seep into your bones. Don't let it go. If he breaks your heart, at least you'll know you still have one. Don't die inside, like me. Let love in. Let it surround you and keep you on your feet when you can't go anymore. Let. Love. In."

The doors to the patio open, and a nurse comes out. "It's time for group," she says, motioning toward my mother.

My mom gets up and turns to me. She hugs me tightly, holding me close. I don't remember her ever doing that before, and I stiffen in her arms. "Let. Love. In," she whispers close to my ear.

She leaves, and I fall back into my chair. My legs won't support me, and I can't leave yet. I'm shaking too badly. It's like everything I never wanted has now fallen into my lap, and I don't know what to do with it.

When I finally can, I get up and go to the only place where I know I can find peace. I go to Matt.

Matt

Paul is in a shitty mood. I don't know what's up with him, but he's been particularly irritating today. Friday's a little bit off, too, but I don't know what's up with her any more than I know what's up with Paul. Paul bangs his tattoo gun on a nearby table, hitting it hard enough that even Logan looks up.

WTF? Logan signs.

I shrug my shoulders. Logan is working on some particularly intricate designs for the catalogs we have pinned to the walls. When he's not at school, at Madison Avenue, or doing tats, he occupies himself by making designs for people to choose from. Some people come in with no idea what they want, and they look through the catalogs until they find something. Other people come in with designs in their heads, and then we have to translate them into real life. I'm glad Friday can draw, too. She's almost as good as Logan. I've seen some of her art, and it's breathtaking.

"Dude, you trying to bust it or fix it?" Pete asks, his brow raising as he stares at Paul. We all have our own equipment, so I don't particularly care if Paul breaks his when he has a tantrum. But I'd rather avoid it if we can talk him through it.

"The damn thing isn't working right," Paul mumbles.

Logan walks over to him and holds out his hand. Paul glares at it and then he rolls his eyes and hands over the tattoo gun. Logan does something to it really quickly and gives it back. He doesn't grin or gloat. He just goes back to the light table, a special table he uses for tracing, and continues his drawing.

"I fucking hate you," Paul mumbles to his back.

I grin. I can't help it.

"What?" Logan asks, looking from me to Paul and back.

"He said thank you," I say.

"I'm sure he did." He glares back at Paul. "What the fuck crawled up your ass?" he asks.

The rest of us go quiet. No one usually messes with Paul when he's in a snit. We step around him and keep on moving until he gets over it.

"He's pissy because he did something stupid last night," Friday tosses out. She doesn't look at him. She just talks about him. She has bigger balls than any of us do, I'll say that for her. "Then he wanted to take it back, but it was too late. So now he feels guilty." She blows out a breath and starts to pack up her backpack. She shoves her books into the bag one by one, using a lot more force than is necessary.

"Where are you going?" Paul barks. Storm clouds are brewing in his eyes.

"I don't know," she barks back. "Maybe I have a date. Maybe I want to get laid. Maybe I just want to have an earth-shaking orgasm and not have to feel guilty about it ten minutes later."

"Oh fuck," Pete says under his breath. I shoot him a look, and he covers his mouth.

"Wait a minute and I'll walk you home," Paul says as he puts his things away.

"No, thank you," Friday chirps. She raises her arm and waves at us from behind her head, her fingers wiggling as she calls, "Good afternoon, all."

"You'll be back tomorrow, right?" Paul yells to her. He's looking a little unsettled, even more than a minute ago.

She doesn't say anything. She just slams the door hard enough that my feet shake under me. Shit. That was awkward.

Paul sinks heavily into a chair and drops his head into his hands, his elbows resting on his knees. He looks so tired. I want to go to him and make him feel better, but I'm afraid I can't.

"You should go after her," Logan says.

Paul looks up. "That's the last thing she needs," he says quietly. He shakes his head. "Never mind." He stands up. "Get back to work," he says to all of us.

Pete opens his mouth to give him a hard time, but I cough into my fist, and he looks at me and throws up his hands. Pete's gaze follows Friday, like he wants to go make sure she's all right. I see him pull his phone from his pocket, and he texts really quickly. He's probably asking Reagan to check on her. He looks up at me and nods. She'll ensure Friday is all right.

There's this crazy tension between Friday and Paul that no one understands, not even them. He can be such a man-whore, particularly now that Kelly is seeing someone. He sleeps with just about everyone, but for the past couple of weeks or so, he hasn't been quite as flirty with girls in the shop, and he hasn't even been on many dates.

The bell over the door tinkles, and I look up. My heart stutters when the woman of my dreams walks through the door. Sky is outlined by the sun as she stands in front of the window, and I've never seen a more beautiful sight. She shifts from foot to foot and crosses her arms beneath her breasts.

"Hi," she says quietly.

She's wearing jeans and a sweatshirt, and she looks so damn pretty that I can't keep from grabbing her. I walk across the room and draw her against me. I lift her arms and put them around my neck. "I'm so glad you're here," I say, and I mean every word. Honestly, she just made my belly flip. I bend my head and kiss her quickly, but her lips follow mine when I start to pull back. Her mouth is soft and warm and wet, and the kiss shoots straight to my center.

My brothers start their catcalling, and I finally have to lift my head. I flip them the bird, and she steps back from me, her cheeks all rosy and pretty. She waves at my brothers. It's a jerky, quick move, and then she buries her face in my shirt. She's so fucking beautiful that she steals my breath, and her blushing is absolutely adorable.

Sky grabs my shirt in her fists and jerks my gaze to hers. "Have you had lunch yet?" she asks.

I just ate, but I wouldn't pass up a chance to sit beside her for an hour for anything. I shake my head. "Do you want to go out?"

She bites her lower lip between her teeth. "Want to go to my place?"

She avoids my gaze, and my heart does that fluttery thing again. "For lunch?"

She nods, but her cheeks go even rosier, and I have no idea what she's thinking. I hope she's thinking what I'm thinking, which revolves around getting her naked and getting me inside her.

"What's for lunch?" I ask as I shrug into my coat. I'm wondering what her plan is, or if we need to stop to pick up sandwiches or something.

She smiles. "Me," she says quietly. Then her smile turns into a grin, and she starts for the front door. I follow like a puppy at her heels because I can't do anything else.

Skylar

Matt trips over his own foot as we step out into the street, and I have to cover my mouth to keep from laughing out loud. He's so damn adorable that anyone who didn't fall in love with him would be an idiot. And I am not an idiot. At least not today. Today, I'm Matt's girlfriend. I am not the daughter of a drug-and-alcohol-abusing mother and a cheating father. I'm done with that for today. I'm just Matt's girl. And Matt just tripped over his own foot to get close to me.

"Oh, you think that's funny, do you?" he asks. He draws me into his arms and nuzzles my neck. Then he pushes back and looks down at me. "Why aren't you at work?" he asks as he threads his fingers through mine. The heat of his palm seeps into my skin and warms me unlike any other touch I have ever experienced. He looks into my eyes. "Everything okay?"

I roll my neck from side to side. I didn't realize how much my shoulders hurt until I saw Matt. I wish I was one of those people who can crack their neck; it always seems like it would help so much. Matt's hands come up to knead my shoulders from the front.

"You're so tense," he says, his eyebrows drawing together. "What's up?" He has only known me for a couple of weeks, and he already can sense my moods. I'm not one hundred percent sure I like it.

"I went to see my mom today," I admit.

His eyes narrow as he walks around my car and opens my door for me. I slide inside and he runs around the front of the car to get in the passenger seat. "How did it go?" he asks after he buckles up. He turns the radio down, because I left the volume a little loud when I parked.

I sigh. "Better than I expected. But now I don't know what to do with it all, you know?"

He nods. But the words that come out of his mouth are, "No, not really." He waits a minute and then says, "I mean, my family has its share of problems. But there's no one who abandoned me and then I had to reach out to in rehab, no."

"She didn't abandon me," I start.

"They both did, Sky," he says softly. "Just as surely as our dad did, your parents did. Just because they have a bunch of money and paid people to do what they should have been doing all along doesn't make them any better."

"Can we talk about something else?" I ask. My head is starting to hurt, and I stretch my neck again.

Matt reaches over and starts to knead my shoulder. "I'll take care of that for you when we get to the apartment," he says quietly.

"What?" I ask, turning my head to look at him.

"That headache," he says.

How did he know I have a headache? "It's nothing," I say.

We pull up at my apartment and park on the side of the street. Matt takes my hand as we walk inside. When the elevator doors close, he pulls me against his front, and I can feel the length of him pressed against my bottom. Goodness. He's ready for whatever we're about to do.

We walk through the door, and I throw my keys onto the kitchen table.

"Why did you bring me here?" he asks. His words whip around the room like lightning, striking me harder than he probably intended.

"I…" I can't verbalize it. I can't tell him.

"You what?" he asks. He walks slowly toward me and cups the side of my neck with his hand. He's gentle and tender, and yet I can feel how much he wants me. I might even be able to feel how much he loves me, even though I'm not sure what that is yet. Is it real? I don't know enough about it to be sure. "Why did you bring me here?"

I dip my head and push my forehead against his chest. I breathe in the scent of him and hold it deep inside me. I don't want to exhale and let it go. It's woodsy and manly and clean, and it's all Matt. "I feel like I have been emotionally assaulted, Matt," I say quietly. "And when it was all over, I needed someone who could make me feel safe." I look up at him, and his blue eyes don't even blink. "I needed someone who cares for me."

Matt scoops me up in his arms, one arm beneath my knees and the other behind my back. I squeal in surprise. He laughs and carries me into my bedroom. He kicks the door shut behind us. "How long do we have before you have to pick up the girls?" he asks. He sits down on the side of my bed and takes off his boots. He's moving quickly, and he grins.

I kick my sneakers off and pull my shirt over my head. "Hours," I say. I unbutton my jeans and push them down my legs, stepping out and kicking them to the side. Matt licks his lips. He tugs my arm when I reach behind my back to unfasten my bra. "Slow down just a little," he says. "I'm not going to rush the first time I get to love you."

My heart trips a beat. "Okay," I say quietly. I sit down on the side of the bed and cross my arms over my chest. I'm feeling a little self-conscious, particularly since I'm not wearing sexy undies. I'm wearing everyday panties and my ratty, old comfy bra.

Matt taps my chin with a crooked finger, and I look up at him. "Stop thinking," he says. He stands up and unfastens his belt, then pulls the belt from the jeans. He shoves his jeans down over his hips, and I can't jerk my eyes away when I see that his boxers are tented by his... God, he's huge. "Stop thinking about that, too," he says over a laugh.

"Lie down on your stomach," he says. He walks into my bathroom and comes back with a bottle of lotion. I crawl across the bed and lay my head on my pillow, my arms crossed beneath it. I watch him as he walks slowly toward me. "God, you're so beautiful," he says quietly. He sits down beside me and squirts some lotion into his hands, then rubs them together briskly to warm it up.

"What are you doing?" I ask.

"Taking care of you," he says. His hip touches mine, and then his warm, slick hands land on my naked shoulders. He applies pressure with his slippery fingertips, and it feels so damn good that a moan leaves my throat. "This okay?" he asks.

I moan again and nod my head, jamming my face into my pillow. "Please don't stop," I say.

He chuckles. "I won't." He does lift his hands for a minute, though, so that he can climb up to straddle my bottom. He doesn't put any of his weight on me, but I can feel him, heavy and hard on top of my lower back. "Can I undo this?" he asks quietly, his voice suddenly rough and abraded when he pulls gently on my bra fastening.

"Yes," I squeak into my pillow.

"What?" he asks with a laugh.

I turn my face and say quietly, "Yes, please." Then I bury my face in the pillow again so he won't see how flushed my skin is.

He unclasps my bra and pulls it out of his way, and then his thumbs begin to do miraculous things up and down my spine. I sink into the mattress after a few minutes, going almost limp as he attacks my muscles one by one, moving from my neck to my shoulder to my back and down to my bottom. He stops when he reaches the elastic of my panties.

"Don't stop," I whimper.

"Tell me what happened with your mother," he says when he has me sated and happy.

"I don't want to," I mutter.

He lifts his hands from my body. "I'll stop now, then," he says. Then he waits.

I draw in a breath. "Please don't stop," I beg. I have never had anyone take such great care with me. I've never had anyone who wasn't paid to give me a massage try to do so. I have never felt such...affection? I don't even know what it is, but I do know it's foreign.

"Talk to me, Sky," he says. He lifts himself, and I immediately turn to see where he's going, but he just moves farther down my legs. I sigh with contentment when he starts to rub the backs of my thighs.

I talk. I tell him everything that happened with my mother, while he works his magic on my body. He grunts when it's appropriate to the story, and his hands get harsh when he's angry, but then they get gentle. He listens. And he takes care of me, all the way down to my toes.

"I knew they'd met, but I didn't know it was a secret," Matt says when I tell him about Kendra and my mother having lunch. "She liked your mom, and she really regretted the situation she was in."

Matt's fingers hook in the hips of my panties, and he gives a gentle tug. He stops. "Is this okay?" he asks as he pulls my panties down under my butt cheeks. He takes in a quick breath, and my heartbeat jumps.

"Yeah," I whisper, smiling into my pillow. I lift my hips, and he pulls them all the way down my legs. I know he can see my ass, and then suddenly his hands are *there*. "God."

He pulls back. "Too much?" he asks.

"Not enough," I tell him.

He sucks in another breath, and his hands settle on my ass cheeks again. He squeezes and lifts and rubs, and he lets out a groan that seems so much like the one stuck in my throat.

My muscles feel like rubber, like I couldn't stand if I wanted to.

"Roll over," he says quietly. He pats my bottom. "Wait," he says when I hesitate. He slides his fingers up my inner thighs and parts my flesh. "Thank God," he says.

"What?" I ask. I look at him from over my shoulder.

"You're wet. I was hoping it wasn't just me," he says. "You got me so turned on that I don't know what to do next." He parts my lower lips with his fingertips and slides a finger inside me. I push back against him.

"You can keep doing that," I suggest. I gasp as he pushes forward, adding another finger. I lift to meet him.

He chuckles. "I can't get to anything from here," he says. He pulls out of me and slaps my butt with his wet hand. "Roll over."

I pull the sheet to cover my middle and roll over. Matt comes up to kiss me. God, he tastes like everything I ever wanted. He tugs playfully at my sheet.

"This has to go," he says with a laugh.

I clutch it to me. "I'll be naked," I whisper.

"That's what I'm going for," he whispers back playfully. He tugs the sheet again, and I let it slide away from me. I pick up the pillow and put it over my face. I'm embarrassed, but I don't want him to stop. I would stab him if he stopped right now. My clit is thrumming so hard that I can feel it in my entire body.

He whistles like a dockworker when my body is bare. His hands slide up and down my sides, gentle and soft, but with an intensity like I've never known. It's almost as if he's memorizing the lines of me. He pulls his hands back and says, "I'm so sorry. I think I just drooled on you."

I laugh and lift the pillow to look at him. But his eyes are on my breasts. He cups them in his big, tattooed hands and plumps them.

"God, they're so perfect," he says. Then he takes my nipple into his mouth. It's not a gentle lick. It's a pull that reaches the very center of me. He laves my nipple, rolling it against the roof of his mouth as he toys with the other breast with his fingertips. I pull the pillow back over my face because if I keep looking at him as he looks into my eyes and plays me, I'll explode.

"Matt, please," I beg.

He lifts the pillow from my face and tosses it off the bed. His eyes are deep blue, his pupils wide and intense as he kisses his way down my stomach. "I told you I'd take care of you," he says. "Patience." His breath tickles my belly button just before his tongue dips inside.

Matt pushes my legs apart and settles between my thighs, his exhales teasing the little strip of hair at the apex of my thighs.

"I like this," he says as he brushes it with his thumb. I arch my hips toward his pressing fingers.

"Matt," I beg. I'm going to be a quivering, pleading mess if he doesn't get on with it. "Please." Oh crap. I already am.

His thumbs part my folds, and he slides two fingers inside me. I lift my head to watch him as he licks across my clit. But it's not enough. I squirm, and he rewards me by pushing his fingers deeper. He crooks his fingers and presses down with his hand just above my pubic bone, and his lips latch on to my throbbing clit.

"Oh my God," I breathe.

He lifts his head just long enough to say, "Nope. Just Matt."

I thread my fingers through his hair and push his head back to where I want it. He latches on again, and licks against my clit in time with the thrusts of his crooked fingers. I grip the sheets in my hands, squeezing tightly, because Matt is about to break me. I can feel the build-up. I keen and cry out and arch my hips to meet him. Then he starts to hum against my tender flesh.

I shatter.

I break.

I fall apart.

I come.

And Matt pushes me all the way through it. He takes me to the top of the cliff, and then he throws me over it. But he's there to catch me when I fall. His fingers pull out of me while his gentle suckle on my clit turns to a solid, secure lick. He coaxes every tremor from me, every quake, every shake, and when I can't take any more, I push his head back. He reaches back and pulls the rubber band from his ponytail. I messed his hair up, but he doesn't seem to mind. He wipes his face on the sheet and then comes up to kiss me. I can smell me on his breath, but it's beautiful. His hair hangs like a veil around us, but I can't even lift my arms to push it back.

"You okay?" he asks.

I moan because words won't even leave my throat. They're stuck somewhere between my sated brain and limp body.

"I'll take that as a yes," he says, and he falls over, landing beside my naked body. I can't even turn my head to look at him. He kisses my cheek and rolls me over so that my bottom is nestled in his lap. "Go to sleep," he says. His arm is beneath my head, and his other arm wraps around my waist.

I want to take care of him, too, but I can't move. "I can't sleep," I murmur. "I have to pick up the girls."

He presses a kiss against my hair. "I'll wake you up in time," he says softly. "Sleep."

"You sure?" I murmur. It's not like I could move if I wanted to.

"Let me hold you," he says. He brushes my hair down between us and pulls the blanket over our bodies.

"Mmm," I murmur. But darkness is already crowding the corners of my vision.

"I love you," he says quietly, just as I let sleep overtake me. I let Matt overtake me. I let peace overtake me for the first time ever.

Matt

I wake up to the feel of a warm, female body draped over mine. I look down and see a blond head as it bends to kiss my chest. I reach down, gathering her hair as I say, "Sky?" and try to blink the sleep from my eyes.

She stills and looks up at me, her brows drawing together. "Who else would it be?" she asks. She's straddling me, and she moves like she's going to get off my hips, but I hitch my hands under her arms and lift her higher so I can kiss her. She resists. "Who else would it be?" she asks again.

She's serious. Fuck. I messed that up.

"No one," I say. I scrub a hand down my face. "I was asleep, and you're kind of kissing my chest and sitting on my dick at the same time, and I woke up and it seemed very strange. That's all."

"You knew who I was, right?"

I don't even need to think about my answer. "Of course." I did. Really, I did. "I was just confirming what a lucky son of a bitch I am by getting you to look at me while you kiss my chest and sit on my dick."

She snorts and buries her face in my chest, putting all of her weight on me. "I'm not quite sitting on your dick," she says quietly. I rock against her center, which is slippery wet against me.

"I know. Can you fix that, please?" I say. I make like I'm trying to adjust her hips, but I know I need to get a condom first. I might have been asleep, but I'm not stupid.

She lifts up a little and points down toward my dick. "I'm a little intimidated by that," she whispers playfully.

I chuckle. "Why? I promise it won't hurt you. I'll make sure he behaves." I hug her to me. My heart is almost full to bursting, and I can't think of anything I'd rather do. Well, I'd kind of like to fuck her, too, but I do have priorities, even right now.

"I wasn't talking about your…parts." Her face gets all rosy.

A laugh bursts from my throat. "Parts? You talk about me like I'm a washing machine."

"Washing machines are not pierced, Matt," she says.

"Oh," I breathe. "You mean *that*." I run my fingers through her hair like a comb. "It won't bite. I promise."

"I was kind of looking while you were sleeping," she admits.

"Looking at my face, I'm sure," I tease. "Was I drooling?"

"Nope." She shakes her head. "Down there. It looked at me first," she says.

"I told him about that shit," I gripe. "Dicks never listen. Just ask any man. He'll tell you the same."

She giggles against my chest. "You always wake up so ready?"

I lift my head and look down at her. "Usually, yeah," I admit. "It's a guy thing."

"And I thought it was just for me."

"Well, no one else is getting him," I say. "So, that would apply." I squeeze her naked bottom in my hand, and she yelps.

"Apparently, I have a lot to learn about men," she says.

"Thank God I'm willing to teach you," I growl as I hook an arm around her waist and flip her over so that I'm above her. I look down into her face, and my heart skips a beat. I want inside her so bad I can taste it, but I'm afraid to rush it.

I know what it's like to have meaningless sex, and I'm afraid she does, too. This isn't meaningless. At least not for me. This is so much more, and I want to savor every second. I also want to be sure that what she's feeling for me is as strong as what I'm feeling for her. If there's anyone who could break my fucking heart, it's her. She's everything I ever wanted.

"You're sure you're in love with me, right?" I ask as I dip my head to kiss her.

She murmurs against my lips. "As sure as I can be."

I lift my head. "What does that mean?" I brace my elbows on either side of her head and use my thumbs to brush her hair from her forehead, sweeping across the delicate arch of her brow.

"I'm still learning what all this is about," she says. "I don't fully understand it, and I wasn't looking for it. I don't know how to analyze it."

"I don't know how to take that," I admit.

"I just...I know I haven't ever felt this way about anybody, particularly not this fast. And I'm scared, Matt. I'm terrified. But I like this. I like these feelings, as much as I dislike them." She bites her lower lip between her teeth. "Can I tell you something?"

"You can tell me anything." I scoot down so that I can touch my lips to her neck. It's there and it's so pretty and soft against my lips. She smells like citrus and soap, and I love every inch of her. I am enamored with the wet parts, and I rock my hips so that I can slide against her heat. She gasps and arches her hips to meet me.

"You're the only one I needed today after I left my mom. You're the one who makes me feel safe. I think I can tell you anything and you won't judge. You dropped everything at Reed's just to come with me, you listened to me, and then you took care of me, until I fell asleep on you." She winces. "Sorry about that."

I chuckle against her skin. "Are you kidding? I enjoyed that as much as you did."

"But you didn't even..." She blushes, and she's so pretty that she makes my belly flip.

"I can get off anytime. Getting you off," I tell her, "that was a dream come true." I cup her breast in my hand and plump it gently. It's barely a handful, but it's mine and I am already in love with it. In fact, I plan to spend a lot more time with it. Along with other slippery parts of her. I take her nipple into my mouth and abrade it with the flat of my tongue. She squirms beneath me, and if she moves one more inch, I'll be inside her.

"Matt," she says, her voice quivering. Her legs come up to wrap around my hips, and I notch my dick at her cleft. I know it's risky, but I want to bump the head of my dick against her clit and see if she'll get even wetter for me.

Her eyes fall closed, and her head turns to the side. A shiver trembles up her spine, and I rock my hips. "I think you like that piercing you were so scared of a minute ago," I say quietly beside her ear. Her eyes fly open.

"That's what that is?" she whispers.

"Well, I take all the credit if you really like it," I whisper, and I drag through her heat again. She trembles in my arms.

"Matt, please," she says.

"Condom?" I ask. She points to her bedside table, and I reach for it. I really don't want to leave her because she feels so fucking good I can barely stand it.

"We need one?" she asks. I sit up on my knees so I can roll it on, and she lies there in the light of day, all exposed and pink and so fucking perfect.

"It would take a miracle for me to get you pregnant," I say. But I do need it because if there's no barrier between me and her, I'm going to go off the second I get inside her. So I roll it down my shaft and hope I can last long enough for her.

She giggles. "Because I want all the children in the whole wide world. Every last one. My three are definitely not enough."

My heart stalls. I fall down beside her instead of on top of her. She rolls toward me.

"What's wrong?" she asks.

"Don't joke about that," I say. "If you want more kids, you had better tell me now because I can't give you any." My heart's beating like I just ran a mile, and I am afraid that it's going to shatter like the glass vase I broke when I was six. There were pieces of it everywhere. I worry for her health if that happens. She'll get stabbed by pieces of my shattered heart. Oh fuck. I throw my arm over my eyes.

Sky climbs on top of me, kind of like she did earlier, her thighs bracketing my hips, her hands on my chest. She kisses through the dusting of hair on my chest. "I'm sorry I ruined it," she says quietly. She lays her face on my chest and rests the weight of her slight little body on me fully. She's warm and soft and…wet? I look down and see her wiping a tear from her eye.

Shit. I fucked it all up. "I didn't mean to make you cry," I say quietly.

"I'm not crying for me, you dummy," she says. She smacks my hands away when I try to wipe her tears.

"Then why the fuck are you crying?" I ask.

"I was crying for you," she whispers.

Shit. She can undo me so easily. "Because I can't have kids?"

She snorts. "Because you want kids." She grins. "I just happen to have three, Matt. I can share them with you, if you'll let me."

Well, I'd planned to do that anyway. She wiggles on top of me, and she's so wet and warm that I can't keep from grinding up into her.

"You ever going to show me what that piercing can do? You said it's magical, right?"

I take her hips in my hands and put her right where I want her. "Sit up a little bit so I can get to stuff," I say.

"You're calling my girly parts *stuff*?" she asks. But she's not crying anymore. She's laughing.

I reach down between us and lift my dick, pointing it toward the center of her. She's wet against my fingertips when I test her to see if she's ready for me. She's ready. I push inside her and she stills, her breaths stopping.

"Okay?" I ask.

Her eyes close, and she puts her weight on her palms, which she lies flat on my chest. She spreads her legs a little wider and slides down the length of me so, so, so slowly.

"Little bit more," I coax. My breath is choppy, and I can barely speak.

"There's more?" she grits out.

I look between us. "Yep." I laugh.

She bounces rather indelicately, and I lift my hips at the same time. I disappear inside her, and all I can see is where her naked skin meets mine.

"God, I hope that's all of it," she says. But she's smiling. She's all silky and soft and hot and so fucking mine.

"Don't move."

"Why not?" she asks. Then she tilts her hips and lifts up, and I can see where we're joined. I'm all wet and shiny with her, and then she falls, taking me back inside.

Sky balances on her hands so she can speed up and slow down as she rides me. Her perfect tits bounce as she finds a rhythm, so I sit up a little to taste them.

She gives me a second but then pushes me back down to lie flat. "Let me love you, Matt," she says.

I lift my hands and lace them behind my neck. It's been a really long time since I've done this, but I can see that she's already close. Her thighs shake, and her rhythm grows shaky. "I want you to come," I say.

Sky takes one hand from my chest and parts her lower lips with it, circling her clit. I push her hand to the side and replace it with mine, catching her clit between my thumb and forefinger. I squeeze gently as she rides me, and her breaths start to catch.

My balls are trying to climb up my throat, but she's close. I know I won't have to wait long when her back arches and her head falls, when her body is racked by trembles. She squeezes my dick inside her, her walls milking me. But I don't stop. I push her through it until she collapses on my chest, spent.

I roll her over and pull her leg up to her chest, tilting her bottom a little higher. Her eyes fall closed as sensations sweep her body, and I lunge once, twice, three times. Then I'm coming inside her. I let her leg fall so I can put my arms under her shoulders and clutch her to me. She turns her head and presses her lips to my neck, and the trembles rack me, too. I groan as I come inside her, and she meets my thrusts until being inside her becomes painful. I have to stop. I pull out of her with a hiss, and when I roll to move off her, she stops me with a hand in mine. "Don't go," she says.

"I'm not leaving." I go to her bathroom and dispose of the condom, then wipe off. I go back to the bed and draw her across me, her head finding that spot that was made for her, where my neck meets my shoulder.

"You were right," she says over a giggle. She's laughing in my arms. Since when did sex become funny? I lift my head to look down at her.

"What was I right about?"

"Your piercing is magical." She laughs out loud, but she's soft and warm and sated in my arms. And nothing ever felt so right.

"That was my dick," I say, and I slap her bottom.

She pouts, her lower lip sticking out. "Ow." She sits up and kisses me, looking into my eyes. "Just for that, I'm going to make you prove it to me later."

"I'll prove it to you right now," I growl as I reach for a new condom and roll her over.

She squeals, laughs, and parts her thighs for me. God, I'm in love with everything about her.

Skylar

"Would you stop fidgeting?" Seth murmurs to me, rolling his eyes as he knocks on the door of Matt's apartment.

I smooth my shirt. "Do I look all right?" I ask.

He rolls his eyes again and shoots me an exasperated grin. "The only complaint Matt might have is that you have too many clothes on." He snorts.

"Seth!" I scold. He really shouldn't talk about things like that.

"What?" he asks. He throws up his hands. "He's used to you greeting him in your jammies at the door is all I meant. He might not know what to do with you in clothes."

His face turns red when he realizes what he just said.

"Never mind," he grunts. He knocks again. The door flies open, and one of Matt's younger brothers motions us forward. The room is completely full of people, but I think most of them are Matt's brothers.

"Which one are you?" Seth asks. That was a little rude, but I was curious, too.

"I'm Sam," he says. "The pretty one."

He clasps hands with Seth the way men do. Then he opens his arms to me. I don't know what to do.

"Don't touch my girl!" a voice yells from over by the TV. I look over and smile when I see Matt sitting on the floor in front of the sofa. He has a game controller in his hand, and he's frantically working it.

"Too late," Sam teases. "You're way over there, and she's way over here all alone." He wraps me up in his arms and squeezes. It probably looks a lot tighter than it feels. I think he's just doing it to get a rise out of Matt.

"Come take over for me, Seth," Matt calls. He doesn't stop the controller.

Seth arches a brow at me. "Go," I say. He grins and goes to replace Matt on the floor. Matt passes him the controller, stopping for a second to watch him.

"He's going to kill all my men," Matt says as he lumbers to his feet.

He walks toward me, and my heart starts to thump. It's Friday, and I haven't seen him since he left my apartment yesterday when I had to go get the girls from school. He had to work late last night, but he's off tonight. I couldn't tell him no when he called and invited us over.

Joey tugs on my hand, and I look down at her. "What's wrong?" I ask.

"I have to go potty," she says.

Matt points toward the bathroom, and I go in that direction with her. *Sorry*, I mouth over my shoulder at Matt.

He grins and shrugs. "When you gotta go," he says.

"I can do it," Joey says when I try to go in the bathroom with her. She shuts the door in my face.

"Okay…" I say to myself.

I turn around and run directly into Matt's chest. He grabs my elbows to steady me, and I find my nose against his shirt. And I like it there, because he smells like Matt. And I like Matt. A lot. "You smell good," I say quietly, my mouth against his chest.

He bends his head and nuzzles the side of my neck. "So do you," he whispers. I tilt my head to give him better access.

Suddenly, there's a loud cough directly behind us. Matt groans and lifts his head.

"Would you knock it off?" he says.

Paul just laughs and nods toward Mellie, who is still holding my hand. "There are kids in the room, numbnuts," he says. He reaches down, and I see a tiny blonde standing beside him.

"Who is this?" I ask and point toward the little girl.

Matt motions her forward as he squats down. She perches herself on his knee. "I'm Hayley," she says. She has blue eyes and blond hair, just like all the Reeds, and she's adorable.

"My daughter," Paul says. He nods toward a door down the hallway. "Do you want to take the girls to play in your room?"

Hayley nods and smiles. They wait for Joey to come out of the bathroom, and then Hayley takes one of Joey's hands and one of Mellie's and drags them into her room. She closes the door behind them with a loud *bang*.

Paul scratches his head. "I guess I should get used to that. But I'm not sure I can," he says. He shakes his head.

"Are they okay in there?" I ask Matt. I kind of want to go see where they're playing.

"We'll check on them in a second," Matt says. His gaze darts around the room, and then he opens a door behind me and pushes me into a bedroom. He closes the door after us and flips me back against the wall with a gentle shove. "I missed you," he whispers.

His hands bracket my face, and his knee slides between my legs, which is kind of good because my knees go wobbly when he grabs me. "Matt," I warn. "The kids."

"Are all taken care of," he says. His lips touch mine, and he groans against my lips as his tongue sweeps inside my mouth. He takes my breath away with every touch. His tongue tangles with mine, mimicking the way he licked me all over in bed yesterday, and my heart starts to thump.

I clench my hands in his shirt and try to keep myself on my feet. He pulls back and looks into my face. "I'm glad you're here," he says quietly. He brushes my hair back from my forehead and then steps back.

"Whose room is this?" I ask. But I know immediately. From the books stacked on the nightstand to the overall neatness, I know it's Matt's.

He grins. "It's mine. Who else's room would I drag you into?" He snorts. "You wouldn't want to see Paul's room. There's some kinky shit in there."

"Seriously?" I ask.

He grins. "No. I'm kidding. But the look on your face is priceless." He laughs, and I love the sound of it.

"Paul's daughter is adorable," I say. I run my finger across the photos taped to his dresser mirror. They're all of him and his brothers and the girls in their lives—Reagan, Emily, and Friday. "Are the girlfriends coming tonight?" I ask. "Or am I the only one?"

"They'll be here soon. Are you kidding? They would not miss a perfect opportunity to grill you." He smiles. "So be ready."

They're going to grill me? I drop the bottle of cologne I picked up, but Matt catches it before it can hit the floor.

"Quit worrying," he says. "They're harmless." He rocks his head back and forth like he's thinking it over. "Well, I wouldn't call Reagan harmless. She can drop-kick the best of us. But with you, harmless."

I don't know what to say to that.

"Don't worry," he says again. "They like you. And they know that I love you, so they'll be on their best behavior. I promise."

My heart swells. I'm not used to Matt's declarations yet.

"You still love me, right?" Matt asks.

I roll my eyes, trying to be nonchalant. "Nothing has changed since yesterday." I look up at him from beneath lowered lashes. "Anything changed for you?"

"Yeah," he says. "I want you more than I did yesterday," he says, his voice soft and harsh all at the same time.

A knock sounds on the door, and it opens a crack. "Are you decent?" a female voice asks.

"Open the door and find out," Matt calls back.

The door opens slowly, and Emily pops her head in. "Oh, thank God," she breathes.

Matt narrows his eyes at her. "What?"

"You're both dressed. I thought that was going to be uncomfortable if I found both of you naked or something."

"Then you should have stayed outside," Matt says, but he pulls her into his side and gives her a noogie. She grins and fends him off. "What did you want?" Matt asks.

"I'm making margaritas for Reagan," she says. "You guys want one?" She looks from Matt to me and back. I don't even know if Matt drinks; I've only seen him drink beer.

"Sky wants one," he says. He nods toward me.

"I have the kids," I protest.

"And they're taken care of," he says. He nods toward Emily. "Make her one."

Emily leaves the room, leaving the door ajar. "I can't get drunk," I whisper. "I have to go home at the end of the night."

He pulls me against him with his fingers hooked in the loops of my jeans. "I was hoping you might want to stay the night," he says. "The girls can camp out with Hayley. Seth can take the couch. I'll sleep with Sam. He has twin beds in there."

He'll sleep with Sam? "Why on earth would I stay over if you're going to sleep with Sam?" I squeak. I shove his chest. "If I stay over, you're sleeping with me."

"I don't want to set a bad example for Seth," he says quietly.

"Is that why you didn't come over after work last night?" I ask. I sound like I'm pouting, and I sort of am. And I hate it, but it is what it is.

"Mmm hmm," he hums right next to my ear. The sound vibrates straight to the center of me.

"We could put Seth in with Sam, and you could start out on the couch," I suggest. I bury my face in his chest to hide my embarrassment.

"Oh, there's an idea," he says. He pretends to mull it over. "I'll think about it."

"Or we could just go home at the end of the night. That's easier."

"Home?" he asks.

I nod. "Home," I say again. "My home. Our home." I look up into his face, and he smiles down at me. His eyes are clear and focused, and I have all of his attention.

"Home," he says quietly. He nods.

I might as well lay my cards on the table, right? "All I can think about since yesterday is the way you feel when you're inside me. It's so…right." I groan. "I sound stupid."

He takes my hand and pulls it down his front until it's pressed over his hardened length. "You sound fucking hot," he says. His lips drag across my jaw toward my hairline. "Are you wet?" he asks, his words a breath by my ear.

"Yeah," I whisper back. Matt unbuttons my jeans and slides the zipper down slowly. The tines *click, click, click* until it's all the way down.

"Can I feel?" he asks.

I nod against his neck. "Yeah," I whisper again. I take his earlobe between my teeth and give it a gentle nip. Just as I do, his fingers slide through my heat and go straight to my clit. I fall back against the wall. "Matt," I whisper, reaching for his wrist. "We shouldn't be doing this."

"I know," he says. "I'll be quick. I just want to feel you come apart."

I can't breathe. "What about you?" I ask.

He chuckles. "This is for me." His fingers slide through my wetness, pressing hard and insistently, and then he hooks two fingers inside me and strums my clit with his thumb. He doesn't have a lot of room to work inside my jeans, so his movements are quick and jerky. I arch my hips, helping him find a rhythm.

I open my eyes and look into his blue ones, which are staring down at me. "Matt," I protest. But it's more pleading than protest.

"I'll make you come, Sky," he says quietly. "I promise."

I nod and lay my head back, barely able to catch my breath. "Okay," I whisper. And then the tremors start. Matt leans into me, pressing his body against mine to hold me up. I turn my head toward him and just as I come, I bite down on the tender skin of his neck. He flinches, but he growls and turns his head to cover my lips with his, drowning my cries of release with his tongue and his lips.

"Shh," he says against my lips.

I'm whimpering, and I didn't even realize it. My body shivers as I come and come and come, and I am nearly wrecked when he finally stops. He pulls his hand from my panties, zips my pants, and buttons me up. Then he chuckles and kisses me quickly.

"I need a minute by myself," he says. His voice is thick and rough and so hot.

"You want me to go?" I ask. "Seriously?"

He kisses me, his mouth lingering. "Why don't you go check on the kids?" he asks. "I'll be behind you in a minute." He turns me around, opens the door, and shoves me out into the hallway. I hear him fall against the door on the other side, and then he pounds it lightly with his fist. He laughs and growls out my name.

Oh crap. I'm still feeling all loose and languid, and he just shoved me into the hallway. Paul rounds the corner and stops suddenly. He puts his hand over his eyes. "I'm not looking," he says. He walks down the hallway and doesn't glance at me again. He opens a door, and I hear a bunch of little girl screams. That's where the girls are, apparently. They were easy to find. I follow on wobbly knees, because really, what else am I going to do?

I stick my head into the room where Paul's on the floor with three little girls climbing on him like he's a horse. He doesn't seem to mind it.

I go sit down on the edge of what must be Hayley's princess bed. I watch as Paul throws the children around, growling and rolling them. Suddenly, he looks up at me. "Hey, Sky," he says quietly. He sets the kids to the side and looks at me. I mean really looks at me.

"Yeah?" I ask. I'm still sort of dazed.

"Be careful with him, okay?" he says. His voice is soft but strong, and I can tell he means it.

"What?" I ask. I force myself out of my haze and focus on him. "I don't know what you mean."

He starts to clean up toys, throwing them into a nearby toy bin. "He's been through a lot," Paul says. "I'm not sure he could survive another heartbreak. Not and stay the same, easygoing guy he is now. Don't wreck him, okay?" he asks. He sighs out a breath.

"I won't," I say. No one ever means to do that, do they?

"He's special," Paul says. "Even before he got sick, he was different from the rest of us. He's good and kind, and he still believes in the goodness of the heart. He needs to stay that way. So, don't hurt him." He says the last part quietly, so the kids can't hear him.

"I won't," I whisper. I want to challenge him and ask how dare he. But I can see the vulnerability in his eyes. I can see that it was hard for him to have this conversation with me.

He nods and gets up, then leaves the room. I sit and watch the girls play while I collect my thoughts. I need a basket to put them all in because my head just isn't big enough.

Matt

When I come out of my room, Sky is with Paul and the girls in Hayley's room. I need a minute to collect myself and wash my hands. I throw some cold water on my face, too. It takes a minute to calm myself down, and if I didn't know that I might be going home with Sky tonight, I would have taken matters into my own hands. But as it stands, the only place I want to come is inside her. Not alone. Not ever again.

I leave the bathroom and go sit down on the couch to see how Seth is doing with my game. He's playing against Logan, and Logan can't hear the game so it's harder for him. But he's a damn fine opponent anyway. He tackles it the same way he does life, by taking cues from everything around him in the game. And he's beating Seth, so it's working for him.

I sit down next to Emily. She scoots closer to me and lays her head on my shoulder. I cuddle up with her for a second, and then scoot to the side. She shoots me a weird look.

"What's wrong?" she asks, her brow furrowing.

I pull her head to me and kiss her forehead. I love snuggling with Emily. I always have. She's like the sister I never had or ever wanted. We bonded after my chemo when she helped me out, saving my life by sacrificing her own freedom, when I didn't want my brothers to know I was sick. She holds a special place in my heart.

She inches closer to me, like she's determined to cuddle. I see Sky walk up the hallway, and her eyes find me on the couch, but

Reagan gets her attention by passing her a margarita. Sky takes it and starts to talk with Reagan.

"Matt?" Emily asks. "What is it?"

I blow out a heavy breath. "You know I love you, right?" I say quietly.

"Yes..." she replies. But she looks flustered. And concerned. And worried. I hate that I'm putting that look on her face. But things have changed.

"And you know how much I love cuddling with you, right?" I say.

She grins and leans toward me. But I push her shoulders back. "Matt?" she asks, shocked.

"Well, here's the deal." I run a hand down my face. "I love you, Em," I say, and I'm not lying. Not a bit. She saved my life by sacrificing everything she held dear two years ago, and she did it without a thought. She will always be in my heart.

"Okay..." she says. "But?" She holds out her hands like she's surrendering to the cops.

I look over at Sky, and she raises her glass to me. She keeps talking with Reagan, and I am glad because I have to have this conversation with Emily. "I love you, Em, but I'm *in love with* her." I nod toward Sky. "Like want to move in with her tomorrow and die together when we're old kind of love."

She sits back a little. "Oh," she breathes. She looks like someone just slapped her. Emily and I don't have feelings for one another, not like that. But we have always cuddled, and I think I'm hurting her feelings, and I fucking hate it because she doesn't understand.

"I'm in love with her, and I'm afraid she'll feel weird about me cuddling with you."

Her brow furrows even more. "So you explain our relationship," she says with a laugh. "She'll understand." She leans like she wants to lie on my side. I push her back a little. "Matt," she protests. "Stop doing that."

"Em," I say. "If you're cuddled up with me, she can't get in that spot, and I really, really, really want her in that spot."

Her face softens.

"Do you get it now?"

She motions toward Logan. "Logan never minded our cuddling. Why would she?"

Honestly, I wouldn't fuck Emily if she were the last woman on the planet. If Logan died tomorrow, and every other woman on the planet did, too, I still wouldn't fuck Emily, that's how much I love her like a sister, but I don't want there to be any confusion. I don't want Sky to feel weird about it. I shake my head because I don't know what more I can say to her.

"Matt," she says softly. I look up into her face, and my heart almost breaks when I see her eyes filling with tears. "You're really in love with her, aren't you?"

I grin. I can't help it. "Yeah," I say. "I am." I nudge her shoulder with mine. "You okay with that?" I ask.

She leans over like she's going to hug me but pulls back. "I can still hug you, right?" she asks. I take her in my arms and hold her tightly to me, and then I roll her over and drop her unceremoniously into Logan's lap. He looks up at her and grins, surprised to find her there.

"We're okay, right?" she asks me, motioning from me to her and back.

I ruffle her hair. "We're just like we've always been," I say. I let my hand rest on the top of her head.

Sky walks over to me and sits down next to me. I put my arm on the back of the couch, and she snuggles against my side. Nothing ever felt quiet as right as this moment does.

Logan turns off the game and the TV. Now that Emily is in his lap, she has all of his attention. Logan signs to me. *Go get Em's guitar.*

I get up and go to the closet where Emily keeps her favorite guitar. Reagan passes out drinks while Emily sets up for a minute, tweaking and twirling as she strums the strings.

Emily leans over, takes my hand off my knee, and kisses it quickly. My heart warms. Sky smiles up at me and looks at me curiously. But she's not angry. I can tell. Then Sky lays her head on my shoulder, her body molding into mine. She fits against me. She fits my life.

Even Pete and Sam stop wrestling when Emily starts to sing. She has a voice that's a thing of beauty, and emotion wells up inside me. The room goes quiet, aside from the sound of her voice.

Sky sucks in a startled breath, and I scoot over behind her, arranging her between my thighs so she can lean against me. She lays her head back on my shoulder and settles into me.

I hear the door open, and Friday walks into the apartment. She looks around, and her eyes land on Paul. He looks everywhere but at her. Her eyes close, and she takes a deep breath. But then she comes and sits on the floor beside Sam, and Paul brings her a margarita. He leans close to her and says something in her ear. She nods and draws her lower lip between her teeth. He smiles, and Paul looks peaceful for a second. Then it's gone.

Emily gets a little louder, and the room starts to ring with the sound of her music. Peace settles over me, and I realize that this is what it's all about. My fight with cancer. My fight with life. My fight with love. All my fighting led me here. And I don't want to be anywhere else. I have my family around me, the woman I love is in my arms, and our kids are scattered around the apartment. It can't get any better than this.

Skylar

I can't figure out why Emily isn't playing on a stage at a huge, sold-out venue somewhere instead of strumming her heart out in the Reeds' living room. She has some amazing talent, and I could sit here all day and listen to her. Her voice is full and rich and so emotional that she almost brings a tear to my eye.

Every few minutes, she looks over at Logan and grins at him. He watches her mouth closely, and I see his fingertips settle on the base of her guitar at times.

Matt's arms tighten around my middle, and his fingers slide beneath my shirt to rest flat on my belly. It's so intimate that it makes me squirm. I cover his hand with mine and he keeps his fingers still for a second. His mouth is right beside my ear when he turns his head, and he whispers, "I bet you're still wet."

Heat creeps up my cheeks, and my belly does that little dance that's all because of Matt. "Stop it," I hiss.

Suddenly, a ball flies through the air and hits Matt on the forehead. He reaches for it and catches it in the air. It's a little, blue Nerf ball and not something that would hurt him. He squeezes it in his fist. "Very amusing," he says to the room.

"You're going to corrupt the kids," one of the twins says. I think it's Sam, but they look so much alike that I can't be sure. Then I see the other one is cuddled up with Reagan, so this one must be Sam.

"The kids are in the other fucking room, dumbass," Matt says. He hurls the ball back at Sam. It bounces off his shoulder, and

Paul reaches up to pluck it from the air. He throws it back at Sam, where it deflects off his ear.

Seth raises a hand tentatively. "I'm a kid, and I'm still here," he reminds us playfully. Any other time he wouldn't be caught dead in the kid category.

Sam raises his hand, too. "I am, too. You're going to corrupt me." He shivers playfully. "All that lovey-dovey shit makes me want to throw up my cupcakes." He burps loudly and covers his mouth with his closed fist after. "And I worked hard on those cupcakes," he reminds everyone.

Matt nudges me. "Did you get a cupcake?" he asks.

I shake my head. "Not yet."

He slides out from behind me and comes back with two. "You'll like it," he says. "Sam makes the best cupcakes." He sits down beside me, the length of his leg pressed along mine.

"Oh, a cupcake," Reagan breathes, and she crawls across the floor on her hands and knees, and then reaches up to take the cupcake from Matt. He laughs and fends her off for a second, but she gets a grip of his wrist and brings the cupcake toward her mouth. Her mouth hangs open wide as she laughs, tugging his arm, and he struggles to keep the cupcake.

"You can take him, princess!" Pete calls from where he's sitting on the floor. "You got this!" Pete laughs, rolling onto his back as he falls over. Sam slaps his palm against Pete's and laughs, too.

"Rea-gan, Rea-gan, Rea-gan," the brothers begin to chat. Reagan is still struggling with Matt's wrist, and he's pretending to fight her off, but he's laughing. Finally, he gives up and lets her take a bite, but just as she pulls back, he smashes her nose into the icing. She looks up, shocked.

"Oh, you did not just do that," she says. Then she wipes a chunk of icing off her nose and holds it out, her palm pointed toward Matt. "You know what that means," she warns, but she's already crawling across his lap toward his face. He passes me his cupcake, or what's left of it, shoves her off his legs, and jumps over the back of the couch. I startle, because Matt is suddenly all broad shoulders and flying limbs. She follows him and chases him around the kitchen island, laughing as he skids in his socks into the counter. He grabs his hip and calls for a time-out, but she's not having it. "You're such a big baby," she sings.

Matt reaches behind him for a fresh cupcake and taunts her with it. "You want to wear this one?" He waggles his brows at her. "Bring it," he challenges.

I cover my mouth to stifle a laugh. I have seen Matt in a lot of situations, but this playful banter and the way they're chasing one another around makes me want to cover my head and duck and laugh out loud at the same time.

Reagan dives for him as he darts back toward the couch and the rest of us. She jumps onto his back and reaches toward his face. He grabs her wrist and holds it away from him, but then he gives up and brings her fingers to his lips, and licks the dollop of icing off them. He hums a little tune while she struggles. Finally, she goes limp on his back and lays her head on the back of his shoulder. His shoulders shake silently as he laughs.

Emily motions to me really quickly, and I pass her my uneaten cupcake. She stands up, and smashes Matt in the face with it as Reagan climbs down from his back. His eyes and mouth open up wide as she grinds it into his face, laughing like hell. Reagan gathers a handful of icing that falls onto his shirt, and she wipes it across his cheek.

"Oh, it's on now," he growls and spins around, bending at the waist so he can toss Emily over his shoulder.

Emily protests, smacking his back, but she's suddenly serious, if the look on her face is any indication. "Put me down, Matt," she cries.

Logan jumps to his feet, and he yells for Matt to put her down, too. Matt's still laughing, though, and he has no idea how serious they are.

"Matt!" Paul yells. The room goes quiet, and Matt spins around with Emily still over his shoulder to face Paul. "Put her down before you hurt her," he says calmly but forcefully.

Logan takes Emily from Matt and lowers her to her feet. "Sorry," Emily says sheepishly.

"What's wrong?" Matt asks. He's suddenly serious, despite the icing that's all over his face. Reagan is wearing some, too, and they all look ridiculous. "Did I hurt you?" he asks Emily.

Emily hangs her head a little and then looks up at Logan like she's asking for permission. She signs and talks to him at the same time. "Should we tell them?" she asks. But she's grinning. Logan smiles, too, and nods.

Emily takes a deep breath.

"You're not sick, are you?" Matt asks, and I can see the love he has for both his brothers' girls in his eyes. And, honestly, it makes me love him even more.

Emily shakes her head. She jerks a thumb toward Logan. "Your brother knocked me up," she says.

The room goes silent. Completely silent. You could have heard a pin drop.

"What?" Matt asks, looking from Logan to Emily and back. He has icing all over himself, yet he's suddenly so serious. He points to Emily's belly. "You're pregnant?" he whispers.

Emily laughs and nods. "We're pregnant!" she cries.

"So no more tossing her over any shoulders," Logan warns, glaring at all his brothers. They're getting to their feet, one by one. Suddenly, Matt jerks Emily toward him and wraps his arms around her.

"I'm so happy for you," I hear him say softly as he swings her around. She giggles and holds him close to her, patting his back.

Matt sets her back from him and looks down at her belly. "You're going to be the best mom ever, Em," he says.

"I hope so," she says quietly, laying a hand on her belly. The rest of the brothers come forward to congratulate them, and they rub Logan's head and jab him in the side, while Emily gets lots of soft hugs. "Maybe she'll be born perfect like her dad," she says. She worries her lower lip.

"Or fucking gifted like you," Matt says vehemently.

Emily sniffs and smiles at him, a watery grin.

"There's just one thing I want to know," Matt says.

He wraps an arm around Emily's shoulders and looks down at her. I flinch when I see what he's about to do, but she does kind of deserve it. His hand inches toward the countertop and he snags a cupcake. "Is the baby going to like chocolate or vanilla?" He brings it up and crams it into Emily's startled face.

She sucks in a jerky breath.

"Booyah!" Matt cries, and he runs away from Emily. Logan drags a finger down Emily's face, scooping up some of the icing and brings it to his lips. He laughs.

"Good cupcakes, Sam," Logan says.

Sam chuckles.

"I'm going to go clean up," Matt says, gesturing toward the bathroom. He goes into the bathroom and closes the door.

"Is he all right?" Emily asks Paul. She looks worried. She picks up a dish towel and starts to wipe her face, her gaze never leaving the direction in which Matt went.

"He's fine," Paul says. But his gaze lingers on the bathroom door.

I can't help but be amazed by their family. They love and care for one another. I look at Seth, who has been watching with amusement. They remind me of how Seth is with the girls. They're playful and loving, and they support one another. I suddenly want to be a part of this family more than I've ever wanted anything. I want to be part of Matt's family. And I want him to be part of mine.

Matt

Emily is fucking pregnant. Logan's going to be a father. Emily is going to be a mother. I'm going to be an uncle. Again. I stare into the mirror and swallow hard to push the feelings back down into my gut, where they can stay nice and hidden. I don't particularly like wearing them on my face.

I leave the bathroom door open, since I'm just washing up. The icing is sticking to my beard stubble, though, and it's a little bit difficult to get off. Emily knocks on the door. She looks ridiculous with her face smeared with icing. Even more ridiculous than I do. She licks her fingers as she walks into the bathroom and takes out a towel. She doesn't say anything as she leans over the sink and gets it wet, and then starts to clean her face off, too.

Her eyes finally meet mine in the mirror. Her gaze darts away.

"You okay, Em?" I ask.

She nods and keeps swiping at her face. "This blue stuff is hard to get off. Need to tell Sam to use a different color next time."

"Or next time, we can try not wearing it." I snort. Like that will ever happen.

She shuts off the water and leans close to the mirror as she continues to scrub.

"Talk to me, Em," I say.

She shakes her head.

"How did this happen?" I ask.

A grin tugs at her lips as her face colors. "Seriously, Matt?" she asks.

I roll my eyes. "That's not what I meant," I say.

"I know what you meant," she says as she turns the water back on. But her face is clean, so I think she's just looking for something to do to keep her hands busy. "You remember when I had my wisdom teeth out a couple of months ago?"

Of course, I remember. She looked like a chipmunk for a week.

"Yeah, antibiotics," she says. She shrugs.

"You're happy, right?" I ask.

"I couldn't be happier." Her eyes meet mine, and I know she's not lying.

I brush her bangs from her forehead and squeegee a piece of her hair with my fingertips, removing a little icing. "What's bothering you, then?" I ask.

She takes a deep breath and closes her eyes. "What if he or she turns out like me?" she whispers. Emily has dyslexia and is nearly illiterate. She has to work really hard to do all the things that people take for granted, like reading street signs and menus in restaurants.

"What if he or she is?" I ask softly. I want to shout at her, to tell her how fabulous she is. I want to tell her how lucky her baby will be to have a mother like Emily and a father like Logan and a whole room full of aunts and uncles who will spoil the baby rotten.

"I'm just scared," she says. She shakes her head like she wants to shake the thought away. "I wouldn't wish my learning disability on my worst enemy."

"If she does, you'll get her the help she needs to succeed." That's something Emily never had. She didn't have the support. She had a father who thought she didn't try hard enough and no one who fought for her, until she met Logan.

She looks up at me. "It'll be all right either way, right?"

Logan lost his hearing because of a fever, so they don't have to worry about a baby of theirs inheriting his hearing impairment. "It'll be all right," I say. And I don't doubt my words, not at all. "You're going to be a great mom, Em."

She nods and throws the towel at my face. I catch it and toss it into the hamper along with mine. She lays a hand on her belly. "It's hard to believe that I have a little person growing inside me," she says softly.

I put my hands on her shoulders and follow her out of the bathroom. But I hear crying coming from Hayley's room and head in that direction. I find Joey and Mellie standing with Hayley, and Mellie has peed in her pants.

"Uh oh," I say. I put my finger to my lips. "Shh," I say. "Don't tell anyone. I'll be right back."

I walk out to the bag that Sky brought with her and get clean clothes for Mellie, and then go back and take her hand so I can lead her to the bathroom. I am not quite sure what to do when she doesn't let my hand go and drags me into the bathroom with her. I let her clean herself up, and she puts on some clean clothes while I sit on the edge of the tub. This is all new to me. Well, I've done it with Hayley, but she lives with us and she's my niece. Her being family makes it easier to know what to do.

I get Mellie to wash her hands and remind myself to tell her to go to the bathroom in a half hour or so. I toss her clothes into the hamper. I'll wash them and take them back to Sky tomorrow. We walk out of the bathroom, and Mellie grins up at me and hugs my leg, just below my knee. She sits down on my foot, and I take a few steps wearing her like a boot, her clinging to me like Velcro. She thinks it's hilarious, and the other girls want to take a turn, too.

After everyone gets a ride and I make sure they all have snacks, I walk out into the hallway. Emily is standing there, and she looks me up and down and nods.

"What?" I ask.

"Nothing," she sings, grinning like a fool.

"Say it," I prompt.

She shrugs. But then she looks up into my face. "You're going to be the best dad ever, Matt," she says.

My heart swells. "Well, at least I don't have to worry about them turning out like me." I scratch my belly. "Being this handsome is quite a burden to bear."

She laughs and punches me in the gut.

I bend in the middle, clutching my stomach, and that's when Sky walks around the corner.

She looks toward Hayley's room. "I was just going to check on the girls," she says.

"I just did," I tell her. Her brow furrows, and she looks so damn pretty that I want to kiss her. "Don't tell anyone, but Mellie's pants peed on her," I whisper dramatically.

She turns toward her bag. "Oh, I better get some clothes," she says.

"Already took care of it," I say, and I wrap my arms around Sky.

She hugs me back. "You took care of it?" She lays her face against my chest and nuzzles against me. I could stand here like this all day long.

"Of course," I say.

She mumbles something against my chest that sounds like, "You're really sexy when you take care of children."

"Hey," I cry. "You should see me when I vacuum. And do dishes. You won't be able to stand the sexy."

She laughs and kisses the center of my chest, just over my heart.

We go back into the living room, and I sit at her feet while she sits on the couch. Emily picks up her guitar again after Reagan gets herself all cleaned up. Or after Pete cleans Reagan up, which takes way longer than it should. Emily starts to play, and I feel Sky's fingers tickle across the back of my neck. I reach up to pull the rubber band from my hair and lean closer to her. She takes the hint and starts to draw her fingers down the length of my hair.

I really need a haircut, but after having been bald for so long, I don't want to cut it off. I feel like Samson, who took his strength from his hair. I know it's stupid, but it's how I feel. My hair being as long as it is means I'm healthy. I'm not going through chemo. I'm not taking lots of meds. I'm just me.

Sky doesn't stop stroking me, not even when the song changes. I have my family around me, and nothing has ever felt quite so right.

"So, who's going to the wedding tomorrow?" Pete asks all of a sudden.

Emily's fingers stumble across the strings, and she slaps her hand down over them to quiet the noise. "Pete," she hisses.

"What?" he asks, throwing up his hands.

"What wedding?" Sky asks.

I look up at her and tangle my fingers with hers on my shoulder. "An old friend of mine is getting married," I say.

Pete makes a blowing noise with his mouth that sounds a lot like the noise we heard a goat make once at a petting zoo. Paul shoots him a look, and he bites back whatever he was going to say next.

"Why would he go to that?" Reagan asks Pete, and she looks at him like he's grown two horns.

"To prove that he's ov—" Pete grunts and shuts up when Reagan elbows him in the stomach. I would have gone for his nuts, honestly. "The invitation was for all of us," Pete grumbles. "We should at least go and eat all their food and drink all their drinks. Just saying."

"Did you want to go?" Sky asks me.

I shake my head. "Not really."

"You said it's an old friend, right?" she asks.

I nod my head. "Sort of."

"I think you should go."

"You could take Sky with you," Pete says. "Rub that shit—" He grunts again when Reagan hits him on the back of the head.

"Go for his nuts next time," I tell Reagan.

"Good idea," she says as she shoots daggers at him with her eyes. "Your nuts are mine the next time you open your mouth," she warns, pointing a finger toward his crotch.

"My nuts have been yours since the day I met you, princess," he says.

Sam makes a gagging noise, pretending like he's going to throw up.

"So, did you want to go?" Sky asks. I wish she'd leave it alone. But I'd have to tell her what's up in order for her to do that, and I'm honestly having so much fun that I don't even want to think about April and Ken. I don't want to let them steal one minute of my happiness.

Emily elbows Logan. "We could go with them," she says. "For moral support."

Logan shrugs his shoulders. He couldn't care less, apparently.

"Well, then, it looks like we're going," I say on a heavy breath. "Yay," I deadpan. "Can you be ready by two?" I look up at Sky.

"Oh, you want me to go with you?" she asks, her eyes opening wide with shock.

I tug her hand until she has no choice but to lean toward my face so I can kiss her. "I wouldn't go without you," I say. "Come with me."

"What about the kids?" she asks.

Friday raises her hand. "I'll babysit. I got nothing better to do."

But Seth steps up. "I'll watch them. No big deal."

"You don't have any plans?" Sky asks.

He shakes his head. "Nope." He avoids her gaze. "Nothing at all." Something is up with that, but I have no idea what. I'll find out later.

"Then it's settled," Pete says. He leans back, a satisfied look on his face.

It's far from settled. The farthest of the far from settled. But at least I'll have Sky with me, which might make it bearable.

Skylar

Matt helps me and Seth as we unload the car and get the girls upstairs. I swear, there's a lot more to being a parent than I ever imagined. There are toys and bags and clothes, and then the kids themselves. Matt has Joey over his shoulder, and Seth carries Mellie.

The girls fell asleep at Matt's apartment, and we decided to scoop them up and bring them home instead of letting them wake up in a strange place. Between that and finding a place for Seth and Matt and me to all sleep, it was just too difficult. I kind of want to wake up in my own bed with Matt tomorrow morning—if he wants to stay over, that is. I haven't asked him yet. But it's what I want.

I know he feels funny about setting a bad example for Seth, but Seth is almost an adult. I think he'll be fine with it.

We go inside, and Matt and Seth put the girls to bed and tuck them in tightly. I give them both a kiss because it's becoming part of our nightly routine. Sometimes I still sneak into their room to watch them sleep, but I get to take part in the bedtime ritual, too. I like putting them to bed, and hearing them talk to their mother when they think I've left the room. It's heartbreaking and uplifting at the same time.

Matt and I walk out into the kitchen, and he gets a bottle of water from the fridge.

"I had a really good time tonight," I tell him as I load the few dishes that are left from dinner.

"I did, too," he says. "My family likes you."

"Did you already know about Emily and Logan? You seemed surprised."

He snorts. "I wouldn't have thrown her over my shoulder if I had known." He winces a little. "Didn't mean to do that."

"You're happy for them, right?" I ask. I watch him closely, because Matt usually wears his feelings on his face.

"Oh yeah," he breathes. "Emily is pretty worried, though."

"About what?"

"She has dyslexia," he says. "Reading is hard for her."

"I know what dyslexia is."

"She's afraid the baby will have it, too, if it gets her genes." He shrugs his shoulders. "She's just worried, like any new mom would be."

"How do you think Logan will do with a baby?" I ask. I have always wondered how deaf people raise hearing children.

"He's been helping Paul take care of Hayley her whole life," he says. "He can do a lot more than people give him credit for."

"Oh, that's not what I meant," I start.

But he cuts me off with a smile. "I know. I get it."

"Is she going to have to quit school?" I ask. I know Emily is in college at Juilliard.

He shrugs. "I have no idea, but they'll work it out. Sometimes I think she went to college just to prove she could succeed. And she has. She's satisfied. All she wants to do is play music."

"She should be playing huge venues with a voice like hers," I say. It really was amazing.

He shakes his head. "She has no desire for fame. She just really loves music. And she loves my brother. So, I love her."

I walk over and wrap my arms around his waist and then lay my head on his chest. My cheek rests over his heart. "My little family fits into your big family pretty nicely," I say quietly.

"Yep." He sets me back from him with his hands on my shoulders. "Were you worried about that?"

I shrug. "Maybe a little."

"Talk to me," he says.

"You guys are just so tight," I admit. "I'm envious of your bond."

"You're part of our bond, now. You know that, right?" he says. The hair on my arms stands up. "Just like Emily and Reagan. You're part of the family."

I nod against his chest. Seth walks into the kitchen and hitches his hip against the counter. "Would you mind if I have a friend over tomorrow night while I'm babysitting?" he asks. He doesn't meet my gaze, and he avoids Matt's, too. Hmm.

"Who's the friend?" I ask.

He shrugs. "I don't know yet. I was just thinking it would be fun to have someone over to talk to."

"Talking?" Matt asks. "That's what you're planning to do?"

Seth's face flushes. "Well, we might play Xbox or something, too."

What would his mother do? "Why don't you come back to me in the morning with the name of the person you want to have over, and we'll discuss it?" I say. "Will that work?"

He scowls, but he nods. He sits down at the kitchen table and starts to flip through a magazine. Matt jams his hands in his pockets and rocks back and forth on his heels. He raises his brows at me. Then he sits down across from Seth and flips open the newspaper until he finds the crossword section. He and Seth start to work it together. Seth laughs when Matt gets a word wrong. And Matt goads Seth incessantly about his penmanship. They look happy and comfy together, though, so I go into the bedroom to shower and get into my jammies.

Matt

I watch Sky's ass as she walks toward her bedroom without a word. I heave a sigh. I want to follow her and grab her ass and lift her shirt and bite the sensitive skin on her side, just above her hip. I want to undress her slowly. I shift in my chair and adjust my jeans. Seth snorts.

"What?" I ask, trying to look innocent.

"Dude, you're so transparent," Seth says. But he's grinning. He's not mad.

"What's transparent?" I ask. How much I love her? I hope that's transparent. How much I respect her? I hope that's obvious. How much I want her? That might be better left between the two of us.

He closes the magazine. "Sorry I cockblocked you," he says.

That hits me in the gut. "Don't talk about your aunt that way," I snap.

Seth's brow furrows. "I didn't say anything bad."

"Don't talk about her like I'm hanging out trying to get in her pants. It's not like that."

He nods his head slowly. "If you say so."

"Seth," I warn.

"What?" he bites out.

I can't think of what I *should* tell him, so I have to go for the truth. "I love her, Seth. I love her a lot. And yeah, I want to get in her pants. But I also want to marry her, and I want to get to love her forever. I want to live with her and share all her ups and downs." I drum my thumbs on the table, trying to figure out what else to say to make him understand. He's a walking hormone, which is what he should be at his age. He's not thinking long-term. But I am. "So, when you talk about cockblocking me, it makes me worry that you might think that's all I'm after. It's not. I respect her. And I want to be sure you know that."

Seth does that slow nod again, like he's thinking it over.

"Would it bother you if I asked her to marry me?" I blurt out. No idea where that came from, but there it is.

Seth's brow rises. "You really want to marry Aunt Sky?"

I nod. I do. I so do.

He looks around, and a little muscle tics in his jaw as he grinds his teeth. "What happens to us if you get married?" he asks.

Huh? "What do you mean?"

"I mean if you and Aunt Sky get married, she's going to be your wife. We were just getting used to her being our mother."

Oh, I get it. Shit. "Can't she do both?"

He shrugs. "Can she?"

"The only difference I see is that you'd have two parents at home instead of one."

Seth's eyes narrow. "Two parents."

I nod. "Seth, I know I'm not your father, and I never will be. But I want to be part of your life. In whatever way you'll let me." It'll probably be in some ways he doesn't appreciate, too, but that's what dads do. It's not always Father's Day and Little League fun. "I don't want to take Sky away from you. I promise." It's important for him to get that last part. He needs to feel safe with her and know that she'll always be there, no matter what. Hell, in two years, he'll be going off to college. I won't have long with him at all, not like Joey and Mellie.

"Your family is pretty cool," Seth says quietly.

"Sometimes they're not." I laugh. Usually they are.

"So, you staying over tonight?" Seth asks.

I shake my head. "No."

"Why not?" He looks confused.

"Because I respect Sky." *Because I don't want you to think poorly of her.*

"Whatever, man," he says as he gets up. "I'm going to bed."

"Good night," I say.

He goes into his room and closes the door. I let out a deep breath. God, there's a lot to consider when there's a teenager in the house. He's impressionable, and he's going to learn how to treat women from the way his mother was treated, and the way Sky is treated around him in the future. I am determined to be a good influence.

Sky walks out of her room, her hair damp around her shoulders. "Did Seth go to bed?" she asks. She fidgets around the kitchen, like she's not quite sure what to do.

"Yep." I stand up and lean against the counter. She turns to set up the coffeepot for tomorrow morning, and I see her ass in those pajama bottoms and I want to just grab it and plump it and sink my teeth into it. But I have to go home. I groan to myself.

"What's wrong?" she asks, turning to face me.

"Nice jammies," I say.

She looks down at herself, grins, and strikes a dramatic pose. "You like them?"

I swipe a hand down my face. "I'd like them more if they were on the floor."

She freezes. The skin I can see through the open vee of her pajama top colors, turning all rosy. "Oh," she breathes. But then she grins and crooks a finger at me. "I think they would really like to be on the floor."

I groan again and toss my head back. "I can't."

She freezes again. "You're not staying?"

I shake my head. I'm stupid. I know.

"Why not?" she asks quietly.

I point toward Seth's room. "Because we have a teenager in the other room, and I need to set a good example for him." I hate this. But it is what it is.

Her jaw falls open. "You're worried about Seth?"

I nod and raise my knuckle to my mouth, biting down on it, trying to take some of the ache out of my nuts.

"I think Seth is old enough to understand."

I shake my head. "I know. But he just said something that hit home with me. I don't want him to think I'm with you because I want to score." I do want to score, but that's beside the point.

She motions from her to me and back. "I kind of hoped to score," she whispers vehemently. She glances toward Seth's closed door. "He's in bed. He'll never know."

I point to my chest. "But I'll know."

She harrumphs, and her shoulders drop. "I put on perfume and everything," she mumbles.

I walk over to her and wrap my arms around her, sniffing her neck. I can smell the sweet scent that's her, but I can't tell where she applied it. "Where?" I ask, hesitant when I hear my own voice quaver.

"Wouldn't you like to know?" she asks with a giggle. She steps onto her tiptoes and wraps her arms around my neck.

I walk her backward toward her room as I kiss her. Her lips are hungry against mine, and she takes greedy little nips at my mouth. I want to stay. I want to be inside her. But I can't.

I grab the hem of her shirt and shove her gently through the doorway of her bedroom at the same time, yanking the shirt over her head.

"Change your mind?" she asks, breathless, as she covers her breasts with her hands. They plump around her fingertips, and I want to kiss her fingers away.

I lift her shirt to my nose and sniff it. "I'm taking this with me because it smells like you."

"Matt," she protests, but it's more of a playful grunt. "Give me my shirt."

"If you want the shirt, you have to give me your panties," I say. I glance down.

"I'm not wearing any panties," she says, taunting me.

I lean forward and kiss her forehead, lingering for just a moment, taking in the feel of her clutching my shirt in her fists. "God, you're killing me," I say. I let my hands drift up and down her naked back, and she purrs like a kitten, pressing her tits against my chest.

"Stay," she says softly.

I shake my head, take her hands in mine, and unravel her fingers from my shirt, then set her back from me. "If it was just us, you wouldn't be able to get rid of me."

"But it's not."

I shake my head. "Good night," I say as I walk away.

"'Night," she calls to my retreating back.

I go out the front door and groan loudly. I want to go back to her. But I also want to do this the right way.

Skylar

Matt's barely out the front door when I call him. In fact, I can hear the *ding* of the elevator over the bad reception in the enclosed space when he answers me with nothing more than a groan.

"Matt," I say quietly.

"What?" he bites out. But I can almost hear the lazy smile in his voice.

"Come back."

He hisses out a breath. Then says quietly, "If you say the word *come* one more time…"

My breath catches, and my heart starts to trip. "Matt." I'm grinning like a fool, and I don't care. My door is shut, and no one can see me.

"Are you still topless?" Matt asks. His voice sounds like it's been dragged down a gravel road and back.

I look down and cross my arms over my naked breasts. I guess I am. "Yeah," I say.

He groans again. "Send me a picture."

"I'm a lawyer. We don't do stupid shit like that." Not to mention that I'm a mom. And moms don't do that. I look down at my chest and unfurl my arms. "My nipples are hard."

"Sky!" he hisses, but he's laughing, too. "Stop it."

"What's wrong, Matt?" I tease. I hear him give his address to a cab driver. "Why are you taking a cab?" He usually takes the subway.

"Because I want to get home quickly," he says.

"Why?" I put one knee on my bed and crawl to the center. I should probably put a shirt on, but I kind of like the naughty feeling of being topless while talking to Matt.

"Because I want to talk you through an orgasm," he says.

"What?" I ask. My heart skitters.

"You heard me." He chuckles. "Unless you don't want me to." He waits for my answer.

"I want you to," I whisper.

He hisses in a breath. "Talk to me about something else for a few minutes," he says over a chuckle. I hear him groan and there's silence, aside from street noises and a gentle sound when he starts to hum in my ear. I grin. I can't help it.

After a short ride, I hear him thank the cab driver and slam the car door. Then he's quiet as he takes the four flights of stairs up to his apartment. He's breathing a little heavier when he gets to the top, but not much.

"Not now," I hear him mutter to someone.

"Who was that?" I ask.

"Paul."

"Do you need to go talk to him?"

"All I need to do right now is make you come. He can wait." I hear his keys clang as he drops them somewhere. Or maybe it's change from his pocket. "Go lock your door," he says.

I scramble across the bed and do what he says. My hand hangs on the doorknob for a second as I think about what I'm about to do. A shiver runs up my spine, but I push the thumb lock. The click shimmers through my hand. I hold on to the doorknob for another second.

"Good girl," he says. His voice is smooth as silk, and it slides up my body, making my knees weak. "Go lie on the bed again."

"You're kind of bossy."

"I know. You like it."

I do. "How would you know?"

"Because you're all wet and slippery and your heart is pounding just like mine is." He waits a beat. "Isn't it?"

This is Matt. Of course, he cares about how I feel. "Yes," I whisper.

He growls. "Take off your bottoms."

I prop the phone between my shoulder and my ear and hook my thumbs in the hips of my pajama bottoms, then shove them down over my feet. "Okay," I say.

"Are you naked?"

"As the day I was born," I say over a nervous giggle.

"God, you're beautiful."

"How would you know?"

"Because every time I close my eyes, you're all I see. You're in my fucking head, Sky, every minute of every day."

I was hot a minute ago, but now I'm breathless.

"Did you tell me your nipples are hard?" His bed squeaks as he talks.

"Are you in bed?" I ask.

"Yeah." He grunts. "Or rather, on it."

"Me, too."

"Good. Now back to your nipples."

"What about them?" I grin. I can't help it.

"I love them. They're all pink and perfect, and when I kiss off all your lipstick, they're the same shade as your lips." He pauses. "Touch them."

"Touch them how?"

"Not soft. Because they probably hurt, they're so hard." He waits. "Am I right?"

"How did you know?"

He chuckles, but it's a pained sound. "Because I'm hurting, too, Sky."

"Oh."

"Pinch them lightly, both at the same time." His breaths grow heavier.

"Matt," I whisper. "I'm not sure I can do this."

"Close your eyes."

I do it.

"Now touch your nipples."

I gasp as I draw a thumb across the turgid peak.

"God, Sky," he whispers.

Matt was right. The swipe of my thumb is not enough. I cup my breasts in my hands and pinch my nipples between my thumb and forefinger. I nearly drop the phone from where it's crammed against my neck.

"If I was there, I would pinch them and then lick the pain away."

"Matt."

"What?" He chuckles.

"What are you doing?"

He laughs again. "What do you think I'm doing?"

"The same thing I'm doing?"

"Well, I don't have pretty tits to play with, but yeah."

"How much longer before I can move down south?" I ask. I squeeze my eyes shut, waiting for him to laugh at me.

But he doesn't laugh. "Now."

"Thank God," I breathe.

"Draw your knees up, and then let them fall open. Please."

I do as he says, and I feel all exposed, even though there's no one in the room with me.

"Such a pretty pussy," he says. "Spread yourself open with your fingers so I can see."

My fingers part my slippery, wet folds, which are swollen and aching.

"Good girl," he says.

"How do you know if I did it?"

"Because I can hear it in your voice, Sky."

I can barely breathe.

"I hear every hitch and every gasp. I even hear what you don't want me to hear."

"Like what?"

"I hear your fears. I hear your aches. I hear your wants and needs. I hear it all."

I squeeze my eyes tightly shut. "No one has ever heard me before." A hot tear tracks slowly down the side of my face toward my hairline.

"I hear everything." He waits another beat. "Touch your pussy, Sky."

I slide my fingers through my wetness.

"Dip inside and get your fingers wet."

"How many fingers?"

He growls. "How many can you take?"

I slide my middle finger inside and pump in and out, and then add my index finger. And just when I think I can't stand it, I stretch myself open by adding my ring finger. I'm too full to crook my fingers, but I don't care. "Three," I tell him.

"Jesus," he breathes.

"What do you want me to do now, Matt?"

"Rub your clit." He grunts, and I hear a slick sound on his end of the phone.

"Are you using lube?"

"Spit." He grunts. "I was in a hurry."

I rub my clit in a small circle. "I won't last long," I warn.

"Thank God," he growls.

My clit is hard and swollen and oh so sensitive. My small circles just leave me wanting.

"Faster," he urges. "I need to hear you come."

"You waiting for me?" My breath stutters along with my heart.

"Always," he sighs.

"Matt," I cry out.

"That's right," he urges. "Say my name."

"Matt, Matt, Matt," I chant.

"It's me making you come, Sky. Only me." His voice is low and soft and hits the very center of me.

"Only you."

"Me. And you."

My legs quiver, and I know it's time.

"Sky," he pleads. "Please come."

A moan leaves my throat as my body bows with pleasure.

"Don't stop," he says. He grunts, and I can tell he's coming, too. "Please don't stop," he begs.

I cry out softly, my body racked with tremors.

"Don't stop," he says, his voice growing softer.

"Unh," I groan. I have to stop. My clit is too sensitive, my body wrecked. I slow my fingers and let the small aftershocks take me. Sensitive and used, I stop rubbing my pussy and listen to him breathe.

We lie like this for a moment, and then I hear him move.

"Stay with me, Matt," I say.

"I'm not leaving you," he says with a chuckle. "I just need to clean up. I'm kind of a mess."

"Oh," I breathe over a laugh. Forgot about that.

"Yeah," he says. He moves around for a second, and then I hear his bed creak again. I imagine him settling back against the pillows, a content smile upon his face. "You okay?" he asks softly.

"Mmm hmm," I hum.

He laughs. "And she's speechless after that orgasm."

I giggle. I can't help it. I'm naked lying on top of my covers, and he just talked me through an orgasm over the phone. "Where did you learn to do that?"

"Learn," he says over a snort. "Shit, I've never done that before. That was all you." He chuckles. "I can't believe I let you corrupt me like that."

I can't bite back my grin. "Will you stay with me until I fall asleep?"

He yawns. "You couldn't stop me."

###

I wake up and look over at the clock. It's two a.m., and I'm naked and cold on top of the covers. I get up and put on my jammies, then go the bathroom and wash my hands. I look in the mirror. I shake my head. A few short weeks ago, I was a single girl living my single life, with a boyfriend who didn't care about me. Now I have three kids who I am learning to love beyond anything I ever imagined, and I have Matt. I never knew I could feel about anyone the way I feel about Matt. I kind of feel sorry for Phillip. He never got me to this point, and I never gave him what I'm willing to give Matt.

I have this irresistible desire to go check on the girls. I walk down the hall and into their room. The night-light they can't sleep without bathes the room in a soft glow. Mellie is on top of her covers, so I gently pull them from beneath her and cover her up. She snuffles into her pillow and rolls over. Joey rarely moves in her sleep, but I tug her covers up to her chin anyway. She doesn't stir.

I want to check on Seth, too, but he's a teenage boy, and I worry about opening his door. I decide not to chance it.

I walk into the living room and startle when I see a light on the end table turned on. Seth looks over his shoulder at me, closes the book he has open in his lap, and jams it into the cushions of the couch.

"Everything okay?" I ask. I sit down on the other end of the sofa and draw my feet up under me.

"Yeah." I realize his eyes are wet, and he swipes a hand beneath his nose.

"What were you looking at?" I ask. My heart breaks for him. He never did cry after his mom's death, at least not that I could see.

"Just some pictures," he says without looking me in the eye.

"Can I see?" I reach for the album, and he shrugs his shoulders. I pull it out and turn to the first page. Seth was adorable as a baby. I smile and look over at him. "You always had those dimples, huh?"

He grins and scoots next to me on the couch.

I look closer, and see my dad in the album. My heart nearly stops. He has his arm around Kendra in a lot of the pictures, and he looks so comfortable with her. "Granddad was here a lot," he says.

I nod. I don't know why that chokes me up, but it does.

I turn the page. "Your mom was so beautiful."

"I know." His shoulder touches mine, and he leans against me, pointing to a picture. "That's my dad."

Well, that's not what I was expecting. His dad is Latino.

"He spoke Spanish to us all the time."

I look up at him. "You know Spanish?"

He nods and turns the page. "That's the man my Grandma eventually married. He was nice."

That's the man who took my dad's place.

"How much do you know about all that?" I ask. I don't know how much I can and can't say around him.

"Enough," he says.

"Your mom was smart *and* beautiful, huh?" I say, turning to a picture of her getting an award for something.

He nods. "But she didn't trust men."

"Men leave," I say. But I want to bite the words back as soon as I say them.

He shakes his head. "Not all of them."

I quietly flip through the book.

"Matt wouldn't leave," he says quietly. "You should trust him."

I heave a sigh. "I do. As much as I can."

He nods. "Sometimes I'm afraid I'll forget what she looks like," he says softly.

"Seth..." I don't know if I should hug him or not, so I just lean more heavily into his side.

"It's okay. It has only been a few weeks, you know, and I can already feel her leaving."

I don't say anything, because I'm not sure he wants me to.

"I thought it was bad when she was dying, but saying good-bye to her afterwards…it's the worst."

"You don't have to say good-bye," I tell him.

"Every day, I have to remind myself she's gone. I get up and I expect to find her in the kitchen working the crossword puzzle. Or cooking. Or dancing with Joey and Mellie. Or me." He grins. "She loved to turn the music on and dance."

He waits while I flip pages. I see my dad in a lot of them. And that makes an ache in my chest that I can't get rid of.

"I can't hear her voice anymore," he whispers. "I want to hear her voice, Aunt Sky." His own voice cracks, and he lays his forehead on my shoulder. A tremor runs through him.

Screw it. I turn and wrap my arms around him. I don't know how to do this because I've never had anyone do it for me. He pulls me close to him and sobs into my shoulder.

When he's finally quiet, I pat him on the back and sit back. I return to the album because he looks uncomfortable. "Life is like a book, Seth," I tell him. "Just like the photo album. Pages go by, but you can turn back to them anytime, even when the last page has been read. All you have to do is open the book back up and pick a page to reread." I don't know if that's true or not, but it sounds good.

"If you could reread any page in your book, Aunt Sky, which one would it be?" he asks me softly.

"This one," I say. I'd relive this one over and over. I take his hand in mine and give it a squeeze. He doesn't pull away.

Matt

I tug on my tie, trying to loosen the son of a bitch. I hate wearing a fucking tie. Logan pops his head into the room. "You about ready?" he asks.

Logan is decked out in Madison Avenue clothes, which Emily's mom sent over for all of us. Her mom likes to dress us up. And since her dad owns the company, we take full advantage of it. Logan looks like he just walked off the pages of a magazine. "Tell Emily to come tie this thing, will you?" I ask. He nods and goes to get her.

She comes into the room, looking like a million bucks. She cleans up nicely. Usually she's in combat boots and jeans. I remember when I met her and she wore a catholic schoolgirl outfit every day and had a blue streak in her hair. Now she totters over on her four-inch heels until she's standing right in front of me. "You sure you want to go to this wedding?" she asks me softly as she starts to knot my tie.

"I don't see why not," I say. I look down at her feet. "Are you sure you should be wearing those stilts? What if you trip?"

She snorts. "I'm pregnant, Matt, not dying. Stop worrying. I swear, you're worse than Logan."

"You want to put on some flatter shoes? It would make me feel better."

She pulls my tie up tight against my neck. "Since when do I care about making you feel better?" she asks, but she's smiling gently at me.

"Always. You started loving me the day you met me."

"You mean when you were puking your guts out?" she tosses back at me. She's the only one who knew how sick I was back then. Or at least I thought she was. It turned out that all my brothers knew; they were just trying to keep it from me.

"You brought me a bucket," I remind her, and the thought makes me grin.

"And ginger ale."

"And you snuggled with me on the couch."

She looks into my eyes. "And I still would if you'd let me."

"Em," I groan.

She holds up a hand to stop me. "I get it. I really do."

I narrow my eyes at her. "Do you?"

She nods. "I do. And I'm so happy for you," she says softly. "When do you go back for more blood work?" she asks. She's the only one who has asked me this.

"Next month," I tell her. "How did you know?" I look at her as I arrange items on my dresser. I just want to keep my hands busy. I hate talking about cancer. I hate that it's such a big part of my life.

She shrugs. "I know you, Matt," she says. "Do you want me to go with you?" she asks.

I shake my head. "It's just blood work, Em," I tell her. Scary, life-changing blood work, but just a needle stick in the grand scheme of things.

She nods. "Okay," she says. "But tell me if you change your mind."

"I will."

"So, you told Sky about April, right? She's not going into tonight blind?"

I nod. "I told her about her."

"And she's okay with going to your ex's wedding?"

"Closure," I say. I put my wallet in the inner pocket of my suit coat.

"Closure," she repeats. "You ready to go?" she asks. She looks me up and down. "You're almost as handsome as Logan, you know?" She grins at me, and I put my arm around her and walk out of the bedroom.

"Get your hands off my baby mama," Logan says.

I laugh because it's the most ridiculous thing I've ever heard come out of his mouth. "Make me," I taunt.

He laughs, and we walk out the door together. They're hand in hand, and I follow. We look ridiculous all dressed up in the neighborhood we're from, and I'm afraid we'll get mugged if we linger too long. But Emily's father let us borrow his driver tonight— and his limo. It was pretty nice of him, and I get to spoil Sky a little.

We pull up to her apartment. She told me to text her when we were close, so she can meet us at the street, but I don't. I go up to her apartment and knock. Seth opens the door. "Damn, dude," he says. "You're all dressed up." He smiles. "I'm glad, because so is she."

He steps back, and it's like he's opening a curtain on *Let's Make a Deal*. Sky steps out of her room and walks toward me. She's in heels that look even higher than Emily's, and she's not a mom right now. She's a classy lawyer who comes from money, and I could never, ever hope to live up to her.

She whistles at me. "You look handsome," she says. She walks toward me with a necklace draped over her fingers. She presses it into my hands and turns her back to me. "Will you put that on me?" she asks. She lifts her hair, which is out of the ponytail I've gotten used to, and it hangs in artful waves down her back. She's wearing a dress that clings to her figure. I know I've already seen everything that's under that dress, but damn if my dick doesn't get happy when she turns her back to me.

I clip her necklace around her neck and bend to kiss the soft skin. She purrs and turns toward me. "Thanks."

"I am so glad you're here," Seth says. "I had to look at 452 dresses. And once she picked a dress, then she had to do the shoe dance."

I quirk my brow at him. "The shoe dance?"

He puts one foot on the floor and stands like a flamingo. He mimics a girl's voice. "This shoe, or this shoe?" he asks, as he switches from foot to foot.

Sky laughs and shoves his shoulder. "I wasn't that bad."

Seth rolls his eyes and goes to flop onto the couch. Mellie and Joey are in the floor playing with Barbies.

"You sure you'll be okay, Seth?" she asks, but he's grinning and typing into his phone. "Seth!" she calls loudly.

He looks up. "What?"

She rolls her eyes. "Are you sure you'll be all right?"

He hangs one arm over the back of the couch. The boy is all skinny arms and legs. "We'll be fine," he says. He goes back to his phone.

"Call if you need anything, okay? Anything at all."

"Okay," he says absently. Something is up, but I don't know what.

"Are you having anybody over, Seth?" I ask.

He looks up, his face flushing. "No, she can't come tonight." He doesn't realize his mistake for a second. Then he rushes on to say, "I mean he. Not she."

Now I get it. He wanted to have a girl over.

"No girls," Sky says. "I'm not ready to be a grandma yet."

Seth doesn't look up from his phone.

"Seth!" Sky cries.

He jerks his head up. "What?"

"No girls in the house unless they're your sisters. Do you hear me?"

He salutes her. "I hear you."

She goes and kisses Joey and Mellie on their heads, and I walk over to Seth. "You heard what she said, right?" I ask.

He looks a little contrite. "Yes."

"Good." I point my finger at him. "Behave yourself."

"You, too," he says with a grin. "What time will you be home?"

Sky opens her mouth, but I cut her off. "In a couple of hours."

"That's all?" Sky asks.

I nod. But that's not all. I put my hand at her lower back and lead her out of the room after she kisses Seth on the forehead. He scrunches up his face and then goes back to his phone.

"Really, just a couple of hours?" she asks as the door closes.

"No," I say. "I just said that so he'll have no idea when we'll be home. He'll be less likely to have that girl over that way."

She smiles. "Oh, very good idea."

"Three younger brothers," I remind her. I look her up and down. "You are so beautiful," I tell her.

Her cheeks get all rosy. "Thank you," she says. She dips her head. "You could have just texted me when you got here. I'd have met you downstairs."

"My mother would roll over in her grave if I didn't pick you up at your door." It's the truth. She would hate it. I adjust my suit coat. "She raised five gentlemen." I lift my nose in the air, being silly.

Sky looks at me. "Yes, I think she did," she says softly.

I hook an arm around her waist and pull her against me as the elevator doors close. I touch my lips to hers. "I'm going to mess up your lipstick," I warn.

"I have more," she breathes softly. Then she throws her arms around my neck and kisses me. I palm her ass and lift her against me. She doesn't seem to mind. She makes a little noise against my lips that shoots straight to my heart.

The doors open, and I pull back. She wipes my lips with her thumb. I take my handkerchief out and swipe my face. "All good?" I ask.

I wipe the corner of her mouth where I smudged her. "Me?" she asks.

"Beautiful," I say.

I take her hand and lead her out of the building. She's so fucking beautiful that I want the whole world to see her. And what makes it even better is she's mine.

She stops short when she sees the limo. "That's for us?" she asks.

I nod and usher her into the car when the driver opens the door. She slides in next to Emily, and Em gives her a glass of champagne. She takes it in one hand, and the other lands on my leg after I get in beside her. Her fingertips draw lazy circles on my thigh. I lay my hand over hers so she'll stop. She looks up at me confused, but it only takes one touch from her to make my dick hard.

Logan laughs from the other side of the car. "Shut it," I say, and I sign it at the same time.

He just laughs a little louder.

Skylar

Matt knows everyone at the wedding, apparently. It's being held at a swanky hotel, and it's truly beautiful. The bride was lovely, and I even felt myself tearing up when she started down the aisle. Matt just squirmed as the ceremony went on, and I guess it was because he's not used to wearing a suit. Now it's time for the reception, which is a sit-down dinner that I wasn't expecting. And then dancing. Matt introduces me to people as they walk up. There are so many of them that I can't even hope to keep up with all the names.

The best man gives a toast that makes the room roar with laughter, and even Matt chuckles and raises his glass in the bride and groom's direction. He leans into me and whispers close to my ear. "Last night, you made this noise on the phone that I can't get out of my head," he says.

My belly flips. "What noise?" I ask. I lean over and kiss his cheek. I just can't help it.

"I can't describe it," he says absently. "But it was when you came."

I choke on my own spit, and he laughs. His hand lands on my thigh.

"I want to hear it again," he says, his words hot on the shell of my ear.

I lay my hand on his inner thigh and hitch it higher. It's a bold move, but so is the way he's talking to me. "Stop teasing," I warn.

"Who's teasing?" he asks. He looks into my eyes.

"You going to stay over tonight?" I ask. I raise my brows at him.

He shakes his head. "Seth," he says.

"Now who's teasing?" I ask. I lean into him, and my breast touches his arm. He lifts a finger to lightly trace the underside of it. I press my legs together to ease the sudden, pounding ache.

He gets up and takes my hand, then pulls me to my feet. "Come on," he says.

"Where are we going?" I ask as he drags me behind him. I run on my tiptoes in my too-tall shoes. He doesn't slow down. We start down a corridor, and he tests doors until he finds one that's unlocked. When one opens, he pulls me inside and immediately backs me against the wall. It's a supply closet. And I don't care.

"I want to hear that noise again," he says against my lips. A thousand butterflies take flight in my belly. "Right now." He stops and looks into my face, his hands bracketing my cheeks. "Is this okay with you?" he asks. "Tell me if it's not."

I nod. I can't even speak.

Matt lifts my skirt, bunching it in his hands until he gets to my panties. He hooks his fingers in them and draws them down my legs. One side hangs over my ankle, and he leaves it there. I don't care. He unbuckles his belt and lowers his zipper quickly, and then reaches into his inner coat pocket and pulls out his wallet. He flips it open and takes out a condom, which he tugs open with his teeth. He rolls it over his length with a grimace, and then he hoists me up, and I wrap my legs around his waist.

He looks into my eyes as he lowers me onto him. My back is pressed against the wall, and one of his hands clutches my naked bottom, opening me up for his penetration, while the other anchors beside my head. He fills me slowly, his blue eyes looking into mine as he impales me. God, I feel so full this way. He doesn't stop until our bodies touch at the hilt of him.

Then he starts to move. His lips touch mine, and he says against my lips, "I love you so fucking much."

I can't speak. I can't think. Matt hits my center, and I adjust my hips a little so that I can take more of him with every stroke.

"Yep, that's the noise," he says, as my breath leaves me. He pulls my hand from where I'm holding on to his shoulder and drags it down to where we're joined. "Rub your pussy, Sky," he says.

"I don't need to come like that," I say.

"I need for you to come like that," he says. "Please." His forehead rests against mine and I can feel his every inhale and exhale. We're sharing the same air.

I reach between us and squeeze the base of his dick as he retreats. He stops moving. "I'm too close," he warns. He growls at me. "Rub your pussy, Sky."

I reach down and rub my clit. I'm already close. I'm so close. He's stroking me from the inside as his big, powerful body holds me tight against the wall. My clit is hard and sensitive, and I rub it quickly, Matt's feral grunts by my ear keeping time with my strokes. They're quick and raw, and I suddenly feel it wash over me. Matt grunts and pushes all the way inside me as I flutter around him, milking his orgasm from him. He stills and pulses inside me, his lips tender against my temple as he finishes.

"Sky," he breathes.

"What?" I whisper back.

"Did I hurt you?" he asks. He pulls back, his brow furrowing. I love that he's asking.

"No, you didn't hurt me. You made me come like crazy, though." I giggle. I can't help it. Nothing ever felt this good. Ever.

"Me, too. I felt like my toes were going to come out of my throat." He chuckles. I untangle my legs from around his back, and he lowers me to stand. My shoes fell off, so I'm on my bare feet on the linoleum floor, and I don't care. My panties are still hanging around my ankle.

I rub my thighs together. Something feels off. "Matt," I say.

"Umm," he says as he pulls the condom off. He looks up at me sheepishly. "We might have a problem."

"Why am I all wet?" I ask. More wet than I would be just from me.

He pulls the condom off and holds it up. "Condom broke," he says.

My heart skips a beat. "What?"

."Yep," he says.

What startles me the most is that hearing that he just came inside me doesn't freak me out. Not in the least. "It's okay, Matt," I start.

"I know." He heaves a sigh and tosses the condom in a trash can, covering it up with the garbage that's already there. "I told you.

It would take a miracle for me to get you pregnant. And I got tested for everything under the sun when I was sick. You're safe."

"I wasn't worried," I say quietly. I want to spend the rest of my life with this man.

He buckles his belt and raises his zipper. Then he bends to unhook my panties from around my ankle. He's suddenly really quiet. More quiet than I want him to be. I don't know what to say to him because I don't know what he's thinking. "Do you want to go and get cleaned up?" he asks.

I nod. "I should." He holds my panties out, and I stuff them into my clutch, which I dropped when he pushed me against the wall. He holds out my shoe, and I step into it. He repeats the process on the other side. He looks up at me from my feet and runs a hand up my leg.

"Matt," I say. But he takes my hand and leads me to the ladies' room. He kisses my temple and lingers there, breathing lightly by my hair.

"I'll wait for you in the banquet room," he says. "That okay?" He's suddenly so quiet.

I nod and go into the bathroom. I let myself into a stall and sink down. My knees are still shaking, and not all of it is because of just having had sex against a closet wall. I'm scared that I don't know what's going on in Matt's head. I don't know what his sudden silence means.

I clean up, and just as I'm pulling my panties up, the outer door opens. Female giggling flows into the room. "Can you believe he brought her?" a voice asks.

"I can't believe Matt even came, much less brought a woman. Maybe he's over April."

"Matt will never get over April. Not after what she did."

"So, who do you think his date is?"

"Just some girl," the voice says. "Someone who will never mean as much to him as April did." She snorts. "They have so much history."

April is the girl who broke Matt's heart.

My gut clenches, and I have to blink back tears.

Matt brought me here to watch April, the woman he loved more than anything, get married. And he didn't even tell me.

I let myself out of the stall when the sound of voices goes away, and I hear the door close. I fix my makeup and wipe my brow. I feel like I just got punched in the gut. But there's nothing I can do about it now.

I walk back out to the table, and I see Emily sitting there. Matt and Logan are talking with a small group of men they know. I sit down beside her, and she eyes me up and down. "Where did you two get off to?" she asks, grinning.

"A closet down the hall, where he fucked me against the wall," I say.

Emily freezes. "For some reason, I don't think that's as good as it sounds. What's wrong?" She looks toward Matt like she wants to get his attention.

I knock on the table, and she looks at my hand. "April doesn't look repentant at all over what she did to Matt," I toss out. I watch for her reaction.

"Oh," she breathes. She lays a hand on her chest. "I wasn't sure he told you."

I smile. "He told me." He told me about the girl who broke his heart. He just didn't tell me April was the one. "Why do you think he wanted to come tonight?" I ask. I take a sip of my water.

"Closure, he said." She looks toward where April is dancing with her new husband.

"He really loved her, didn't he?" I ask. I say it casually.

"He even wrote her a letter when he was dying. He made me promise to give it to her. I'd sooner rot in hell. But he made me promise, because his brothers refused to give it to her."

I smile even though my insides are roaring.

Matt comes to the table and takes my hand in his. "Come dance with me," he says.

I nod and let him pull me to my feet. There's a slow song playing, and he leads me onto the dance floor and then draws me into his arms.

"Something wrong?" he asks.

I shake my head and smile up at him. His brow furrows. "Did you get a chance to congratulate the bride yet?" I ask.

He shakes his head. "Not yet." His gaze roams to where she's dancing with her new husband. I maneuver us in that direction and then pull myself from his arms. I turn and lay my hand on April's husband's arm.

"Can I cut in?" I say with a huge smile. He looks down at his wife, and she shrugs. Then he sees Matt beside me and his grin falls, but he puts it back as quickly as he loses it.

"Matt," he says.

Matt nods at him, a quick jerk.

As though he understands, the groom passes the bride to Matt, and he takes me in a dance. I watch out of the corner of my eye as Matt says something to April, and then he reluctantly takes her in his arms. He scowls at me and looks in my direction, but I give the groom my attention.

"A lot of history there," the groom says.

"So I hear," I say back.

"Mighty big of you to give her to him."

"Yep," I say, and I let out a little pop on the *p*.

"They're done, you know?" he says.

I look over and see them talking while they're dancing. "No, they're not."

He heaves a sigh. "I know," he says. "It doesn't bother you?"

I shake my head. It fucking kills me.

The song stops, and I turn on my heel. I need to get out of here before I fall apart. I nearly run down the hall toward the exit. I jump into a waiting cab and give the driver the apartment address. But I don't want to go home. When did the apartment with the kids become home? I don't know, but it is. But I know Matt will go there and wait for me.

I pick up my phone and dial. "Hey, Dad," I say when he answers.

"Sky?" he asks. "Are you all right?"

"Oh yeah," I lie. "I'm fine. I'm a little embarrassed to say that I've had too much to drink, though. Would it be possible for you to go and stay with the kids tonight? I want to go to my own apartment and crash there."

Dad pauses for a second. "You want me to stay with the kids."

"Would you mind?" I lay my head back against the seat. "If it's too much trouble, don't worry about it."

"It's not too much trouble," he rushes to say. "I'll go. I'll go right now."

"Thanks, Dad. Text me when you get there, will you, so I know everything is okay?"

"Sky," he says, his voice hesitant. "Are you all right?"

"I'm fine, Dad. Really I am. Text me when you get there. I have to go." I hang up on him. And then, and only then, do I let myself cry.

Matt

Why the fuck did she do that? One minute, I had Sky all nice and warm in my arms, and the next I'm holding April. April, I can ignore. But the fact that Kenny has my Sky in his arms, that tears me apart inside.

"I'm glad you came," April says softly.

I look down at her, and she blinks her pretty brown eyes at me. There was once a time when I could get lost in her gaze. Hell, I got lost in *her*. "I'm glad you invited me," I say.

I am glad. I didn't think I would be, but I am. Because what was between us can now be considered closed.

"Do you think we could ever be friends?" she asks.

I can't answer that. I don't possibly see how, but saying that could hurt her feelings.

"I'd like to at least not be enemies," she says, instead.

I stop dancing. "I don't think you understand. I would have to care about what you do from here on out for that to matter, and I can't really say that I do."

"You did once," she says. People are looking at us.

"I did, and then you stomped all over my fucking heart. It took me a long time to get over it. Much longer than it should have. But I did realize one thing: I was in love with the idea of being in love a lot more than I was in love with you."

She sucks in a quick breath.

"I don't mean to hurt you. Heaven knows, I would have done that long before now if that was my intention. But what I felt for you wasn't strong enough to last a lifetime. I know that now." I take her forearms in my grip. "Thank you for leaving me. I appreciate it more than you know. Because what we had for one another was nothing compared to what I feel for someone else. So, if you invited me here to be sure you still had my heart on a fucking string, let me confirm for you that you do not." I set her back from me, even though she's still protesting. "I need to go find Sky."

"Matt," April says, clutching onto my arm. "Wait." I turn back to her. "I didn't mean to fall in love with him," she says.

I get close to her. I shouldn't do this, and I wouldn't if I didn't think she really, really needed to know. But there's already a buzz about it in the crowd. She's the only one who doesn't know. I lean down close to her ear. "I'm sorry you fell in love with him. He's not the one for you."

"And you were?" she sneers.

I toss my head back and laugh. "No, I wasn't. But one thing is certain. I would have never, ever cheated on you." I close my eyes and steady myself with a deep breath. "He fucked your maid of honor last night," I blurt out.

"That's low, Matt."

"He's been sleeping with her for the past six months. Everyone knows it but you." Then I leave her standing there in the middle of the floor.

I can almost feel her behind me, devastated and broken. Her pain radiates through the air, but I don't stop.

My heart is heavy when I get back to my table. Devastating her wasn't nearly as freeing as one might think. I take my jacket from where it's draped over the back of my chair and put it on. "Have you seen Sky?" I ask Emily and Logan. They both stare at me with their mouths hanging open.

Emily recovers first and looks around the room. "She was dancing with the groom a minute ago."

What the fuck was that about? Logan signs vehemently. He doesn't talk.

That was closure, I sign back. *Are you ready to go? Meet me outside. I'm going to find Sky.*

I walk around the ballroom, looking for the blue dress that matches her eyes. I smell for her scent. I listen for the sound of her voice. But she's gone. She's not there.

I finally end up outside, and a valet approaches me. "Cab, sir?" he asks.

I shake my head. "I'm looking for a woman," I say. I hold my hand up, indicating how small she is. "A little blonde, dressed in blue."

"Oh, yes, sir," he says with a nod. "I put her in a cab a few minutes ago."

"A cab?" I parrot.

"Yes, sir. She was going to the city."

"Why would Sky be going to the city?" I ask myself. "Her apartment is downtown." But he must have heard me.

"She was a little upset, sir," he says.

"Why was she upset?" I clutch his shoulder.

He shrugs. "That I'm not sure about, sir," he says.

Logan motions to me. He gets into the limo with Emily, and I lean inside. "I can't leave yet. I don't know where Sky is," I tell him.

"Get in the car," Emily says. "We need to get out of here."

I get in and the car pulls out. "The valet said she was going uptown."

"What did you do to her?" Logan asks.

Emily punches me in the shoulder. "Seriously, couldn't you wait to get home to have sex with her? You had to do it at April's wedding?"

"You had sex at April's wedding?" Logan asks. He chokes a little, so I kick him in the shin.

"Shut up," I grumble.

"You didn't tell her who April was, did you?" Emily asks, her voice soft.

"I told her all about April," I protest. "I told her all about the girl who broke my heart right after we met."

"But did you tell her this was her wedding?" Emily snaps at me. "Did you ever say her name?"

I can't answer because I don't know. She punches me again. "Stop hitting me," I mumble. I rub my arm because that shit hurts. "I don't know if I ever said her name." I throw up my hands. What the fuck else am I going to do?

"She must have figured it out," Emily says. "And then she quizzed me when you were gone." Her eyes close and she grimaces. "I thought you told her everything."

"I did, just not the important part, apparently."

"It's all a big misunderstanding," Logan says. "You'll go to her and explain."

"I accidentally told her about the letter," Emily says quietly.

"What letter?" I ask. I take my phone out and text Sky.

Me: *Where are you?*

I stare at the phone like it holds the secrets of the universe.

"The letter you wrote to April when you were dying. The one you made me promise to give to her after you kicked the bucket."

I raise my brow. "Kicked the bucket?"

"Bite the big one? Meet the Holy Ghost? Pushing up daisies?" She punches my arm again. "Why does it matter?"

"Why did you tell her about the letter?" I ask. I'm not angry. I'm just confused.

"She was talking about April. And I wanted her to know how very much I hate her, so I told her about the letter." She groans. "It seemed relevant!" she yells.

"What do you think was in that letter?" I ask.

"You professing your undying love as you lay on your death bed…" she says.

I snort. "Okay," I say. "Have your driver take me to the apartment. I need to get something."

"Then what?" she asks.

"Then I'm going to get Sky."

She grins and pats my arm. "Good."

I just hope she'll see me.

My phone bleeps.

Sky: *I went home. Leave me alone.*

Me: *You don't get to run off and hide. Not right now.*

Sky: *Yes, I do.*

Me: *I'm coming to see you.*

Sky: *I won't let you in.*

Me: *I'm very persistent.*

Sky: *I'm very hurt.*

Me: *Let me fix it.*

Sky: *You can't.*

Me: *I will.*

I will, if it's the last thing I ever do.

Skylar

My apartment smells stale and unused. I open a window and look around. It's too clean and too empty. There are no dolls lying around. There are no board games littering my kitchen table. There are no kids anywhere. I should be at home with my kids. But if I go there, I'll have to face Matt.

I take a shower and put on my old, unattractive, single-girl flannel pajamas. I don't put on any makeup because my eyes are all swollen and I look like shit anyway. It's not like I'm going to see anyone. Matt doesn't know where my apartment is.

In my freezer, there's a half a gallon of Chunky Monkey and it's still good. I take it out and don't even get a bowl. I just grab a big soupspoon and take it to the couch. I flip the TV until I find something mindless, something that will not require any thinking at all.

I've eaten about half the carton when a knock sounds on my door. I startle. I don't go to the door. No one I know would come here.

My phone bleeps.

Matt: *Answer your door.*

Me: *No. Go away.*

My heart starts to trip. He's here. Shit. I uncurl my feet from under me and perch my bottom on the edge of the couch. He'll go away if I wait long enough.

He knocks again, and I jerk, dropping my spoon to the floor. I get up and toss it in the sink as I walk past. It clatters loudly. I walk over to the door, press my ear against it, and listen. I don't hear anything.

Matt: *I'm not leaving.*

Me: *How did you find me?*

Matt: *Your father felt sorry for me.*

Me: *Traitor.*

I hear a chuckle through the door.

Matt: *He loves you.*

Me: *What did you tell him?*

Matt: *I told him that I'm an idiot.*

I wait.

Matt: *He agreed.*

A grin tugs at my lips.

Matt: *You're laughing, right?*

I don't respond.

Matt: *Please tell me you're not crying.*

Me: *Not anymore. You should go home, Matt.*

Matt: *You first.*

I hear Matt speak softly through the crack in the door. "You should go home, Sky."

I sink down onto my bottom and lay the back of my head against the door. "I can't go home," I say.

"Why not?" he asks, his voice soft, and I think he is sitting down now, too, just on the other side of the door.

"Because you'll go there."

He chuckles. "I'm here."

I sigh heavily. "Go home, Matt. My feelings are hurt, and I don't want to see you right now."

"It wasn't what you thought it was. I thought you knew who she was, and you obviously didn't. I never meant to hurt you."

"You still love her, Matt," I say.

"No," he protests. "I don't. And I made that very clear when you forced me to dance with her tonight."

"You wrote her a fucking letter when you were dying," I say.

"Ugh!" he cries. "That letter will haunt me until the day I die."

"Only because it tells how you really feel."

He chuckles. "It does tell how I really felt when I wrote it."

I bang the back of my head against the door. I want to stop talking about it.

"I want you to read it," he says.

"I don't want to read it."

"Yes, you do."

I hear a rustle, and an envelope slides under my door. It has the word *April* written across the front. I push it back to him. He laughs and shoves it through again.

"I need to tell you something," he says.

"What?" I ask. I don't touch the letter. I just let it lie there on my carpet.

"Seth and Mellie and Joey, they depend on you. They don't deserve for you to leave them."

That hits me like he just kicked me in the chest. "I didn't leave them."

"You're here so you can avoid me, and they're there."

I don't say anything because he's right. I did leave them.

"I'll go away if you'll go home," he says. "I won't like it, but I love you, and I love them enough to give up for tonight so you can go back to them. They need you. And you need them."

Tears burn my eyes, and I blink them back. "Matt," I say.

"Will you read the letter?" he asks.

"Maybe," I grouse.

He chuckles, and I hear a sniffle from his side. "Will you call me when you're ready?"

"Maybe," I say again.

"Go home to the kids, Sky. I promise to give you some space. Read the letter, though. It might help."

With everything that's going on, he's still thinking about my kids. My belly flips. He's just on the other side of the door. I could open it up and jump into his arms, if I wanted to. But I don't. I just sit there. I sit there until my butt gets tired. I sit there until my foot falls asleep. I sit there until the letter taunts me to pick it up. I sit there long after Matt is gone.

I take the letter in my hand and hold it out so I can see the name on it. It's not for me. It's for April. It's for the love of his life.

I tear into it and unfold it. It's short, not even half a page.

I start to read.

Dearest April,

When I met you, I immediately felt like the sun rose and set in your eyes. I went to bed thinking about you at night, and I woke up with you on my mind in the morning. We had some really good times, didn't we? I relished the long walks we took. I looked forward to seeing you at night and sleeping with you in my arms.

Then I got the diagnosis. I found out that I was sick, and when I needed you to be there for me, you fucked my best friend. You weren't there to hold my hand through chemo. You weren't there to help me get to and from doctors' appointments. You weren't there when I was so sick I couldn't hold my head up. You were with him. You were under him and on top of him and with him instead of me.

I asked my brothers to give you this letter in the event of my death, so if you're reading this, I'm gone. I've lived out my days, and even though you've moved on, I need to tell you how I feel.

A good man might want to ease your conscience.

A good man might want to give you some peace.

But good wasn't important to you.

I fucking hate you. I hate that you're breathing. I hate that you're alive. I hate that you're able to laugh and that you're going to go on and procreate and make more sorry-ass human beings just like yourself.

I hope that your heart leaped when you got this letter. Final words of love from me. Hahahahahaha! I am dead, so I can say whatever I want.

And what I want to say is:

I fucking hate you. I hope you get exactly what you deserve in life.

With the utmost hatred and disdain,
Matthew Reed

PS – I still hate you.

I lay my hand over my mouth to stifle the noise that wants to come out. I'm not sure what it is. It might be a laugh. It might be a gasp. But whatever it is, it takes my breath away. I get up and go get my coat. I don't even get dressed. I put on my jacket and pad downstairs in my bedroom slippers. It has started to rain heavily, so I call a cab and get in it and go home. I go back to my kids because that's where I belong. And there's no doubt in my mind that I want to go to Matt.

But I can wait until tomorrow. He was willing to give up and go home so I could do what was in the best interest of my kids. He will be willing to wait until morning. I need to talk with my dad anyway. And I need to go watch Joey and Mellie sleep. And maybe even Seth, too.

Matt

I let myself into the apartment. I should have known that they would all still be up. There wasn't a chance in hell I would come home and not be bombarded with questions. One: there was the wedding. Two: there was April. Three: April and Sky were in the same room. Four: I kind of did Sky in the supply closet, against the wall.

Shit. Paul is going to skewer me.

My brothers are draped across the furniture like building blocks. Pete's feet are on the back of the couch, and Sam's head is just below them. Paul is in the lazy chair, and Logan is stretched out on the other sofa by himself. He sits up first and turns off the TV. I look toward the hallway. Where are Reagan and Emily?

"We sent them baby shopping." Paul says, swiping a hand down his face.

Baby shopping? Oh yeah. I keep forgetting that Emily is pregnant. Logan is such a lucky bastard. I know it sounds resentful to call him that, when he has to deal with being deaf every day, but still. I survived fucking cancer. I should get a perk. Like fatherhood.

"Thank you," I breathe. I'm so glad they're not here. They're as nosy as my brothers, but not nearly as subtle.

"You had a big night, I hear," Paul says.

"We had a little misunderstanding. That's all." I go get a beer and then sit down beside Logan.

"Where is Sky now?"

"I hope she's at the apartment with the kids."

"Logan told us what happened," Paul says. "Tough luck."

I throw my beer bottle cap at Logan. "You just couldn't keep your mouth shut, could you?" I'm joking. Sort of. I throw my hands up. "It's not like you guys haven't had sex in some strange places."

Paul's brow furrows. "Sex? What about sex?"

Logan laughs out loud. It's more of a bark. But I hear it. "Shut up," I grumble, and I kick his leg.

He laughs again. "I didn't tell them about that." He cups his hands around his mouth and says, "He did her in the coat room."

I take a sip of my beer. A grin tugs at my lips. Hell, they already know. "Supply closet, actually."

"How was it?" Pete asks.

I scowl at him. "None of your fucking business."

Sam puffs his chest out and pretends to be Paul. "Did you use a condom?" He laughs. I don't. I'm not going to tell them that part, regardless.

"I'm shooting blanks, man. We all know that. I couldn't get her pregnant if I wanted to."

"You don't know that," Paul says.

"I do, too. I know in the very marrow of my bones that I will never have a child of my own." I hold up a finger. "But," I say, "Sky just happens to have three already, and they all need a dad, so I'm a pretty happy guy."

"Are you really?" Paul asks. His brow furrows. He grabs my knee and squeezes it. "You going to be satisfied with that?"

I take another sip of my beer. "I'll have to be, won't I?"

"You want a kid, man, we'll all donate sperm for you. We could mix them all together so we have no idea who the father is." Sam laughs.

"There's no fucking way I'd let one of you get Sky pregnant. No." Absolutely not.

"You ever need my sperm, you let me know," Sam says. "Hell, I don't have a girlfriend. I'd be happy to participate. Give me a magazine and a little plastic cup." He makes a crude gesture with his hand.

What's bad is that he's half serious. Any of them would do it for me, I'm pretty sure. "I'll be happy with the kids we have. I already love Seth and Joey and Mellie."

"Do you worry at all about people's perception of them, and of you when you're with them?" Paul asks. He's playing devil's advocate, I'm sure, because we weren't raised to see a difference in color. We see people, the way it should be.

"I don't worry about it at all. None whatsoever." That's the God's honest truth. "I'm humbled by the very idea of being their dad." I have to swallow past the lump in my throat all of a sudden. Paul squeezes my shoulder. That doesn't help.

"So what happened at the wedding?" Sam asks. He rubs his hands together like he's excited.

"Sky got scared. She took off when she thought I still have feelings for April. I had to go to her and prove that I don't."

"Did Emily fuck it up for you by mentioning the letter?" Logan asks. He winces.

"That letter saved me," I say, chuckling.

"What letter?" Sam and Pete look at one another.

"I wrote a letter to April when I was dying," I tell them. They had no idea. "I wrote one for all of you."

Sam raises his hand. "I want mine."

"Nope." I shake my head. "I didn't die, so you don't get a letter. Deal with it."

"Em knew about the letters, but we didn't?" Logan asks. He pretends to pull a knife from his chest.

"She promised to deliver them for me."

He nods. "You trusted her. I'm glad."

"She's trustworthy." I shrug my shoulders. He just smiles.

Sam stands up and stretches. "Well, if we're not going to talk about jizzing in a cup, I'm going to bed."

"Me, too," Pete says. He gets up and pulls his keys from his pocket. "Emily's going to drop Reagan off at home."

Logan drops his feet to the floor. "I better go, too, then," he says. He jerks on my ponytail as he walks by me. But then he walks back to stand in front of me. *I'm happy for you*, he signs.

I grin at him. *Thanks*. I need to talk to him about something. *Tomorrow, do you think you can draw up a new tat for me?*

Any idea what you want?

I know exactly what I want. We'll talk about it tomorrow.

He nods and ruffles my hair because he knows how much that shit bothers me.

Then it's just me and Paul.

"I'm really proud of you," he says.

I jerk my head up. "What brought that on?"

He shrugs his shoulders.

"It was the sex in the supply closet, right?" I pat my chest. "You know I got mad skills in the sack."

He chuckles. "You got mad skills in life, Matt." He closes one eye and looks at me. "You ever think about going to college?" he asks.

I shake my head. "I like what I'm doing." I think about it for a second. "I might have to make my appointments a little earlier in the day, though, so I can be home at night." Paul already does that when he has Hayley. He works late one week and comes home early the next.

"We can cover." He nods. "Whatever you need to do, we'll make it work, just like always."

"Thanks."

"You know she makes more money than you do, right?"

I laugh. "Yeah, I know."

"Does it bother you?"

"That she's successful and educated? No. Doesn't bother me at all. Hell, maybe I'll stay home and be Mr. Mom."

"You'd be good at that." He lays his head back and closes his eyes.

"*You* ever think about going back to college?" I ask. He never even got a chance to go; he was too busy taking care of us.

He shrugs, suddenly looking really uncomfortable. He plays with a string on his jeans. "Never had time to give it much thought."

Oh, he's thought about it, if his avoidance is any indication. "You should go. When I move out to go live with Sky, it'll just be you and Hayley here. You won't know what to do with all the quiet."

He snorts. "Like I could ever get rid of you guys. You're all here more than you're at home."

"Can I ask you something?" I say quietly. I try not to get into his personal business, but I can't help it.

"You can ask. I can't promise I'll answer."

"What's going on with you and Friday?"

He groans. "Nothing. Why? What did she tell you?"

I try to play it off. "She didn't tell me anything. There's just, like, this undercurrent when you're in a room together. What did you do to her?"

"I kissed her," he blurts out.

I choke. "You kissed Friday?" I thump my fist against my chest, trying to restart my heart.

"Well, we kind of kissed each other."

I grin. "How was it?"

"Amazing," he breathes. But then he realizes what he said, and he sobers. "I mean, it was okay."

He's such a bad liar. "You should ask her out," I say.

He shakes his head. "I did. She told me no. She's been telling me no for years."

"You know she's not a lesbian, right?" I ask.

He raises one brow. "No thanks to you, yes."

I chuckle. "Sorry about that."

"No you're not." But he's grinning. "She's got some issues," he finally says. "I would love to know what they are."

"What kind of issues?" I ask.

"I don't know. The I-don't-have-any-family kind. The girl is completely alone. You know she doesn't even go home in the summer?"

"Well, she didn't get picked out of a cabbage patch." I stay quiet for a minute because it looks like he's thinking. "What happened when you kissed her?"

"Sparks," he says. "Fucking sparks." He blows out a breath.

"What about Kelly?"

His gaze jerks up. "What about her?"

"I'm guessing that Friday wouldn't like kissing you when you're still sleeping with Kelly. Was that the problem?" Getting information out of Paul is like pulling teeth.

"I haven't slept with Kelly since you and I talked about it that morning. Haven't slept with anybody since I kissed Friday. I can't get her off my fucking mind."

"So go for it."

He shakes his head. "She said no way. Her exact words were *no fucking way, Paul, you stupid son of a bitch.* Then she told me to go fuck myself."

That's Friday for you. You have to love her.

Suddenly, there's a knock at the door. I jump to go answer, hoping deep in my heart that Sky has come to see me, to be sure everything is all right. To tell me she loves me and can't wait another minute to see me. I open the door and my heart stalls, but for a completely different reason.

It's not Sky at my door. It's April. She has her arms crossed, and she's all wet. Her makeup streaks down her face, making her look like a semi-drowned raccoon. She's still in her wedding dress, and a puddle is forming on the floor beneath her.

"Can I come in?" she asks.

I step back and let her walk by me, right into the house, and right back into my life.

Skylar

Dad is still up washing dishes and cleaning up the kitchen when I get home. I toss my keys onto the table, and he turns to face me, rubbing his hands on a kitchen towel. "I didn't think you'd be home until morning," he says.

I shrug my shoulders. "I missed my kids," I say. I smile, because it's true. I really did miss them.

"Never thought I'd hear you say that." He lays the towel down on the counter and crosses his arms. "Did Matt find you?"

I nod. I don't need to tell him more than that.

"What was that all about?" he asks.

"Just stuff," I say. "It doesn't matter."

"It does matter, Sky," he protests.

I don't like that he's acting like this. I don't like it at all. He has no right. "What gives you the right to ask me questions, Dad?" I say. The words hang there in the air between us, visible and palpable, almost living and breathing. "I did what you wanted. I took on your responsibility. That doesn't mean that you get a free ticket into my life."

"I don't want a free ticket," he says. He turns away. "Never mind," he mutters.

I let out the breath I was holding. "What *do* you want, Dad?" I ask.

"I don't want a free pass, Sky," he says. "But I do want to earn a ticket. I'm trying. And I know I've done a brilliant job of walking away my whole life, but I don't want to walk away right now." He holds out his hands like he's surrendering. "So, what happened with Matt?"

"He came to see me," I admit. "He came to my apartment. Why did you give him my address?"

He chuckles. "The boy was wrecked. I couldn't sit here and let him suffer."

"Why would you care about Matt's suffering?" I cross my arms and glare at him.

"I walked away from your mother's suffering for a long time. And yours. And now that I'm trying to be aware of all of it, you don't get to give me a hard time about it."

"Yes, I do." I sound like Mellie when she doesn't get her way.

He chuckles. "You can. But it won't get either of us anywhere." He waits a beat. "You know he came to see me, right?" he asks.

I roll my eyes. "I'm not deaf, Dad. You just told me that."

"Not today, Sky. Yesterday. He came to see me."

I go to the fridge and get a bottle of water. Chunky Monkey makes me thirsty, apparently. "Why would Matt come to see you?"

"He wanted to ask for my permission to marry you."

I drop my bottle, and it rolls across the floor. "He wanted what?"

"You're not deaf, Sky," he says.

"Not funny, Dad." But a grin steals across my face. "He really asked you that?"

He smiles, too. "Yeah, he did. I told him you guys should just shack up like young people do, but he told me he couldn't do that as long as there are impressionable kids in the house. He said that Seth will learn how to treat women from the way he treats you, and that Joey and Mellie will learn how to treat men from the way you treat him. And vice versa. So, he wants to marry you and make it all legitimate."

My heart warms at the very idea of it. "He hasn't asked me yet." But I know what my answer would be. I feel for my ring finger with the pad of my thumb. I want to wear Matt's ring. I want him to be my husband.

Dad takes in my grin. "He's the one, huh?" he asks.

"Yeah," I say. "He's the one."

"I had a feeling he would be. I met him when Kendra was sick. He seems like a wonderful person. Good and kind. And persistent." He narrows his eyes at me.

I laugh. "He's definitely persistent. But you know what I love about him most, Dad?" I ask.

He quirks a brow instead of responding.

"I love that he was willing to give up tonight and walk away for the good of the kids."

"I don't get it." He looks confused.

"I ran to my apartment because I didn't want to face him. He came there and told me he would give up if I would just go back to the kids, because they didn't deserve for me to leave them. He quit our argument. He walked away. And that makes me love him even more than I did before."

Dad walks over and gives me an awkward hug. He's not nearly as good at it as Seth is, but he's trying. He gets points for trying.

I look up at my dad. "Did you tell him yes, Dad?" I ask quietly.

He brushes my hair back from my face. "Yes, Sky. I did."

I grin. "I'm glad."

"Me, too. Glad you met him. Glad he's capable of loving you like you deserve." He kisses my forehead. "Well," he breathes, "since I'm here, do you want to go see him? I was planning to stay the night."

Go see Matt? I chew on my lower lip and think about it. "Would you mind?" I ask quietly.

He pulls me close and kisses my forehead again. "I'd mind if you didn't. Go get your happiness, kiddo. You deserve it."

Before I go, I look in on Mellie and Joey, and Seth's door is half open, so I look in on him, too. He stirs when I pull the ear buds from his ears.

"Aunt Sky?" he says, sitting up on his elbows. "What's wrong?"

"Nothing," I whisper. "I was just checking on you."

"My mom used to do that," he murmurs as he rolls over. "Love you, Aunt Sky," he says quietly. Then I hear a snore erupt from his throat.

I grin. I can't help it.

Dad is waiting by the door on my way out. "Take your raincoat. It's pouring."

I take it from him and shrug into it. "Thanks for being here, Dad," I say.

He nods and rocks back on his heels.

I let myself out so that I can go to Matt. I just hope he wants to see me as much as I want to see him.

Matt

Fuck my life.

I close the door behind April. I have no idea what to say to her. She looks like she got hit by a makeup truck. And left. On the side of the road. In the rain.

"I'm sorry to bother you," she says.

I see Paul get up and start toward the hallway to his room. "Don't you even think about going anywhere," I say to him. He freezes. He goes and gets a beer instead.

"April," he says with a nod. "You look like shit."

"Thanks," she mutters. She sniffles.

He doesn't linger. He goes back to the lazy chair. Fucker.

"Why are you here?" I ask. She's dripping all over the fucking floor.

She hugs her arms around herself and shivers. I look closely at her face. Her lips are a little blue, and her teeth are chattering.

"Go get her a fucking towel, asswipe," Paul calls. But he doesn't get up to help me. I turn toward the linen closet, but suddenly there's a knock on the door.

Shit. If that's Kenny, I'm going to shove her out into the hall and straight into his arms. I steel myself and open the door.

My heart clenches when Sky raises her little hand at me, waves, and says, "Hi, Matt."

I have never been so happy to see anyone in my life. "I am so glad you're here," I say. I hook my hand behind her neck and draw her to me, because I have to kiss her. I just can't wait another second.

She mumbles against my lips. "I couldn't wait until tomorrow," she says.

I lift my head and look down at her. "I'm so glad you couldn't wait," I tell her.

Paul chuckles from his chair and slaps his knee. He's enjoying this too fucking much. Sky looks over my shoulder and freezes. "What is she doing here?" she asks. Her eyes search mine like she's going to find the answer in my gaze. But she's not going to find anything there because apparently I have shit for brains.

"I don't have a fucking clue," I whisper vehemently.

She stares at April for a minute, and then her face softens. "You have to help her," she says.

"Help her with what?" I ask fiercely.

"Get her a fucking towel," Paul calls again. "Duh."

I grind my teeth together. I don't want to get her a towel. I want her to leave. And to take all her waterworks with her.

Sky lets me go and walks to April. She takes her elbow and guides her toward the bathroom. "Come on," she says gently. "Let's get you cleaned up."

April lets Sky push her into the bathroom, her sopping-wet dress dragging along the floor like a wet seal is sliding across our carpet.

Sky shoves her into the room and turns around to glare at me. But then she shakes her head, sighs heavily, and then goes into the bathroom.

"That's fucked up," Paul says over a maniacal laugh.

"You're fucked up," I say. "You could have helped."

"What did you want me to do? She's your girlfriend."

"Ex-girlfriend," I correct.

"Well, your ex-girlfriend is in the bathroom with your current girlfriend." He laughs again. "Go get me another beer when you go clean that water up." He *thunks* his feet onto the end table. "And get your balls out of April's pocket when you go in that direction."

"My balls are not in April's pocket." They're in Sky's pocket. Happily.

"Mmm hmm," he hums.

I take him a new beer and start to clean up the water.

Sky opens the bathroom door a crack and sticks her head out. "Can I get some towels? And something for her to wear?"

"What are you doing in there?" I hiss.

She looks back in the door. "She's a mess," Sky whispers. She steps out and closes the door behind her. "She was freezing, so I put her in the tub."

"Emily left some girl shampoo here. It's under the sink."

"Can you find some clothes? Just some shorts or something will work."

Sky disappears back into the bathroom. I get a pair of athletic shorts and a T-shirt that I don't like. Hell, I think it's one April bought. I knock gently on the door. Sky comes back out. "How's it going in there?" I ask.

"It's going," she murmurs, rolling her eyes. "She's had a hard day."

Good. She should. She made her bed, and now she gets to lie in it. "Sorry to hear that," I say instead.

She rolls her eyes and disappears back into the bathroom with the towels and clothes.

I pace for twenty minutes, until Paul barks at me. "You're going to wear a hole in the carpet."

"Who gives a shit?" But I sit on the couch next to his chair.

"What do you think they're talking about?" Paul asks, grinning like an idiot.

"No idea."

"I bet they're discussing the length of your dick," he taunts.

"Shut up."

"Or all the ways you never learned to use your tongue."

"Fuck you." I have a lot of skill with my tongue.

"The way you shave your balls."

"Asshole." But a grin tugs at my lips.

He laughs out loud and shoves my shoulder. "Quit worrying."

I look down at my thumbnail, which I have gnawed down to a nub.

The bathroom door opens, and I jump to my feet. Sky walks out first, with April behind her. April looks a lot better. Her face is free of makeup, and her hair is damp but combed into a tidy mass. She's wearing an old pair of my shorts and that shirt I hate. She crosses her arms in front of her chest. What happened to that monstrosity of a dress?

What happened to her marriage?

What happened to her baby? I look at her belly and realize that I can see a small swell there. What the wedding dress hid, these clothes do not. But it's not mine, so I couldn't feel more removed from it. I force my eyes back up to her face.

"Thank you for letting me in," April says quietly.

"Why are you here?" I ask finally. I do need to know.

"I didn't know about Kenny and my maid of honor. Thanks for telling me. Apparently, I was the only one who didn't know." Her voice is quiet and a little hoarse, like she spent a lot of time crying.

"Where's Kenny?" I ask.

She shrugs. "Probably at the hospital."

Hospital? "What?"

"I sort of hit him over the head with a vase." She holds out her hands to show me how big. "A big one." She rotates her arm at her shoulder. "It was kind of heavy. My arm still hurts."

Paul laughs. I shoot him a glare, and he shuts up.

"Hi, Paul," she says.

"April," he mumbles back. He turns the TV up.

"I should go," April says. She turns to Sky and holds her arms out for a hug. "Thank you," she says to her. "I appreciate it very much."

I watch the two of them. Sky pulls her in and holds her close, rubbing her back softly for a second. What the fuck happened in the bathroom?

April steps back and wipes her eyes.

"I'm glad you hit him," I tell April.

She smiles a watery smile. "Me, too." She takes a breath. "Matt, I'm sorry for everything," she whispers.

"I know." What else can I say?

I pull Sky in to my side and drop my arm around her shoulders. "It all turned out okay," I say. "For me, anyway."

April blows out a breath. "I got what I deserved."

I nod. What the fuck else am I supposed to say?

Sky elbows me in the side.

"What?" I ask. I rub my ribs.

"I know I got what I deserved." April lays a hand on her belly, and my heart clenches for her. "I picked passion over love, and look where it got me. I could have been stable and happy."

Yeah, but she wouldn't have been pregnant right now. That part I don't share with her because it's none of her business.

April holds out her arms. "Can I hug you, Matt?" she asks tentatively.

Sky and I both say "No" at the very same time. April lets her arms drop, and she smiles.

"I don't blame you," April says. "For what it's worth, I wouldn't want to hug me, either."

"I'm not mad at you, April. Not anymore." I can tell her that much. And I don't mind letting her know.

"Now you feel sorry for me?" she asks.

"I feel hopeful for you," I say. I squeeze Sky to me. "Take care of that baby, okay?"

"I will," she says with a nod. She walks to the door, and Sky opens it for her. "Thanks again, Sky."

Sky nods, and April walks out of my life, hopefully for the very last time.

I draw Sky into a hug and whisper to her, "I'm so glad you got here when you did."

Skylar

It feels really good in Matt's arms. I let him hold me for a second and then I step back, shove him gently, and shake my finger at him. "What would you have done with her if I hadn't shown up?"

He scratches his chin. "I have no idea." He laughs.

Paul chuckles. "Damn," he says. "Talk about looking like what the cat dragged in…"

I shoot Paul a look, and he rolls his shoulders in, trying to make himself smaller. But he's not truly contrite. I know that much.

"I kind of feel sorry for her," I admit. "You didn't see her in the bathroom."

"Thank God," Paul mutters. "She had a lot of fucking nerve coming here."

"She didn't have anywhere else to go," I tell him. "She lives with Kenny now, as of last week. And she just hit him over the head with a heavy object." I laugh. That part makes me laugh.

"But she couldn't possibly think that she would be welcome here," Paul says.

"She's made a lot of enemies. She's not welcome in many places." I point toward the bathroom. "Her dress is still in the tub. She said to burn it."

"Can I just toss it out the window?" Paul asks.

I shrug. "She doesn't care what you do with it."

"You okay?" Matt asks, his gaze as soft as his fingertips, which drag across my forehead, pushing my hair from my face.

I jerk my thumb toward the door. "April and I had a long talk. Well, I talked, and she listened. I think she got it."

His eyes narrow. "What did you tell her?"

I look toward his bedroom door. "Can we talk privately?"

He takes my elbow, much like I took April's, and he leads me toward his room. Paul makes a coughing noise. He looks like he's about to hock up a lung. He jerks his thumb toward the kitchen, and Matt rolls his eyes, goes to the kitchen, and comes back with a handful of condoms. They have a drawer full of condoms? In the kitchen? What?

Matt laughs as he closes the bedroom door behind us. He tosses the condoms onto the dresser. There are about twenty of them. "You were feeling kind of ambitious, huh?" I ask.

"A man can hope," he says over a chuckle. "So what did you tell April?" he asks as he sits down on the edge of his bed.

"I told her that I appreciated her need for help this time, but that I'd appreciate it even more if she never sought you out again."

He nods and makes a noise low in his throat. "Nice," he says. "I like it."

"I think she understood what I was talking about."

"What else did you tell her?" He kicks his shoes off and reaches behind him to pull his shirt over his head the way men do. I look at the frog on his belly.

"I told her your frog prince has met his frog princess."

He laughs. "You did not."

"It was something like that."

"I was just talking with Logan tonight about drawing a frog princess for me to put beside this one. I want your name inked on my skin, too. Something permanent."

"That's sexy," I say.

"So are you," he says quietly. He shoves his pants down over his hips.

"Is there a reason you're taking your clothes off?" I ask. My heart is tripping like mad, though.

"I like your jammies," he says, eying me from head to toe in a slow sweep that makes my blood pound in my veins. "Did you wear those in the cab?"

"I didn't think you'd mind."

"I don't. I'd like them more if you took them off, though." He's wearing nothing but his boxers now, and he shoves those down, too, and kicks them across the room. His dick bobs like it wants my attention. I grin. I can't help it.

"Why are you here, Sky?" he asks.

I pull my shirt over my head. I'm not wearing a bra. "I guess I missed you."

"Which part of me?" he asks. He lies down on his bed, his manhood arching toward his belly.

"The whole package," I say.

He takes his dick in his hand and squeezes. "Me or my package?" He chuckles.

I roll my eyes. "You can be so silly."

"Come sit on my face, and I'll shut up."

I laugh. But my panties are suddenly wet. "Don't tempt me."

"I've been trying to tempt you since the day I met you. I sat down beside you in that church, and you were trembling. I wanted to know you. Immediately. It hit me like a speeding train."

I push my pants and my underwear down my legs and step out of them. I'm completely naked, but I don't care.

"You took on all that responsibility without blinking an eye, just because those kids needed you. And I fell in love with you a little bit because of that. Because if you could love three kids you'd never met, you could maybe love me a little, too." He beckons me forward. "You got room in your heart for me, Sky?" he asks. "I did warn you that I was going to make you fall in love with me."

I crawl across the bed until my chest touches his. I straddle his hips and look down into his beautiful face. "You win. I can't live without you." I kiss him. His lips are warm and soft and feel so right under mine. "I hope you're ready for a big family."

"I'm ready for anything you give me." He arches his hips under me, rocking into my naked heat.

Matt rolls us over, and he settles between my thighs. He bends his head and toys with my nipple, rolling it gently between his lips, tugging lightly and abrading it with his tongue. "You ready to marry me?" he asks when he lifts his head. He stares into my eyes, and I swear I can see the very depths of his soul. He's good and kind, and he loves me with an intensity I never could have hoped for.

"Yeah," I whisper to him. "I'll marry you."

"I'm going to ask you again when I can do it right."

"It won't be as wonderful as this time." It won't. There's no way.

Matt reaches for a condom and rolls it down his length. He pushes inside me until he can't push any further. Then he stills and brushes my hair back from my face. "I never thought I'd be so lucky," he whispers.

His arms slide under my shoulders, and he holds me close to him as he begins to pump his hips. He slides in and out, in and out, in and out, each move punctuated by little grunts by my ear.

Suddenly he stops and pats my thigh. "Roll over," he says.

I grin and comply. We've never done it this way, but I'm willing. I'm so willing. Matt slides one hand beneath me and dips into my curls, teasing my clit, and from behind me, he spreads my cheeks and sinks inside me. It's fast and hard and so so perfect. I push my bottom back toward him, and he adjusts his angle until he makes me tremble. "Found it," he gloats.

I cry out because I feel so full and so tight and Matt's moving just right inside me. "Shh," he whispers beside my ear.

Shit. Forgot. "Matt," I whisper.

"I love how you say my name right before you come. Right before you get that little hitch in your breath and make that little gasping noise." His fingers move against my clit, rubbing fast as he powers into me.

"Matt, Matt, Matt," I chant. Then I suck in a breath as he pushes me over the edge.

"There it is," he whispers, and then he grunts and comes inside me while my walls clamp down around him. My release flutters through me, and he works my clit until I'm spent. Then he drops onto my back, heavy and warm like a blanket, as his fingers thread through mine, holding me to the bed. He stills, and his breaths blow hot against my neck, where he buries his face. He hisses as he pulls out of me, and I can't even move. I lie there naked and exposed and so well worked that I don't care.

Matt shuffles around behind me, disposing of the condom. Then he crawls across the bed and kisses my shoulder. "So glad you're here," he says.

Matt's the most sincere man I've ever met. He tells me how he feels. And what he doesn't tell me, I can ask about and then he'll tell me. He doesn't hold back.

"I love you," I tell him, and I climb up to lie on his chest. I turn my head so that my ear is directly over his heart. It's steady and strong and…mine. "Will you love me forever?" I ask. I lift my head to look into his face.

"And a day," he affirms.

"Matt," I start. I don't know how to say what I want to say. "You mentioned that it would take a miracle for you to get me pregnant."

"Yeah," he says quietly.

"What if I said that I believe in miracles?"

"I'd say you're wishing for things you can't have." He doesn't stop touching me, so he's not mad or sad. He's just resigned to it.

"But—" I start.

He puts a finger over my lips. "But nothing, Sky," he says. "You're my fucking miracle. Not a baby. I don't need a baby to make me whole. I just need you." He laughs. "And I get your kids as a bonus. What more could I ask for?"

"Matt, could you move in with me?" I ask. I hold my breath as I wait for the answer.

"What about Seth?" he asks.

"We could have a talk with Seth."

"I'll talk to him when we go home in the morning." He yawns. "You can sleep here tonight."

"You want to go to my house now?" I ask.

He looks at the pile of condoms on the dresser and shakes his head. "We still have about nineteen condoms to use." He lifts me up and pulls the covers down, and then pulls them over us. I settle into his arms.

"I think we should do away with the condoms and see what happens," I suggest.

He shakes his head. "Not necessary."

I find that spot between his chin and his shoulder that's all mine and snuggle into it. "We'll talk about it again later." I yawn and close my eyes. Nothing ever felt quite this right.

Matt

I wake up with Sky in my arms. I want to wake up like this every day for the rest of my life. She's turned so that her bottom is in my lap, and we're lying like two spoons in a drawer. I reach behind me and get a new condom. We used four more during the night. I might just have to take her suggestion and dispense with them entirely. See what happens. But not yet. Not until I marry her. I want her to have my name. I want it to be permanent.

She stirs and murmurs encouragement at me when I push into her from behind. "Matt," she whispers. I reach around her, trying to get to her, but she shoves my hand away. "I can't come anymore," she protests. "You wore me out."

I stroke inside her, my movements lazy and slow. She clenches around me, and while she might not be able to come again with me touching her clit, she can certainly take the warm wash of pleasure that I want to give her. She squeezes me tightly, so tight that I want to come already. Her breath hitches and she makes that noise, and my own completion hits me faster than I thought possible. I come holding on to her shoulder, pushing in lazy strokes, and she rides it out with me.

I stop moving and hold her close, not even wanting to pull out yet. She's so perfect, and everything I've ever wanted.

"Good morning," she whispers.

I chuckle. "I'm almost ashamed of myself," I say. "I haven't come that fast since I was a teenager." I roll her onto her back so I can look into her face. "See what you do to me?"

"I'll take it as a compliment," she says over a giggle.

"Are you ready to go home?" I ask her.

She smiles and nods. "Can we?"

I smack her naked bottom and laugh. "Of course, we can. Get up. Let's go take a shower."

We shower quickly, and she protests that she's sore. I wash her gently and wrap her in a towel, and then sneak her across the hallway back to my bedroom so she can get dressed. The sun is barely up, and we're moving around like teenagers. Her hair is wet, and she's still in her jammies. I pack some clothes this time because I won't be coming back here. I'm going to sleep at her house, provided Seth doesn't mind.

We stop for breakfast and take donuts back for the kids.

As we walk into her house, I realize that I've just come home. Her dad is puttering around the kitchen, and Mellie is helping him flip a pancake. He looks up and scowls. "Hi, you two," he says. He glares at me. I laugh. Fuck, he's her father. He's supposed to glare at a man with lustful intentions. I also know I have his blessing, and that's all I need.

"'Morning," Sky chirps. Mellie scurries over and straight into Sky's arms.

"I was afraid you weren't coming back," Mellie says. "Like my mom."

Oh fuck. I never even thought of that. Emotion chokes me and I have to swallow hard to push it back.

"I'm not going anywhere for long," Sky explains. "Neither is Matt. We're both going to be here, kind of like a mom and dad for you."

Mellie looks over at me like she's curious. "A mom *and* a dad?"

Sky blinks her blue eyes. "Yes. A mom *and* a dad. Is that okay with you?"

Mellie takes Sky's face in her little hands and looks into her eyes. "And you won't go away?" she asks.

"Never," Sky says.

"Matt, either?" Mellie asks. Her gaze is skeptical.

"Matt, either," Sky affirms.

I walk toward Seth's room. He has a wrestling meet today, I'm pretty sure, so he should be up. I knock on his door.

"Come in," he calls.

I stick my head in. He's getting dressed. "You almost ready?"

"Yeah," he says. "Are you going?"

"Of course," I say. I approach him and sit down on the edge of his bed. "Can we talk? Man to man?"

"Dude, I used a condom," he blurts out.

"What?" I say. I stand up.

His eyes go wide. "Oh, I thought you figured it out," he says. He winces. "Shit," he says. "I messed that up."

"You're having sex?" I ask.

"Just…like…once." He looks everywhere but at me. Hell, he's sixteen.

"You're being careful, right?" I ask. "Do we need to go shopping for more condoms?" I'd hate to think he just got *one* from the school nurse or something.

"Umm, no…" he says. "I got some."

"Well, when you need some more, let me know."

He nods and lets out a breath. "You're not going to tell Aunt Sky, are you?" he asks.

I bite my lips together. "Sorry, but I can't keep secrets from her." He nods. "How did it go?" I don't want details. I just want to know he's okay.

He keeps packing his bag with his uniform and equipment. "Okay, I guess." His face gets red.

The first time is usually fantastic for a young man, not so much for a young lady. "Who is she?" I ask. "You need to bring her by to meet us."

"She's not quite that kind of girl," he says with a wince.

"If she's worth fucking, she's worth bringing home to meet your family, dumbass," I bite out. That shit pisses me off. But I can remember having this same talk with Sam and Pete, too. And Logan for that matter. Logan was a bigger man-whore than either of the twins. "But that's not what I wanted to talk about."

He looks up. "What did you want?"

This time, it's my turn to fidget. I don't know why I feel so out of place asking Seth about this. "I want to marry Sky," I say.

"Okay…" he says.

"That okay with you?"

He nods slowly and then with more speed. "It's okay with me."

"So, I was thinking, while we wait for a wedding, that I might move in here." I wait and watch his face. "How would you feel about that?"

"You already asked her to marry you, right?"

"Yeah."

"You're not going to change your mind?"

"She couldn't chase me off with a really big stick."

He chuckles. "It's fine if you want to move in, Uncle Matt," he says. My heart stalls. He just called me Uncle Matt. I'm one step closer to being part of his family.

"I like that," I say softly.

"Me, too," he says back. "We had better go."

Sky has already changed clothes, and she's getting the girls into their coats. This will be an all-day event, so she's packed snacks and toys, too.

We all go out together, going to our first event as a family. Her dad isn't going with us today, though. He's going to visit Sky's mom.

Seth wins in back-to-back matches, and he advances to the final round.

Every time Seth wins, he stops after the match and raises his hand toward the sky, like he's reaching for heaven. It brings a tear to my eye.

His last match isn't like the others. He's up against a boy who's really good. Seth comes up in the stands to talk to me. "Uncle Matt," he says, "I don't know what to do."

I go and retrieve Joey from the bottom of the bleachers because she is getting a little too close to the wrestling mat. One fling of a fully grown boy in her direction, and she'll get hurt. I go to get her and bring her back up. I blow on her belly and then toss her over my shoulder. She laughs and hangs there, giggling. "About what?" I ask.

He nods toward the bottom of the bleachers. "You see that guy in the wheelchair?" he asks.

I do. I saw him when we first came in.

"He's my next opponent's dad."

"Oh," I breathe. "Is he sick?" He's wearing a stocking cap over his bald head, so I can guess what's wrong with him.

"Final stages of cancer," Seth says quietly.

"And you're worried about whether or not you should let his son win?" I weigh it in my mind. I can see why Seth is conflicted. And to be honest, I'm conflicted, too.

"Yeah."

"Do you think it would make his dad happy for this match to be handed to him?"

Seth shakes his head and gnaws on his lower lip. "Probably not."

"Seth, if I were his dad, I would want him to do his best, and may the best man win."

Seth nods.

"Just be prepared." I squeeze his shoulder. "He might be in it to win it." He's a few pounds heavier than Seth, too.

"Okay," he says. And he goes down to the clock to sign in when it's his turn.

"What's wrong?" Sky asks when I sit down beside her. She takes Joey from over my shoulder and sets her beside Mellie, and then puts a crayon in her hand and gives her a piece of paper.

I point with my chin and tell her what's up. She looks sympathetic. "This one has to be hard for him after what happened with his mom."

I nod. It fucking hurts me, and it's not even my match.

"Do you think he'll throw it?" she asks.

I shake my head. "I doubt it."

He doesn't.

He goes at it just like he goes at everything else. He kicks ass. The boy is strong, and he has Seth almost pinned once, but the clock has ten seconds to go. The referee swipes his hand beneath Seth's lifted shoulder to show the other boy that Seth isn't pinned yet. It's close, and I hold my breath. Sky is squealing beside me, and the whole auditorium starts to count down with the clock. It goes off and Seth rolls over, and they move on to round two.

Seth holds his own, and he gets some back points when he lays the boy out flat. It's now almost the third round, and he's up by one point. Just one point. Seth looks over at his opponent's dad, and the man gives him a thumbs-up. Seth smiles at him and goes back to it.

Seth makes a crazy move, one that I have never even seen, one that might just be dumb luck, and he gets the boy on his back. His opponent can't wiggle free, no matter what he does. All Seth has to do is hold it.

Suddenly, the ref calls a pin. Seth reaches down and helps the boy to his feet, and they share a back-thwacking hug. The ref raises Seth's fist, and Sky whoops and yells beside me. Seth stops at the edge of the mat and raises his hand to the sky. He closes his eyes and says something under his breath that I can't quite make out. But then he turns and goes to his opponent's dad.

He squats down in front of him and says something to him. Seth's eyes fill with tears, and he's so fucking emotional all of a sudden that I have to blink mine back, too. Sky doesn't even try. She just wipes her face.

Seth goes to the locker room to clean up, and it's not until we're on the way home that Sky turns to him and says, "What did you say to that boy's dad, Seth?"

Seth blows out a breath. "I told him to keep fighting. That's all."

I have to blink back tears again. Seth is going to make one hell of a man. Sky reaches back and takes Seth's hand in hers and gives it a squeeze. He leans forward and kisses her cheek.

"I love you, Aunt Sky," he says quietly.

"I love you, too, Seth," she breathes.

"Me, too?" Mellie chirps.

Joey follows with, "And me?"

Sky laughs and reaches back to tickle their feet. "You two, too."

Then she takes my hand in hers and says, "You, too."

I give her a squeeze because it's all I'm capable of right now.

Skylar

Two months later

My mother stands in front of me and fluffs my veil. It has been a long time coming, but we're making progress. She got out of rehab a couple of weeks ago, and we've actually been spending some time together. We pop popcorn and talk about...nothing. It's nice. It's something she's never been capable of before. Neither was I. I had to set aside my doubts and my distrust. Sometimes, if you choose to walk the same road, you have to keep filling in the holes so you can find your footing. But other times, it's safe to take a new path altogether, and my mom and I are on a new path, completely. We're discovering one another like we've never met.

When I got my news yesterday, she was the only one I told. I'm going to tell Matt after the wedding. We got his good news last month when his blood work revealed that he is still in remission. Now I'm going to give him some more good news.

"You look so beautiful," my mom says. She has adjusted my hair, and she even held my dress up when I had to pee one last time. She has really been here for me today.

"Thank you," I breathe. My nerves are frayed, not because of the wedding but because of what I have planned afterward. "You have Matt's gift, right?" I ask.

She pats her clutch. "I have it. It's safe."

We found out last week that Joey and Mellie's dad is willing to give up his parental rights and let us adopt them. They'll have the Reed name. Matt has never been happier, but I have a feeling the news today will top even that. We'd like to adopt Seth, too, but he says he doesn't need it. He says he wants to keep his mother's name. That's fine with me, as long as he knows he's ours, too. And I'm pretty sure he does.

My mother gives me one last hug and goes to take her seat.

I hear the wedding march begin, and Dad comes to collect me. "It's not too late to back out, if you want to," he says.

I shake my head. "Never."

He laughs. "I didn't think so." He sticks out his elbow. I slide my arm inside. I only have three bridesmaids, and they're all standing at the front of the church already. Friday, Reagan, and Emily are family, but they agreed to get all dressed up and stand with me. Of course, Matt had to have every one of his brothers and Seth stand with him. He couldn't leave a single one out, so our sides don't match. But that's okay with me.

I step up to the walkway and look up. The guests all rise to their feet. But I don't look at them. I look at Matt. I can tell the moment he sees me because his eyes get glassy and his mouth falls open. I watch his face the whole way down the aisle. Paul punches him on the arm, and he still doesn't break my gaze. My dad kisses me on the cheek, and the rest of the service is just a dream. I look into Matt's eyes and say my vows, and he says his. When it's time for rings, I let him slide mine on my finger, and nothing ever felt so right. Until I slide his on, too. And then it's perfect.

"You may kiss the bride," the preacher says.

Matt takes my face in his hands, his fingertips splayed toward my ear, and he lays a kiss on my lips that steals my breath.

Paul starts to cough indelicately to break us up. When Matt finally lifts his head, he stares into my eyes. I hold his wrists and can't break away.

The preacher says, "I'd like to introduce Mr. and Mrs. Matthew Reed!"

The crowd goes nuts, and we walk out amid a shower of birdseed. We both close our eyes and let it rain down on us, soaking up every second.

Friday has Mellie by the hand and Reagan has Joey, so we scoop them up in our arms, each of us taking one of them, and we run toward the reception hall. We accept a ton of well wishes, and then it's time for a toast.

Paul stands and holds up his glass. "If there was ever anyone deserving of love, it's my brother." He stops to clear his throat. "I'm just glad he found it. Sky, you make my brother even better than he already was, and I know he'll do the same for you. You know everything about him, and you love him anyway." The crowd laughs, and Matt scowls playfully. "To you, to your love, and to your life and your family. May you continue to be blessed."

He tips his glass and drinks. So does Matt. And everyone in the crowd. Except me. "What's wrong?" Matt asks.

"Nothing," I say. I motion my mother forward, and she puts a box in my hands. It's small, but it's weighty at the same time. "I have a present for you."

"I thought our honeymoon was our present to each other," he reminds me with a scowl. We're leaving for the Carolina coast for a week with the kids tonight. I can't wait.

I motion for him to take my package. "The vacation is our gift. This is just extra." I blink back the tears that are already forming in my eyes.

He makes a face and opens up the box. He looks inside and then gets confused. He pulls the tiny little item out of the box. It's a onesie that has tattoo designs all over it, and on the back, it has the name Reed. "What's this?" he asks, confused.

Then his eyes grow wide. Friday gasps when she realizes what's going on, and the rest of the crowd rumbles and fidgets. "Is this...?" he asks. He stops, because he's choked with emotion.

"Yes," I say. Tears roll down my face, and I don't care. I lean close to him. "You knocked me up."

He takes me in his arms and pulls me close, and a sob rolls through him. "Are you serious?"

"Completely serious, Matt," I say. "But wait." I look down and shake the onesie out. A second one falls out, and Matt catches it in the air.

"Two?" he asks.

I nod, so broken by his reaction that I can't speak. "Two tiny little heartbeats," I say as soon as I can.

"Holy fuck," he breathes into my ear. He squeezes me so tightly that I chirp. "I love you so fucking much," he says to me.

He takes a second to breathe me in and compose himself, then he drops to his knees and lays his forehead on my belly. He says something quietly to his unborn children, and I'm not even sure what it was, but I do know it was between him and them. Or him and God. I'm not sure which.

Then he stands and looks up at the crowd. Half of them are as teary-eyed as we are. "Do you know what this means?" he asks our friends and family.

They rumble, but he can't hear one voice over another.

He points to Logan. "This means my sperm are better swimmers than yours, little brother!" he says. He signs while he talks, and Logan flips him off. But he's laughing. He wraps his arms around Emily and lays his hands on the small swell of her belly.

I slap his shoulder. "What if it's my eggs that are amazing and not your sperm?"

"What if it's just us?" he asks quietly, and he kisses me. "Us together."

"I told you I believe in miracles, Matt," I say when I can finally lift my head.

"You're my miracle," he says. "You. Just you."

Joey tugs on his pant leg so he scoops her up. He kisses her cheek soundly. She whispers in his ear. He turns and says, "Oh, someone has to go potty." He holds up a finger. "I'll be right back." And he stops the celebration right there to take her to the bathroom.

Miracles.

Yes, I believe.

More by Tammy Falkner:

More from Tammy Falkner in the Reed Brothers series

Tall, Tatted, and Tempting

Smart, Sexy, and Secretive

Calmly, Carefully, Completely

Just Jelly Beans and Jealousy

Finally Finding Faith

Reagan's Revenge *and* Ending Emily's Engagement

Maybe Matt's Miracle

Proving Paul's Promise

Only One

Beautiful Bride

Zip, Zero, Zilch

Christmas with the Reeds

Good Girl Gone

While We Waited

Holding Her Hand

Yes, You

Always, April

I'm In It (coming soon)

Made in the USA
Columbia, SC
05 July 2021

41407872R00172